SNOOPY™

JOE
COOL

kaboom!™

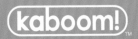

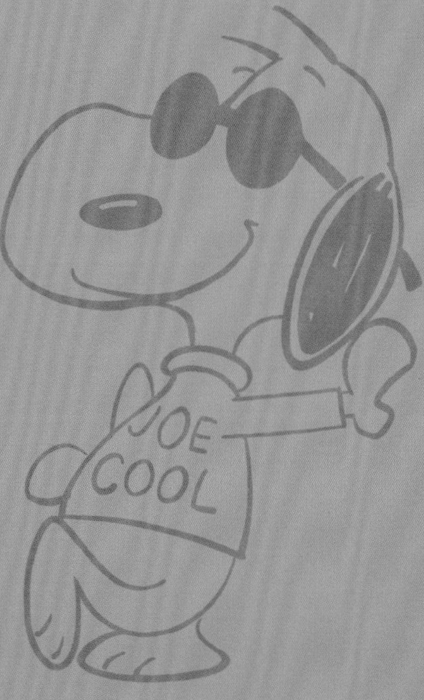

Cover
Art by **Charles M. Schulz**
Design by **Kara Leopard**

Designer: **Kara Leopard**
Associate Editor: **Alex Galer**
Editor: **Whitney Leopard**

For Charles M. Schulz Creative Associates
Creative Director: **Paige Braddock**
Managing Editor: **Alexis E. Fajardo**

Special Thanks to the Schulz family, everyone at Creative Associates, and Charles M. Schulz for his singular achievement in shaping these beloved characters.

ROSS RICHIE CEO & Founder • MATT GAGNON Editor-in-Chief • FILIP SABLIK President of Publishing & Marketing • STEPHEN CHRISTY President of Development • LANCE KREITER VP of Licensing & Merchandising • PHIL BARBARO VP of Finance
ARUNE SINGH VP of Marketing • BRYCE CARLSON Managing Editor • MEL CAYLO Marketing Manager • SCOTT NEWMAN Production Design Manager • KATE HENNING Operations Manager • SIERRA HAHN Senior Editor • DAFNA PLEBAN Editor, Talent Development
SHANNON WATTERS Editor • ERIC HARBURN Editor • WHITNEY LEOPARD Editor • JASMINE AMIRI Editor • CHRIS ROSA Associate Editor • ALEX GALER Associate Editor • CAMERON CHITTOCK Associate Editor • MATTHEW LEVINE Assistant Editor
SOPHIE PHILIPS-ROBERTS Assistant Editor • AMANDA LaFRANCO Executive Assistant • KATALINA HOLLAND Editorial Administrative Assistant • JILLIAN CRAB Production Designer • MICHELLE ANKLEY Production Designer • KARA LEOPARD Production Designer
MARIE KRUPINA Production Designer • GRACE PARK Production Design Assistant • CHELSEA ROBERTS Production Design Assistant • ELIZABETH LOUGHRIDGE Accounting Coordinator • STEPHANIE HOCUTT Social Media Coordinator • JOSÉ MEZA Event Coordinator
HOLLY AITCHISON Operations Assistant • MEGAN CHRISTOPHER Operations Assistant • MORGAN PERRY Direct Market Representative • CAT O'GRADY Marketing Assistant • LIZ ALMENDAREZ Accounting Administrative Assistant • CORNELIA TZANA Administrative Assistant

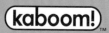

SNOOPY, November 2017. Published by KaBOOM!, a division of Boom Entertainment, Inc. Peanuts is ™ & © 2017 Peanuts Worldwide, LLC. Originally published in single magazine form as PEANUTS: Volume One No. 4, PEANUTS: Volume Two No. 4, 7, 8, 14, 17-19, 24, 28, 31, 32, PEANUTS: FRIENDS FOREVER No. 1. ™ & © 2012-2016 Peanuts Worldwide, LLC. All rights reserved. KaBOOM!™ and the KaBOOM! logo are trademarks of Boom Entertainment, Inc., registered in various countries and categories. All characters, events, and institutions depicted herein are fictional. Any similarity between any of the names, characters, persons, events, and/or institutions in this publication to actual names, characters, and persons, whether living or dead, events, and/or institutions is unintended and purely coincidental. KaBOOM! does not read or accept unsolicited submissions of ideas, stories, or artwork.

BOOM! Studios, 5670 Wilshire Boulevard, Suite 450, Los Angeles, CA 90036-5679. Printed in Canada. First Printing.

ISBN: 978-1-68415-161-5, eISBN: 978-1-61398-945-6

Classic Peanuts Strips by

Charles M. Schulz

Colors by **Justin Thompson & Katharine Efird**

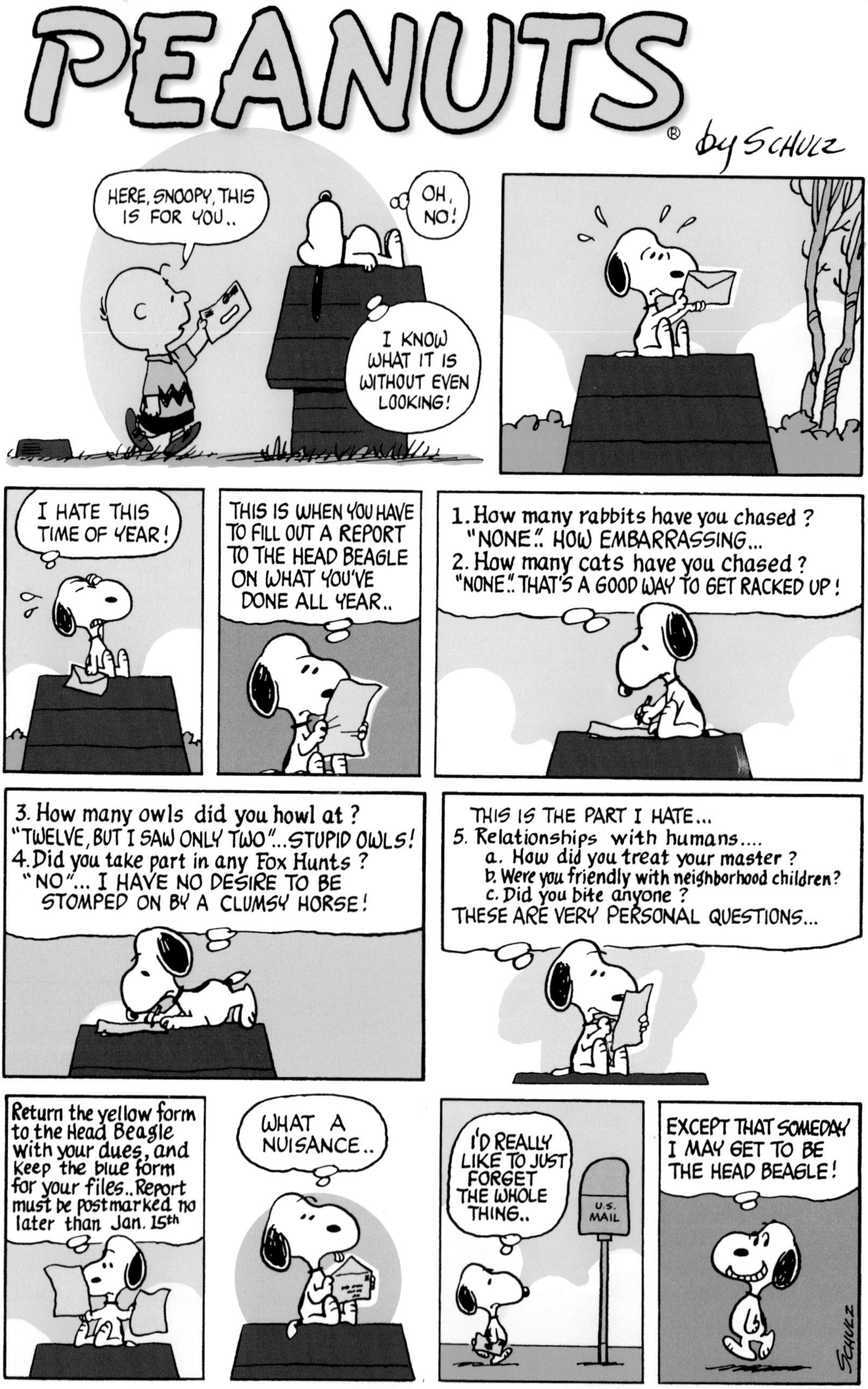
PEANUTS
by SCHULZ
HERE, SNOOPY, THIS IS FOR YOU..
OH, NO!
I KNOW WHAT IT IS WITHOUT EVEN LOOKING!
I HATE THIS TIME OF YEAR!
THIS IS WHEN YOU HAVE TO FILL OUT A REPORT TO THE HEAD BEAGLE ON WHAT YOU'VE DONE ALL YEAR..
1. How many rabbits have you chased? "NONE".. HOW EMBARRASSING...
2. How many cats have you chased? "NONE".. THAT'S A GOOD WAY TO GET RACKED UP!
3. How many owls did you howl at? "TWELVE, BUT I SAW ONLY TWO"... STUPID OWLS!
4. Did you take part in any Fox Hunts? "NO"... I HAVE NO DESIRE TO BE STOMPED ON BY A CLUMSY HORSE!
THIS IS THE PART I HATE...
5. Relationships with humans....
a. How did you treat your master?
b. Were you friendly with neighborhood children?
c. Did you bite anyone?
THESE ARE VERY PERSONAL QUESTIONS...
Return the yellow form to the Head Beagle with your dues, and keep the blue form for your files.. Report must be postmarked no later than Jan. 15th
WHAT A NUISANCE..
I'D REALLY LIKE TO JUST FORGET THE WHOLE THING..
U.S. MAIL
EXCEPT THAT SOMEDAY I MAY GET TO BE THE HEAD BEAGLE!
SCHULZ

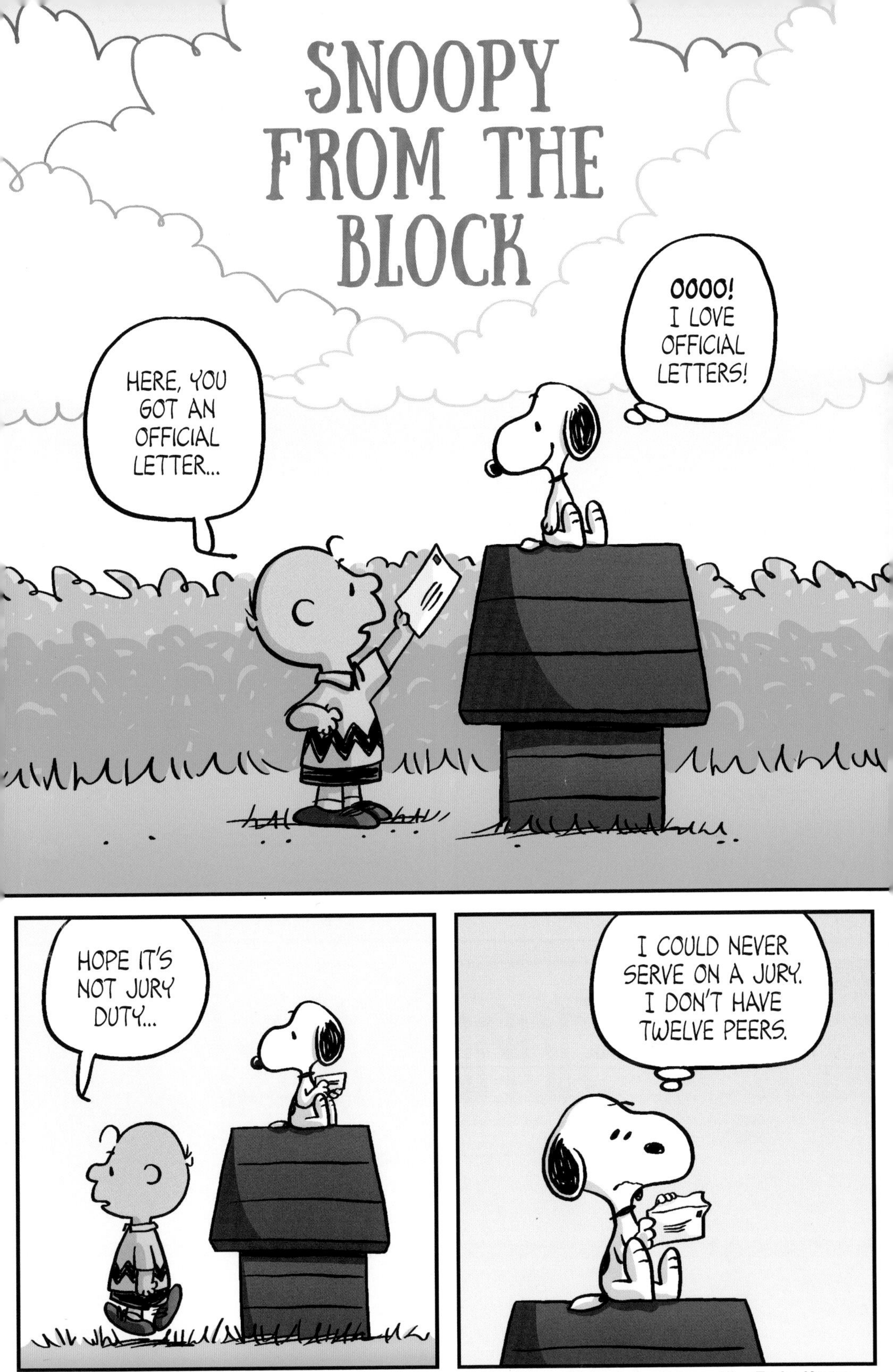
SNOOPY FROM THE BLOCK
HERE, YOU GOT AN OFFICIAL LETTER...
OOOO! I LOVE OFFICIAL LETTERS!
HOPE IT'S NOT JURY DUTY...
I COULD NEVER SERVE ON A JURY. I DON'T HAVE TWELVE PEERS.

Story by **Charles M. Schulz** Adapted by **Jason Cooper** Art & Letters by **Donna Almendrala** Colors by **Nina Taylor Kester**

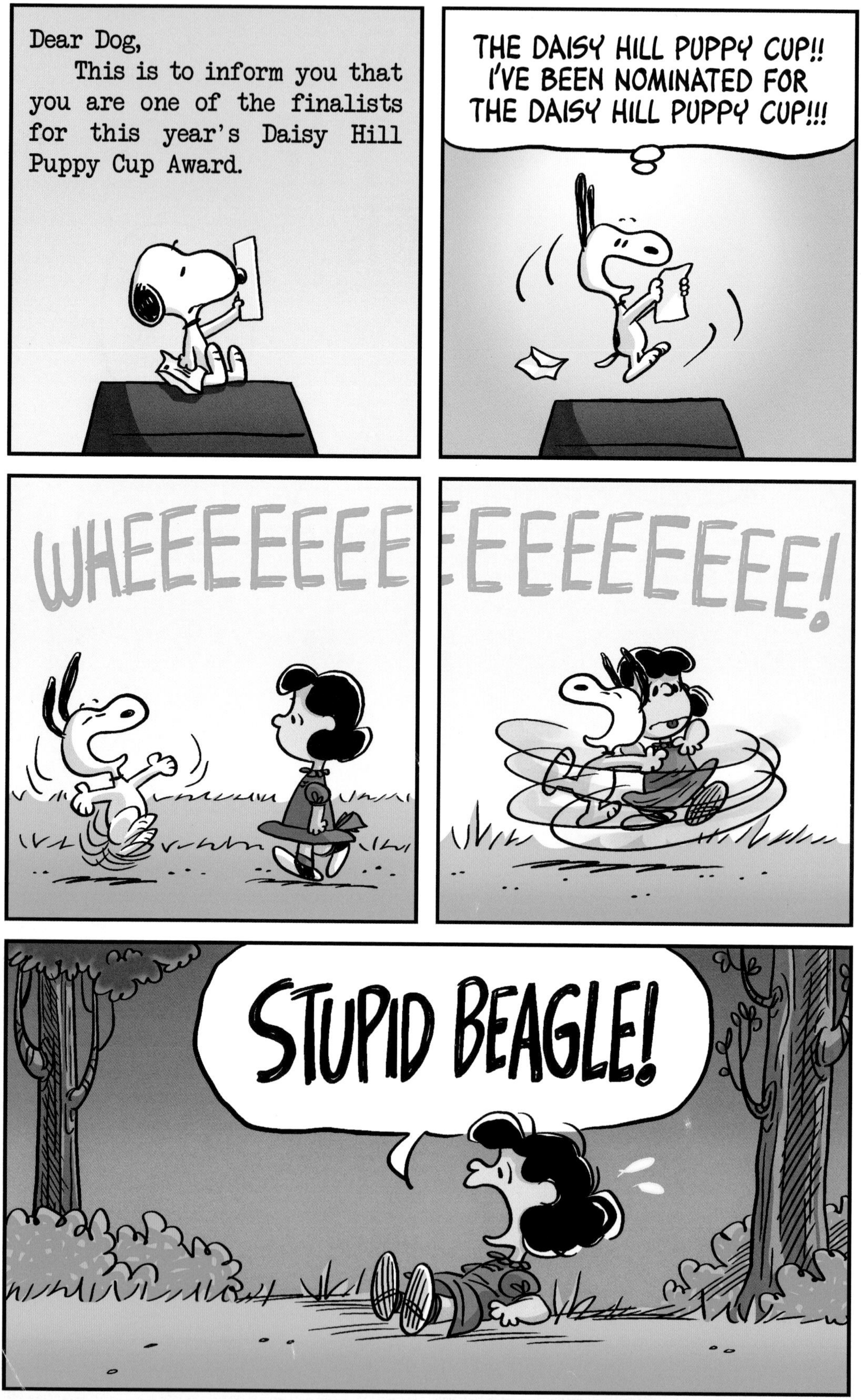
Dear Dog,
This is to inform you that you are one of the finalists for this year's Daisy Hill Puppy Cup Award.
THE DAISY HILL PUPPY CUP!! I'VE BEEN NOMINATED FOR THE DAISY HILL PUPPY CUP!!!
WHEEEEEEEEEEEEEEEEEE!
STUPID BEAGLE!

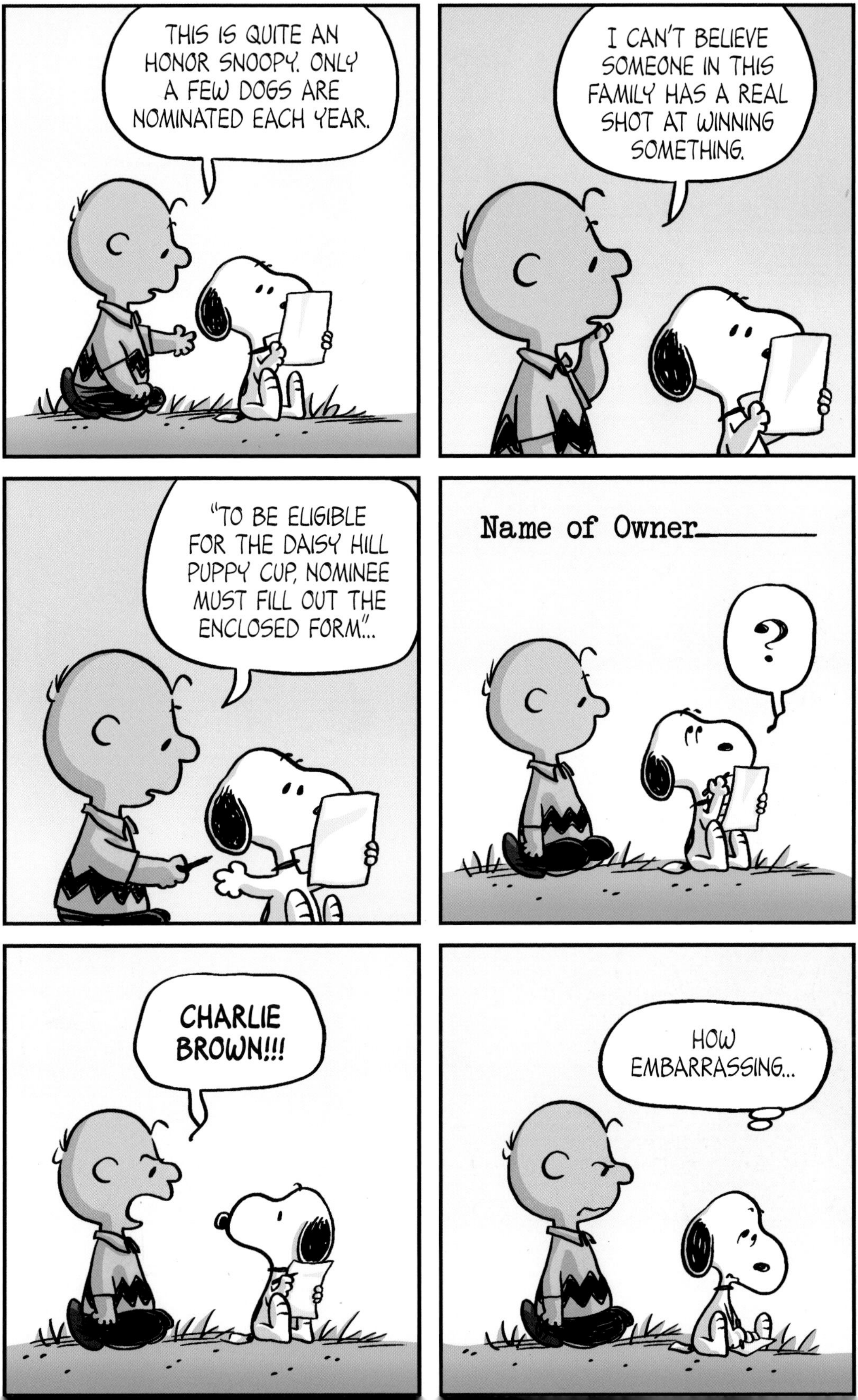
THIS IS QUITE AN HONOR SNOOPY. ONLY A FEW DOGS ARE NOMINATED EACH YEAR.
I CAN'T BELIEVE SOMEONE IN THIS FAMILY HAS A REAL SHOT AT WINNING SOMETHING.
"TO BE ELIGIBLE FOR THE DAISY HILL PUPPY CUP, NOMINEE MUST FILL OUT THE ENCLOSED FORM"...
Name of Owner
?
CHARLIE BROWN!!!
HOW EMBARRASSING...

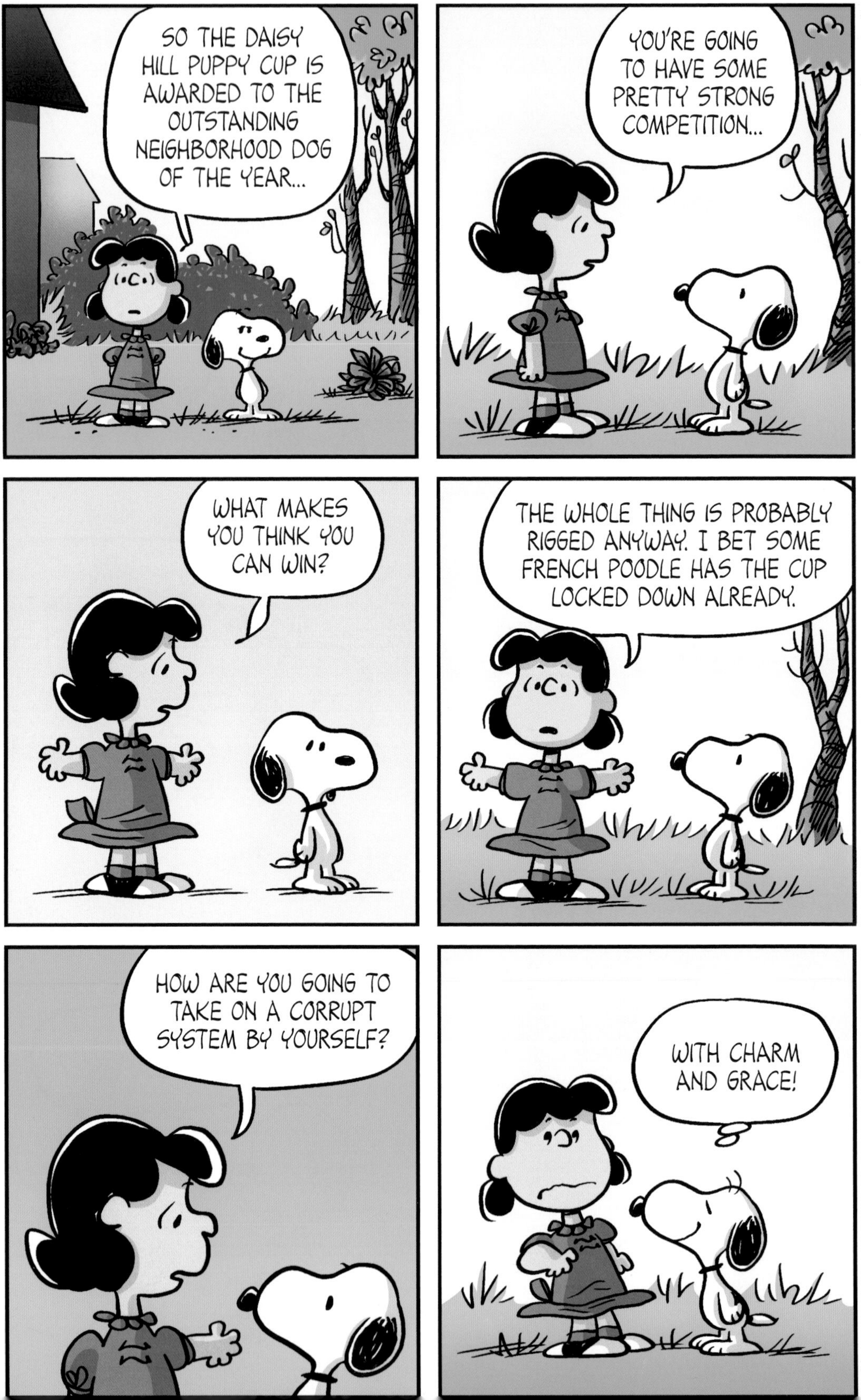
SO THE DAISY HILL PUPPY CUP IS AWARDED TO THE OUTSTANDING NEIGHBORHOOD DOG OF THE YEAR...
YOU'RE GOING TO HAVE SOME PRETTY STRONG COMPETITION...
WHAT MAKES YOU THINK YOU CAN WIN?
THE WHOLE THING IS PROBABLY RIGGED ANYWAY. I BET SOME FRENCH POODLE HAS THE CUP LOCKED DOWN ALREADY.
HOW ARE YOU GOING TO TAKE ON A CORRUPT SYSTEM BY YOURSELF?
WITH CHARM AND GRACE!

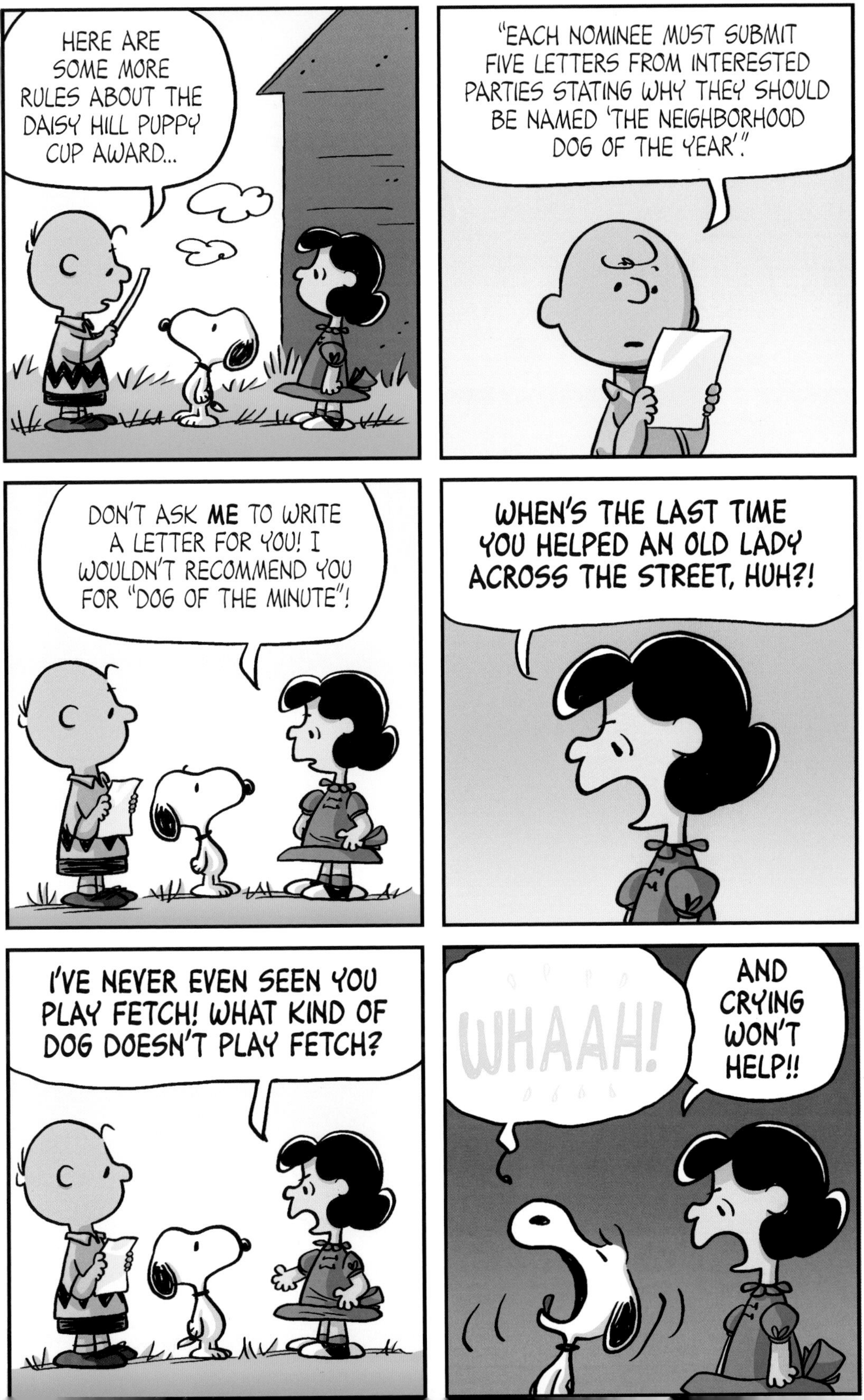
HERE ARE SOME MORE RULES ABOUT THE DAISY HILL PUPPY CUP AWARD...
"EACH NOMINEE MUST SUBMIT FIVE LETTERS FROM INTERESTED PARTIES STATING WHY THEY SHOULD BE NAMED 'THE NEIGHBORHOOD DOG OF THE YEAR'."
DON'T ASK **ME** TO WRITE A LETTER FOR YOU! I WOULDN'T RECOMMEND YOU FOR "DOG OF THE MINUTE"!
WHEN'S THE LAST TIME YOU HELPED AN OLD LADY ACROSS THE STREET, HUH?!
I'VE NEVER EVEN SEEN YOU PLAY FETCH! WHAT KIND OF DOG DOESN'T PLAY FETCH?
WHAAAH!
AND CRYING WON'T HELP!!

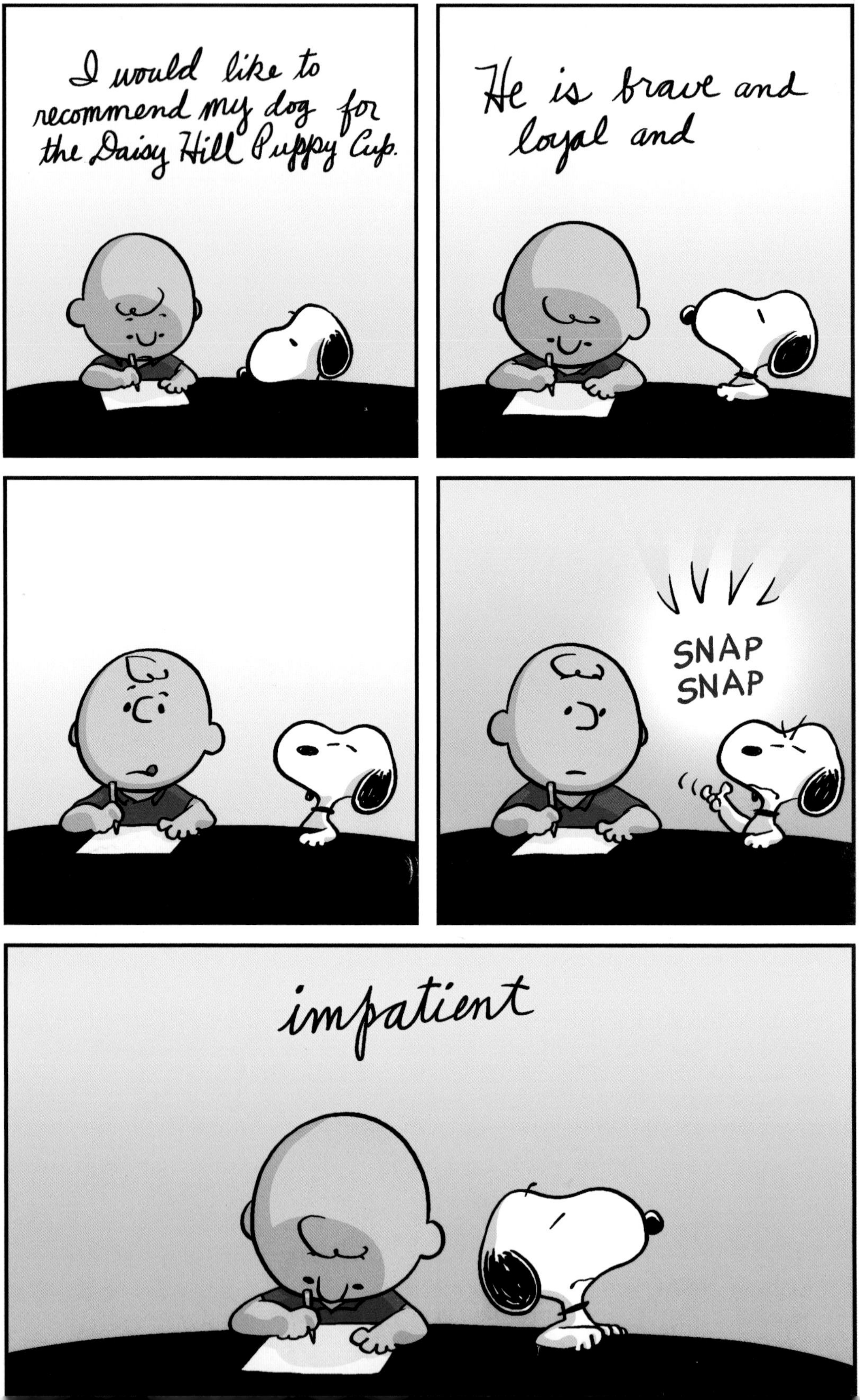
I would like to recommend my dog for the Daisy Hill Puppy Cup.
He is brave and loyal and
SNAP
SNAP
impatient

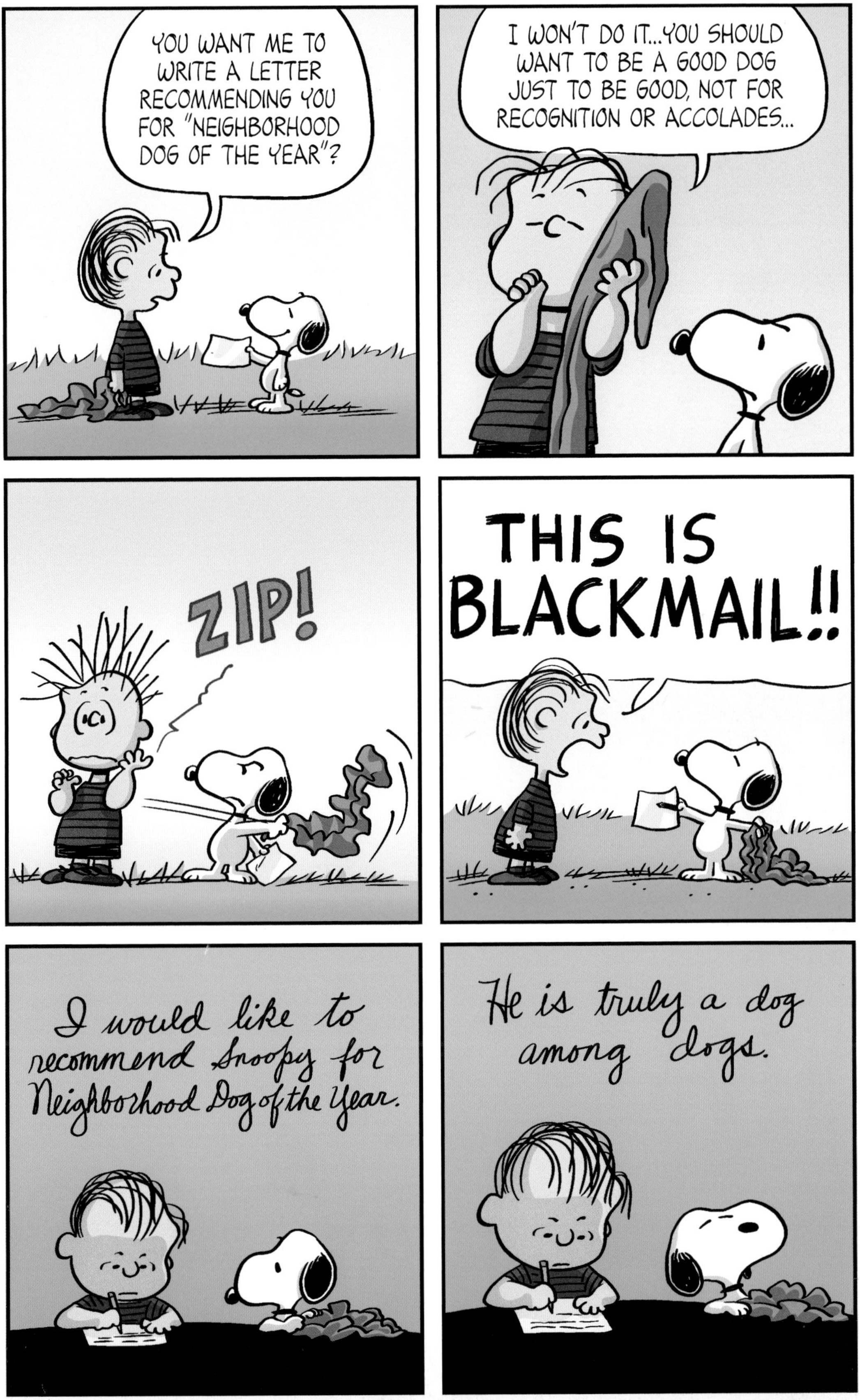
YOU WANT ME TO WRITE A LETTER RECOMMENDING YOU FOR "NEIGHBORHOOD DOG OF THE YEAR"?
I WON'T DO IT...YOU SHOULD WANT TO BE A GOOD DOG JUST TO BE GOOD, NOT FOR RECOGNITION OR ACCOLADES...
ZIP!
THIS IS BLACKMAIL!!
I would like to recommend Snoopy for Neighborhood Dog of the Year.
He is truly a dog among dogs.

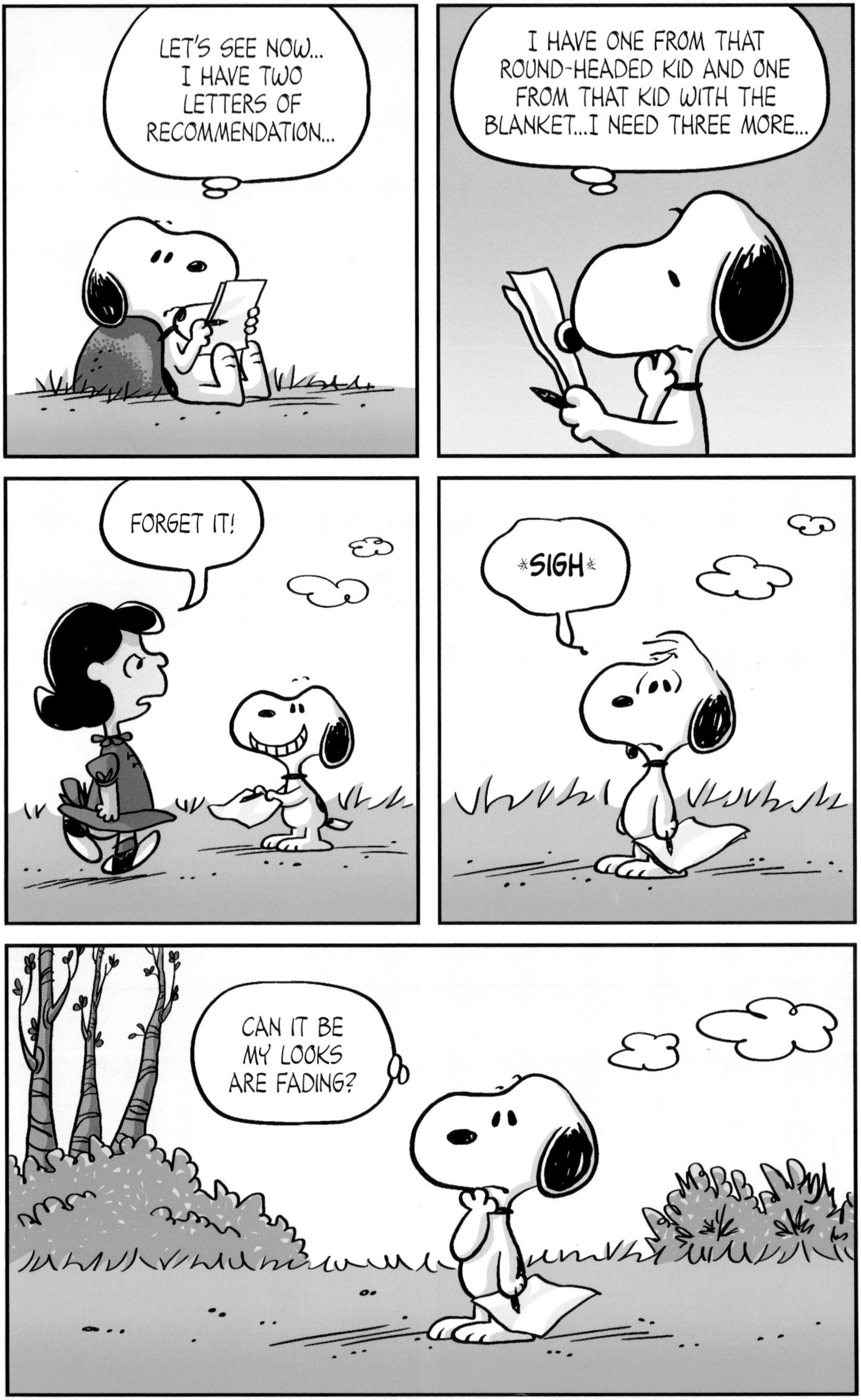
LET'S SEE NOW... I HAVE TWO LETTERS OF RECOMMENDATION...
I HAVE ONE FROM THAT ROUND-HEADED KID AND ONE FROM THAT KID WITH THE BLANKET...I NEED THREE MORE...
FORGET IT!
SIGH
CAN IT BE MY LOOKS ARE FADING?

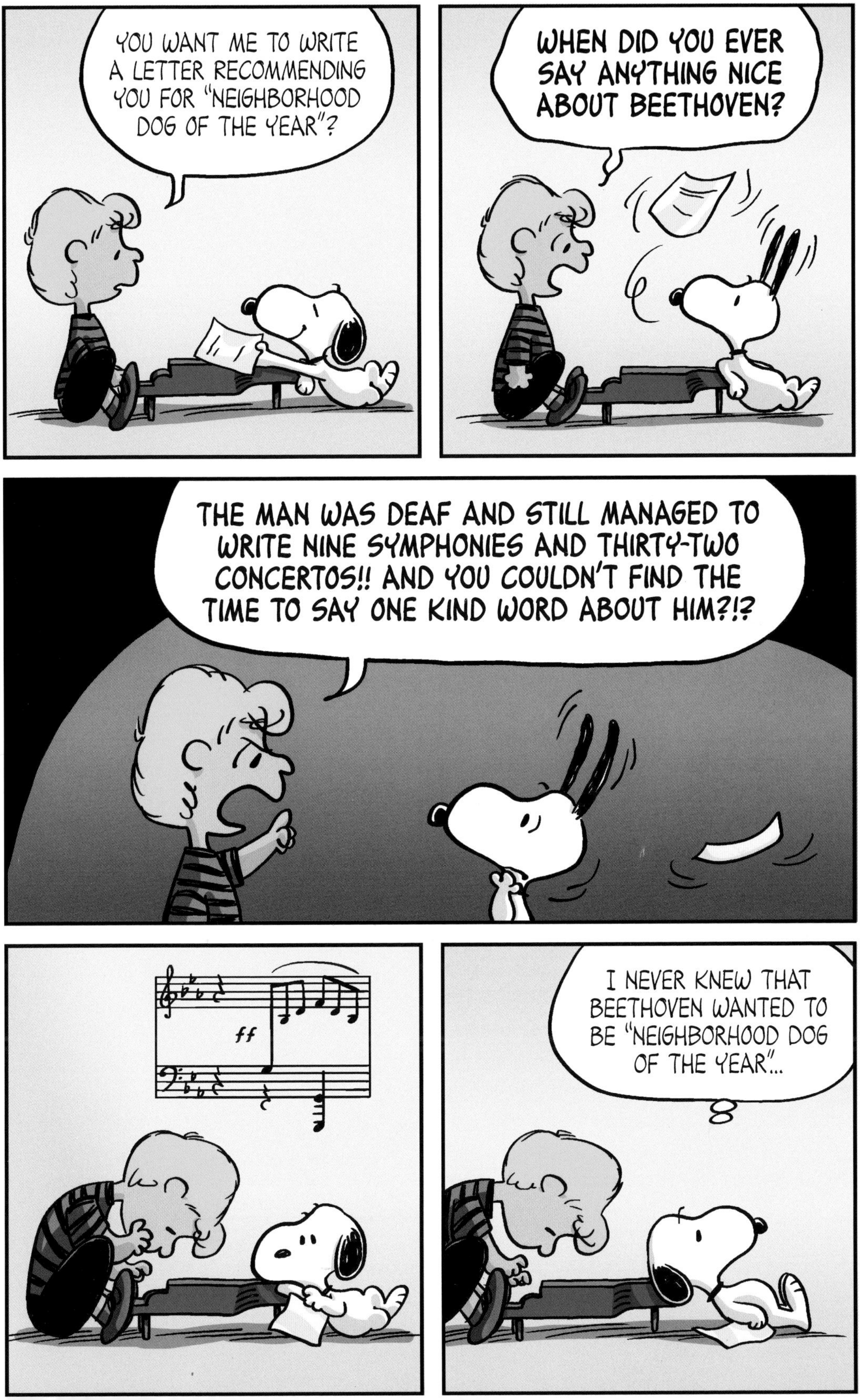
YOU WANT ME TO WRITE A LETTER RECOMMENDING YOU FOR "NEIGHBORHOOD DOG OF THE YEAR"?
WHEN DID YOU EVER SAY ANYTHING NICE ABOUT BEETHOVEN?
THE MAN WAS DEAF AND STILL MANAGED TO WRITE NINE SYMPHONIES AND THIRTY-TWO CONCERTOS!! AND YOU COULDN'T FIND THE TIME TO SAY ONE KIND WORD ABOUT HIM?!?
ff
I NEVER KNEW THAT BEETHOVEN WANTED TO BE "NEIGHBORHOOD DOG OF THE YEAR"...

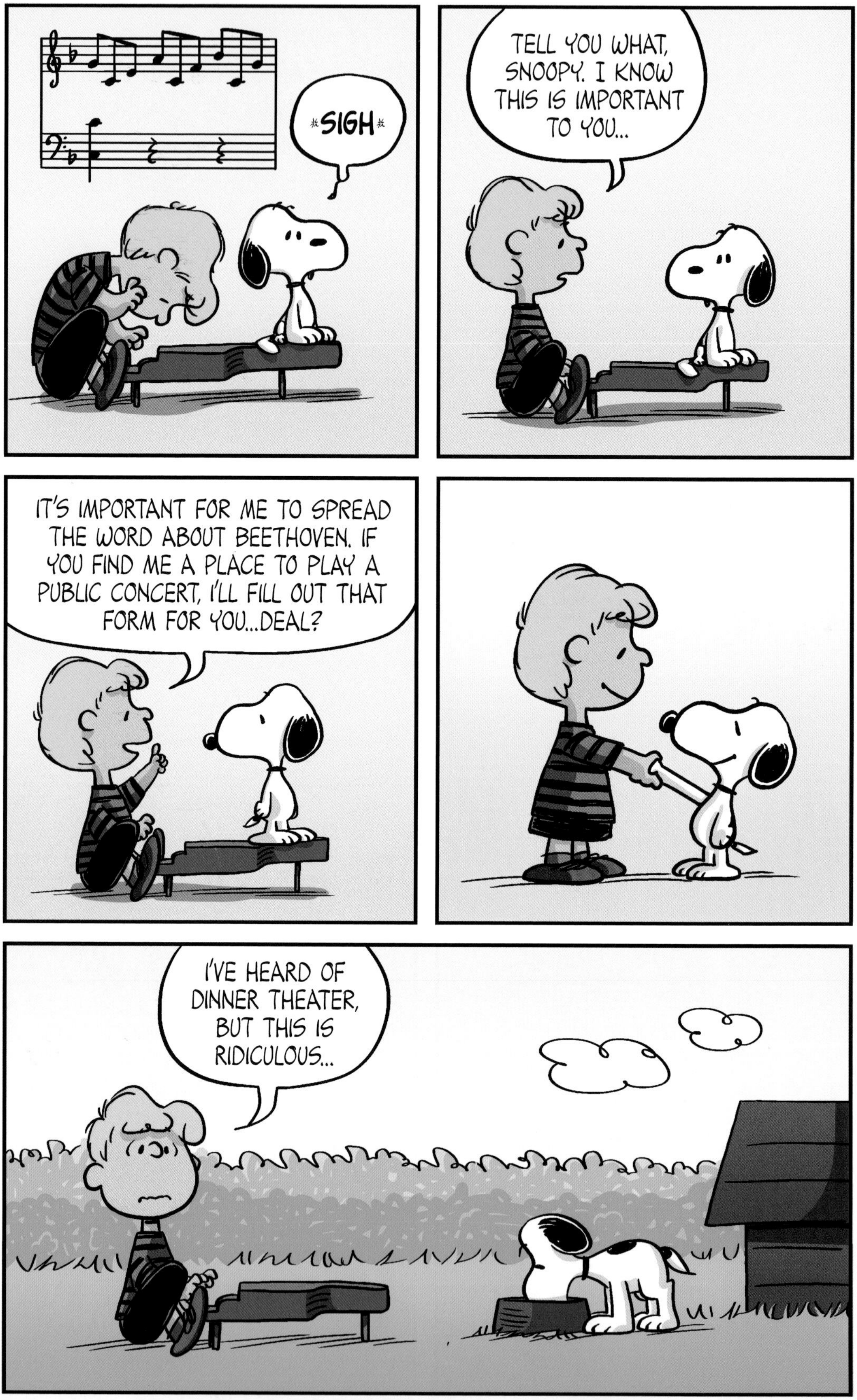
SIGH
TELL YOU WHAT, SNOOPY. I KNOW THIS IS IMPORTANT TO YOU...
IT'S IMPORTANT FOR ME TO SPREAD THE WORD ABOUT BEETHOVEN. IF YOU FIND ME A PLACE TO PLAY A PUBLIC CONCERT, I'LL FILL OUT THAT FORM FOR YOU...DEAL?
I'VE HEARD OF DINNER THEATER, BUT THIS IS RIDICULOUS...

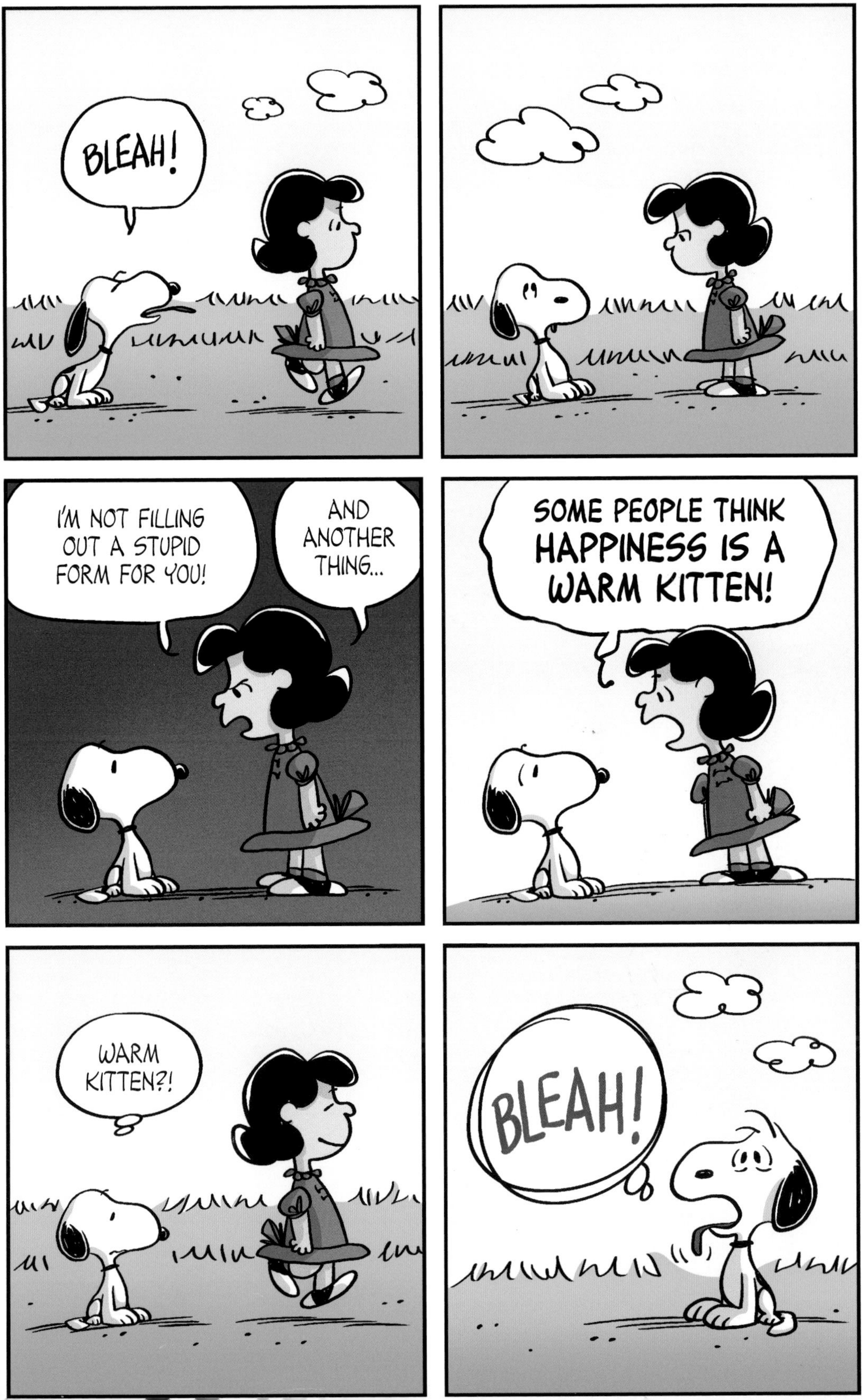
BLEAH!
I'M NOT FILLING OUT A STUPID FORM FOR YOU!
AND ANOTHER THING...
SOME PEOPLE THINK HAPPINESS IS A WARM KITTEN!
WARM KITTEN?!
BLEAH!

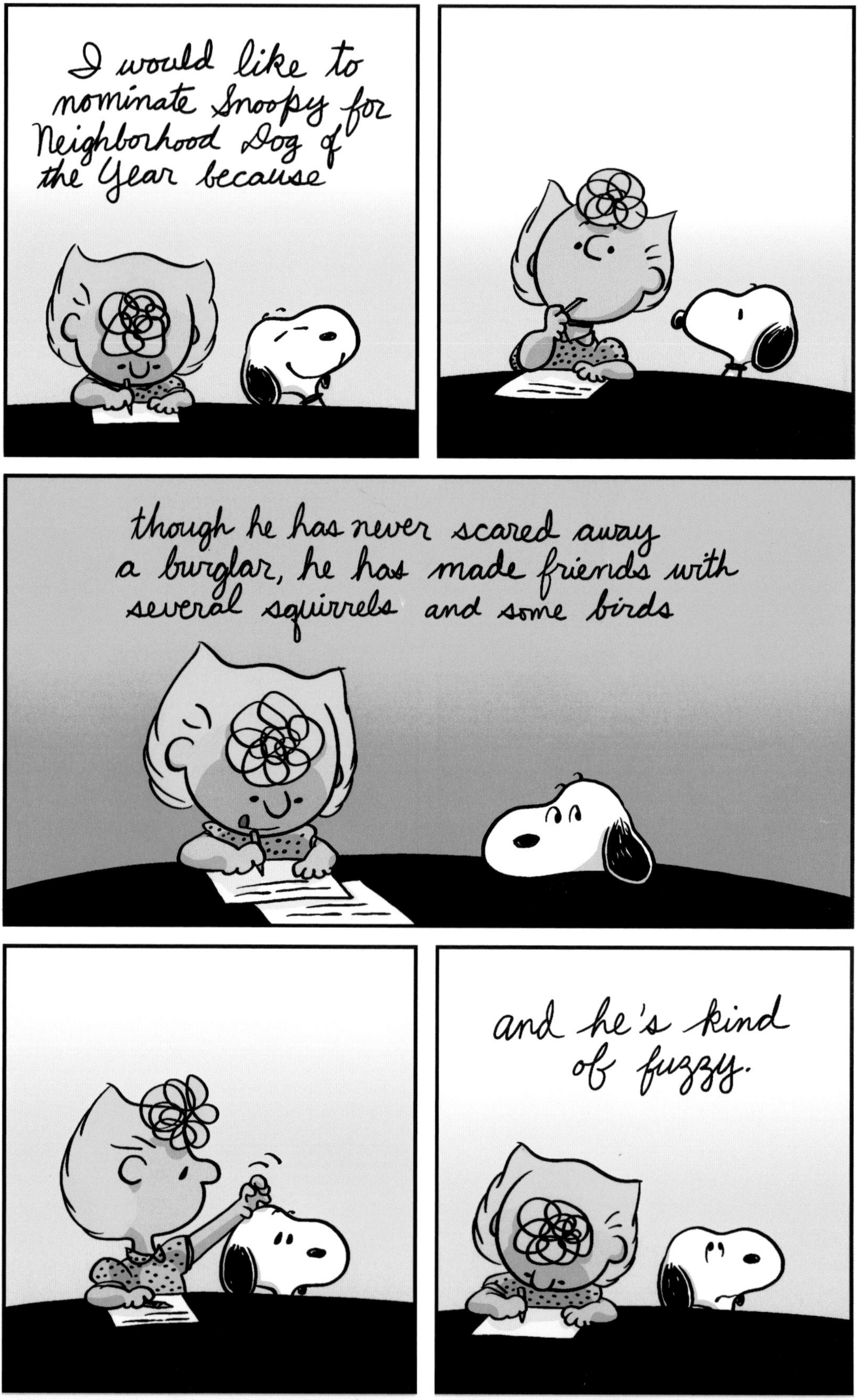
I would like to nominate Snoopy for Neighborhood Dog of the Year because
though he has never scared away a burglar, he has made friends with several squirrels and some birds
and he's kind of fuzzy.

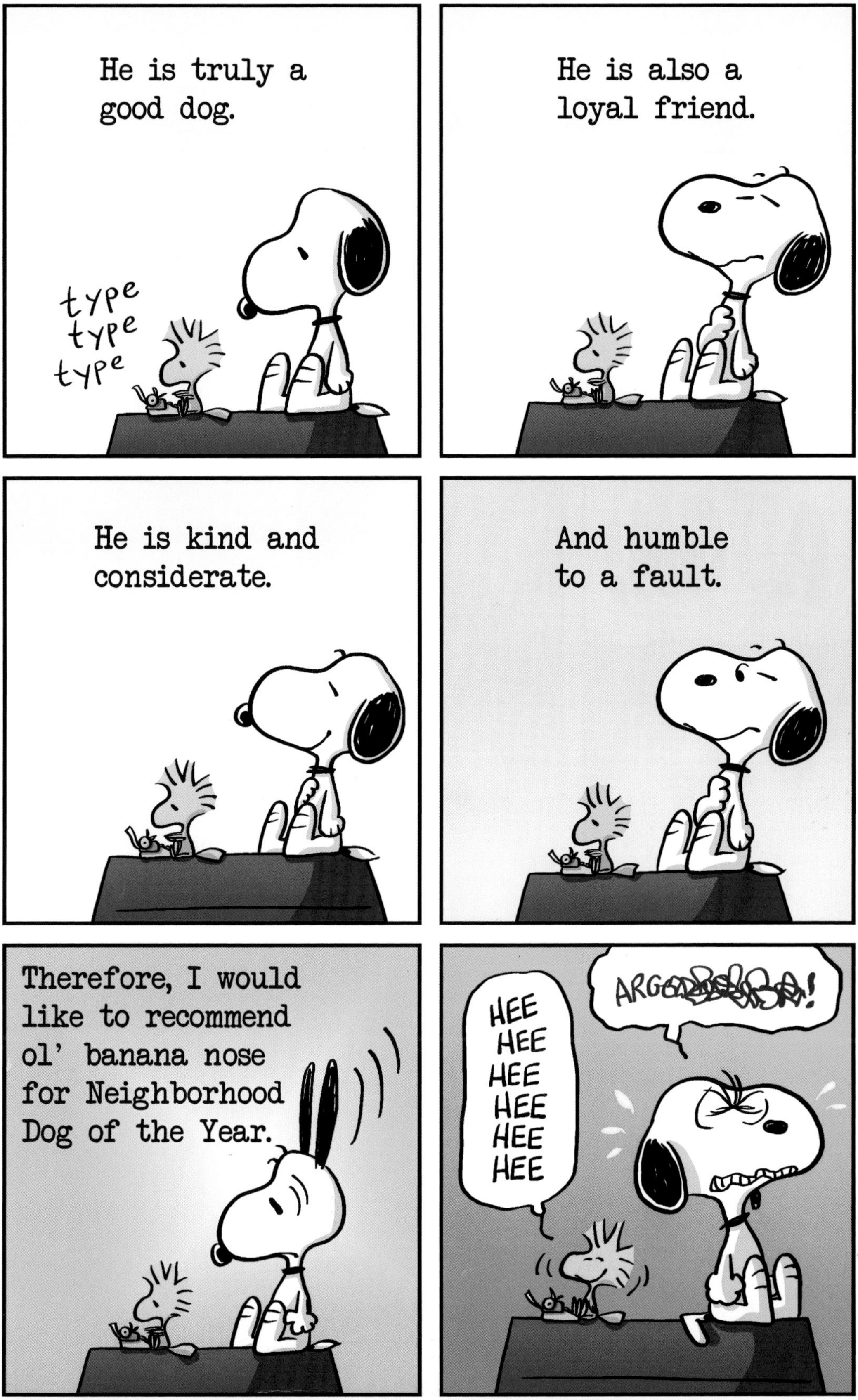
He is truly a good dog.
type type type
He is also a loyal friend.
He is kind and considerate.
And humble to a fault.
Therefore, I would like to recommend ol' banana nose for Neighborhood Dog of the Year.
HEE HEE HEE HEE HEE HEE

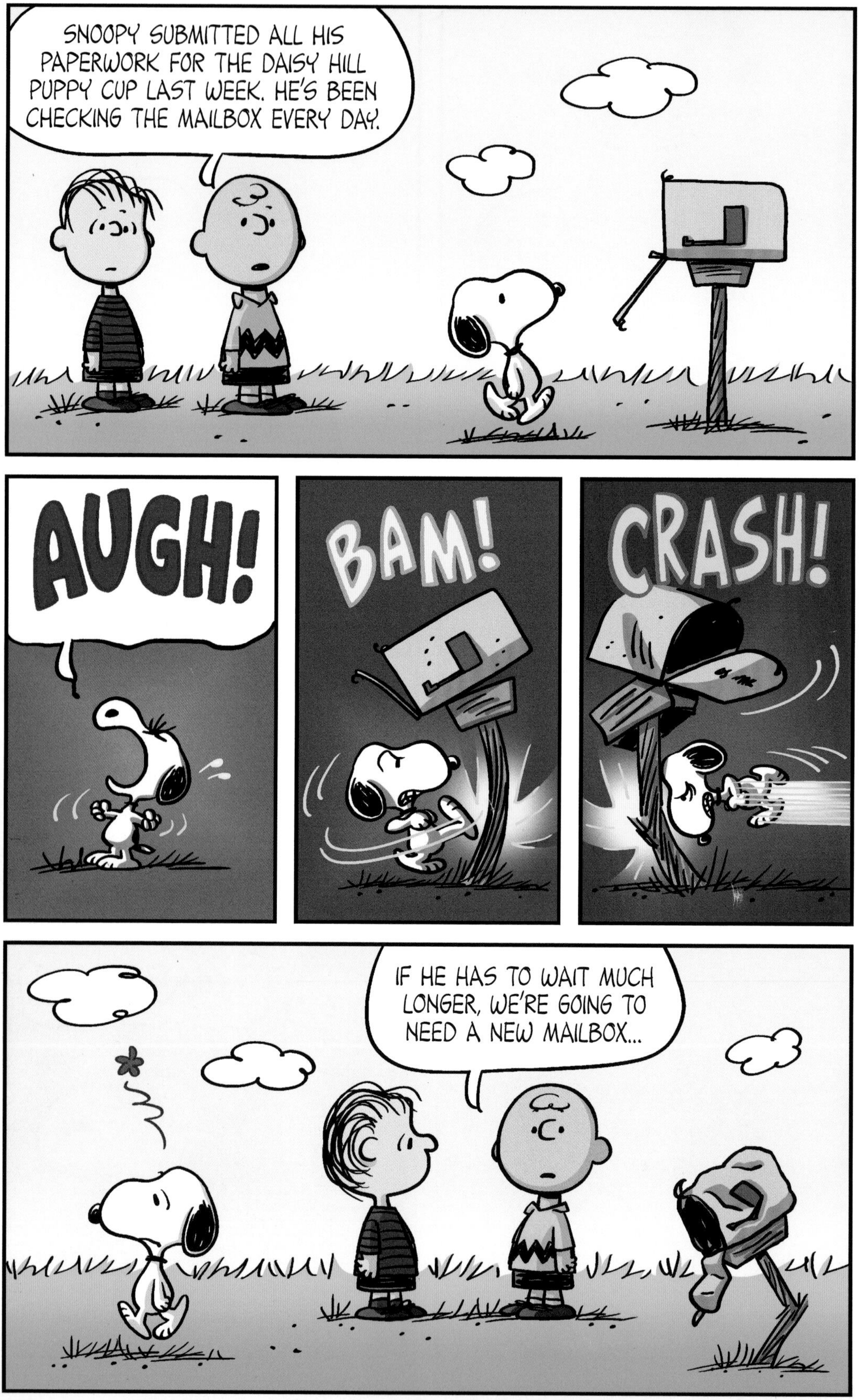
SNOOPY SUBMITTED ALL HIS PAPERWORK FOR THE DAISY HILL PUPPY CUP LAST WEEK. HE'S BEEN CHECKING THE MAILBOX EVERY DAY.
AUGH!
BAM!
CRASH!
IF HE HAS TO WAIT MUCH LONGER, WE'RE GOING TO NEED A NEW MAILBOX...

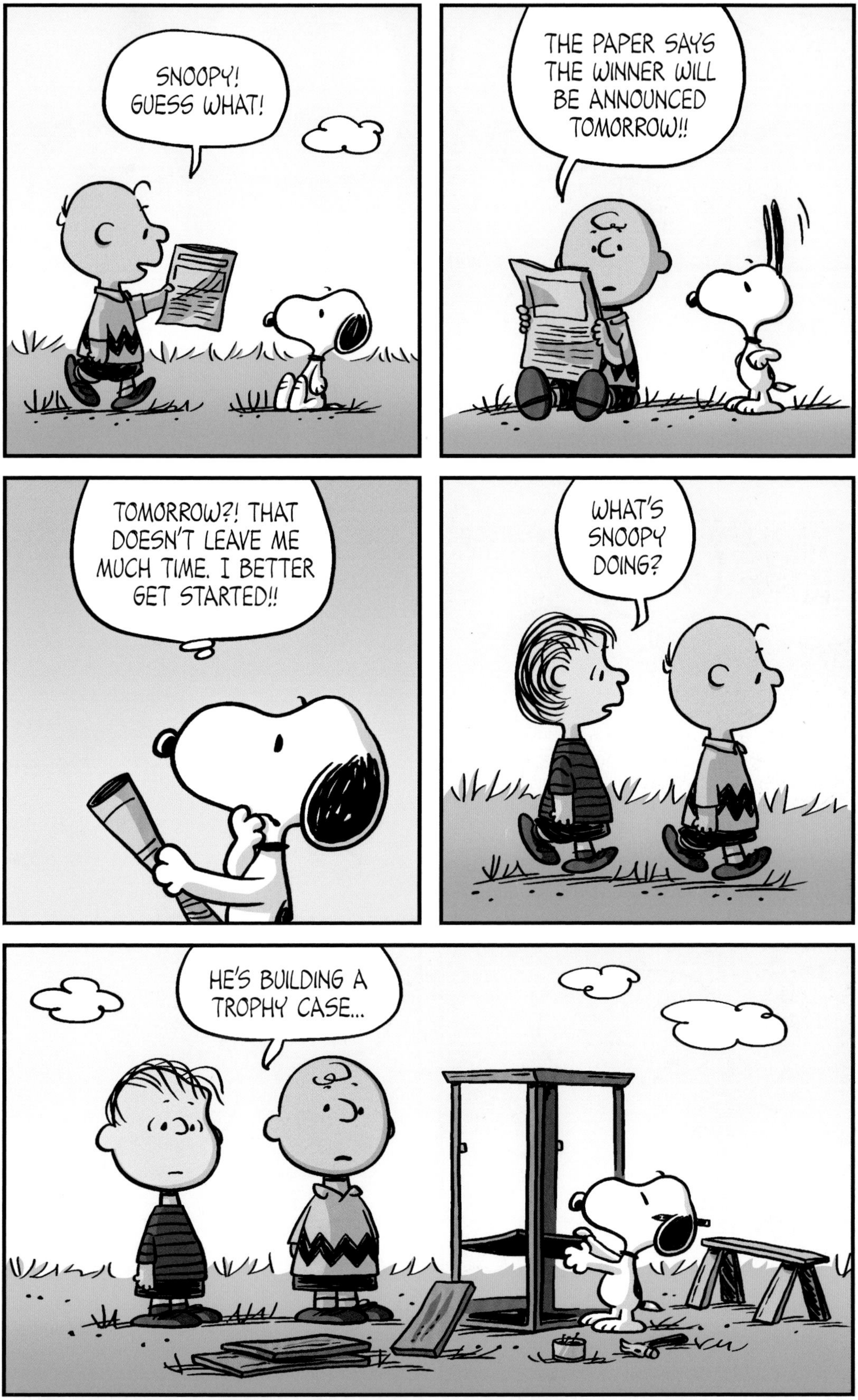
SNOOPY! GUESS WHAT!
THE PAPER SAYS THE WINNER WILL BE ANNOUNCED TOMORROW!!
TOMORROW?! THAT DOESN'T LEAVE ME MUCH TIME. I BETTER GET STARTED!!
WHAT'S SNOOPY DOING?
HE'S BUILDING A TROPHY CASE...

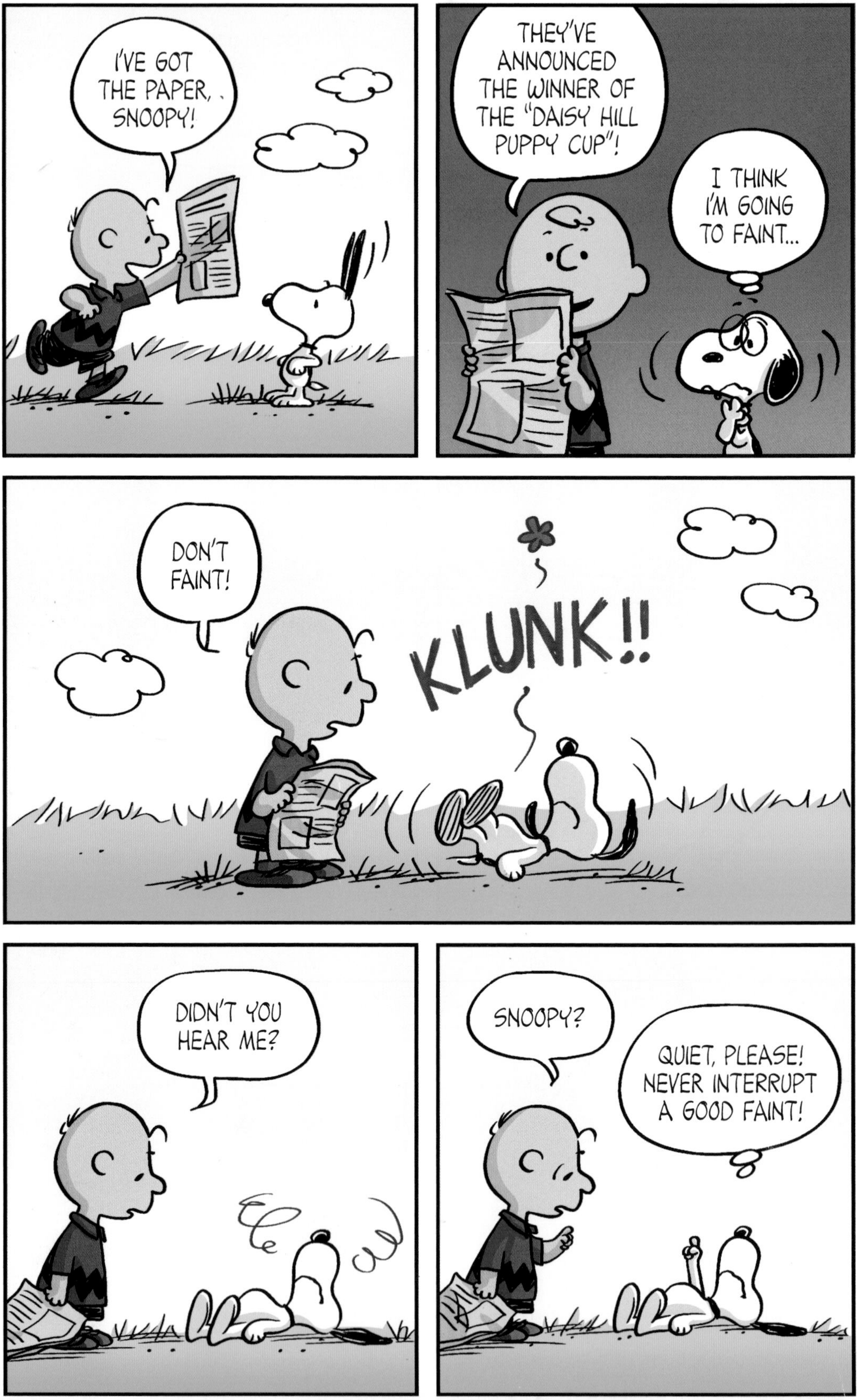
I'VE GOT THE PAPER, SNOOPY!
THEY'VE ANNOUNCED THE WINNER OF THE "DAISY HILL PUPPY CUP"!
I THINK I'M GOING TO FAINT...
DON'T FAINT!
KLUNK!!
DIDN'T YOU HEAR ME?
SNOOPY?
QUIET, PLEASE! NEVER INTERRUPT A GOOD FAINT!

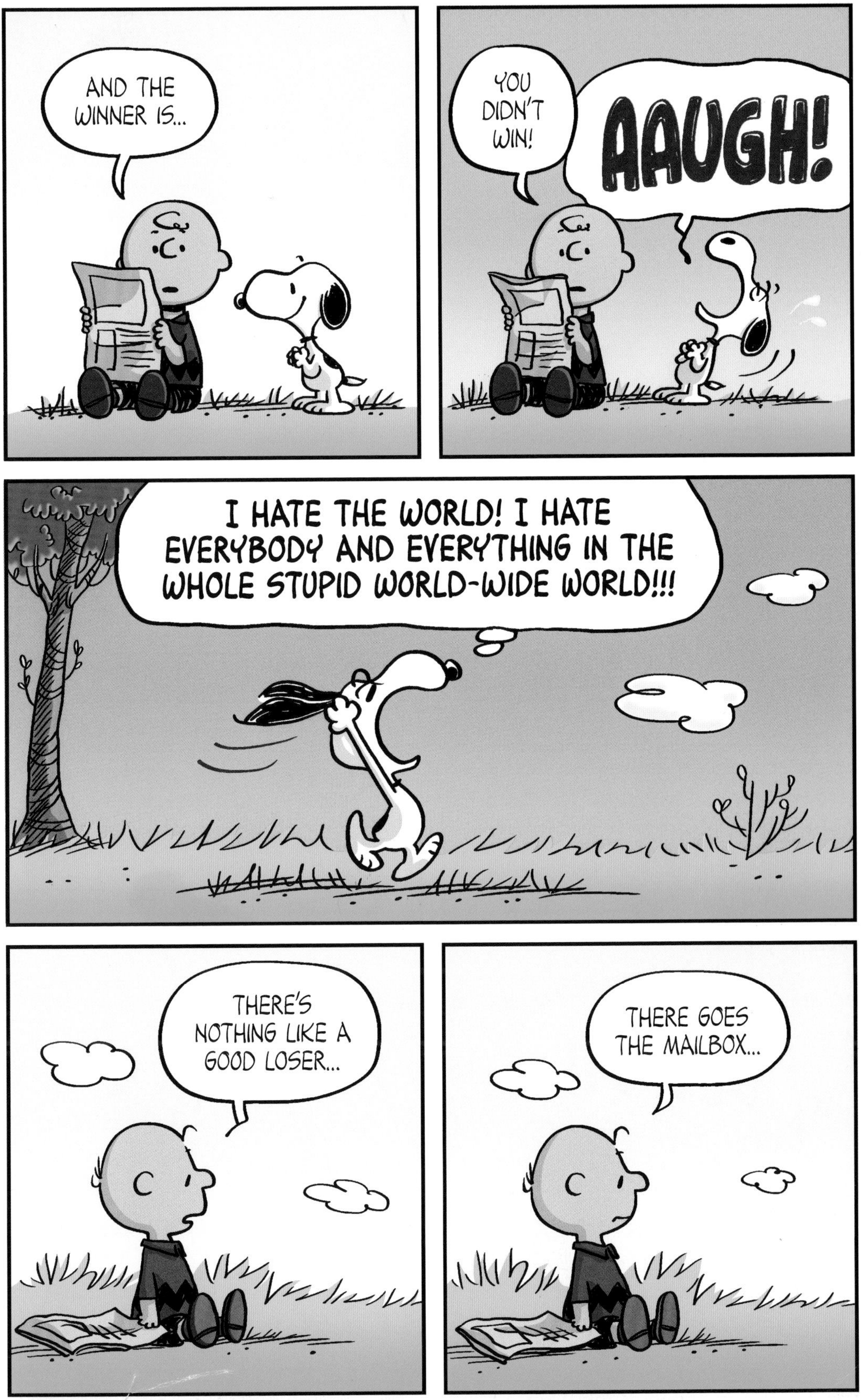
AND THE WINNER IS...
YOU DIDN'T WIN!
AAUGH!
I HATE THE WORLD! I HATE EVERYBODY AND EVERYTHING IN THE WHOLE STUPID WORLD-WIDE WORLD!!!
THERE'S NOTHING LIKE A GOOD LOSER...
THERE GOES THE MAILBOX...

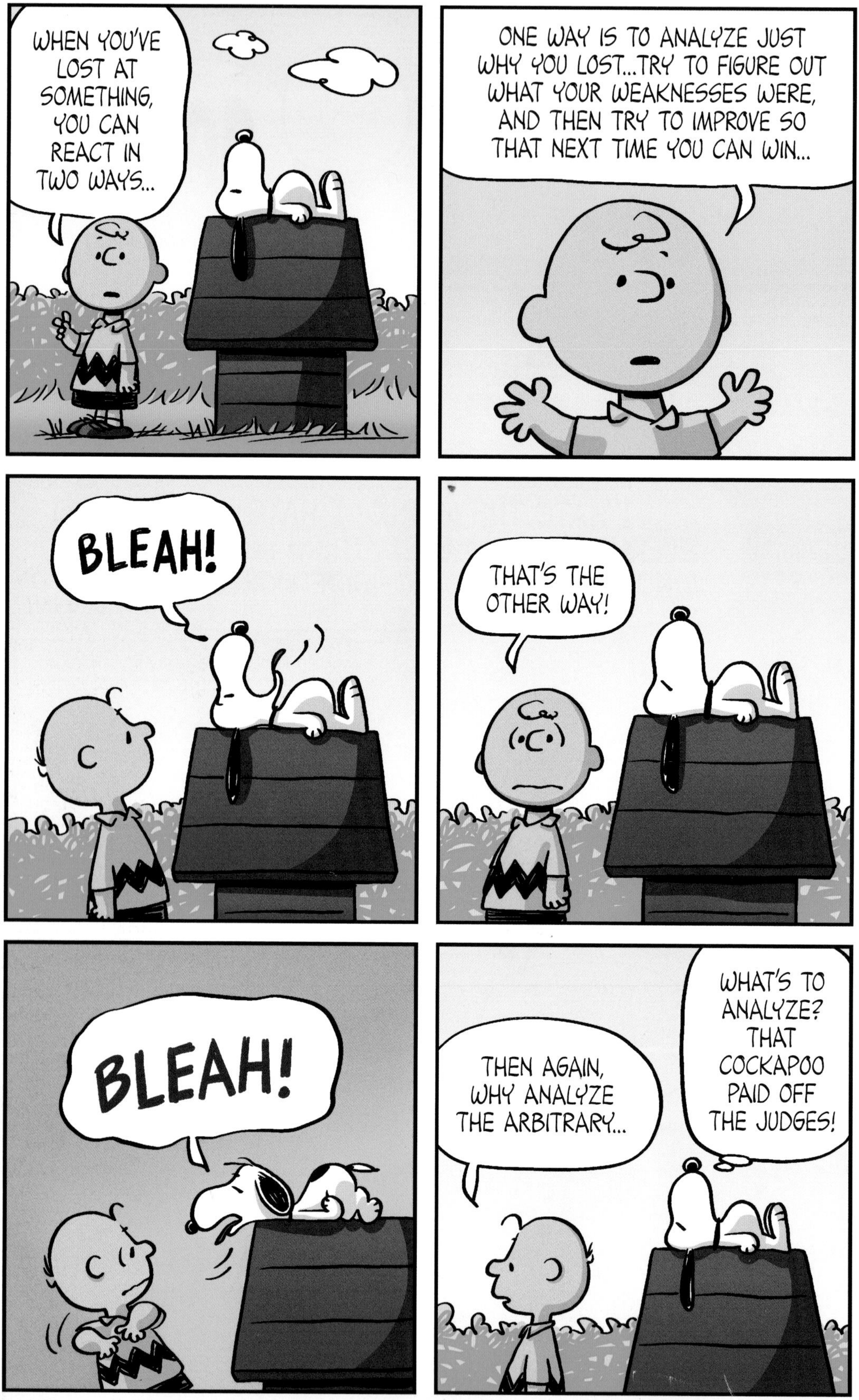
WHEN YOU'VE LOST AT SOMETHING, YOU CAN REACT IN TWO WAYS...
ONE WAY IS TO ANALYZE JUST WHY YOU LOST...TRY TO FIGURE OUT WHAT YOUR WEAKNESSES WERE, AND THEN TRY TO IMPROVE SO THAT NEXT TIME YOU CAN WIN...
BLEAH!
THAT'S THE OTHER WAY!
BLEAH!
THEN AGAIN, WHY ANALYZE THE ARBITRARY...
WHAT'S TO ANALYZE? THAT COCKAPOO PAID OFF THE JUDGES!

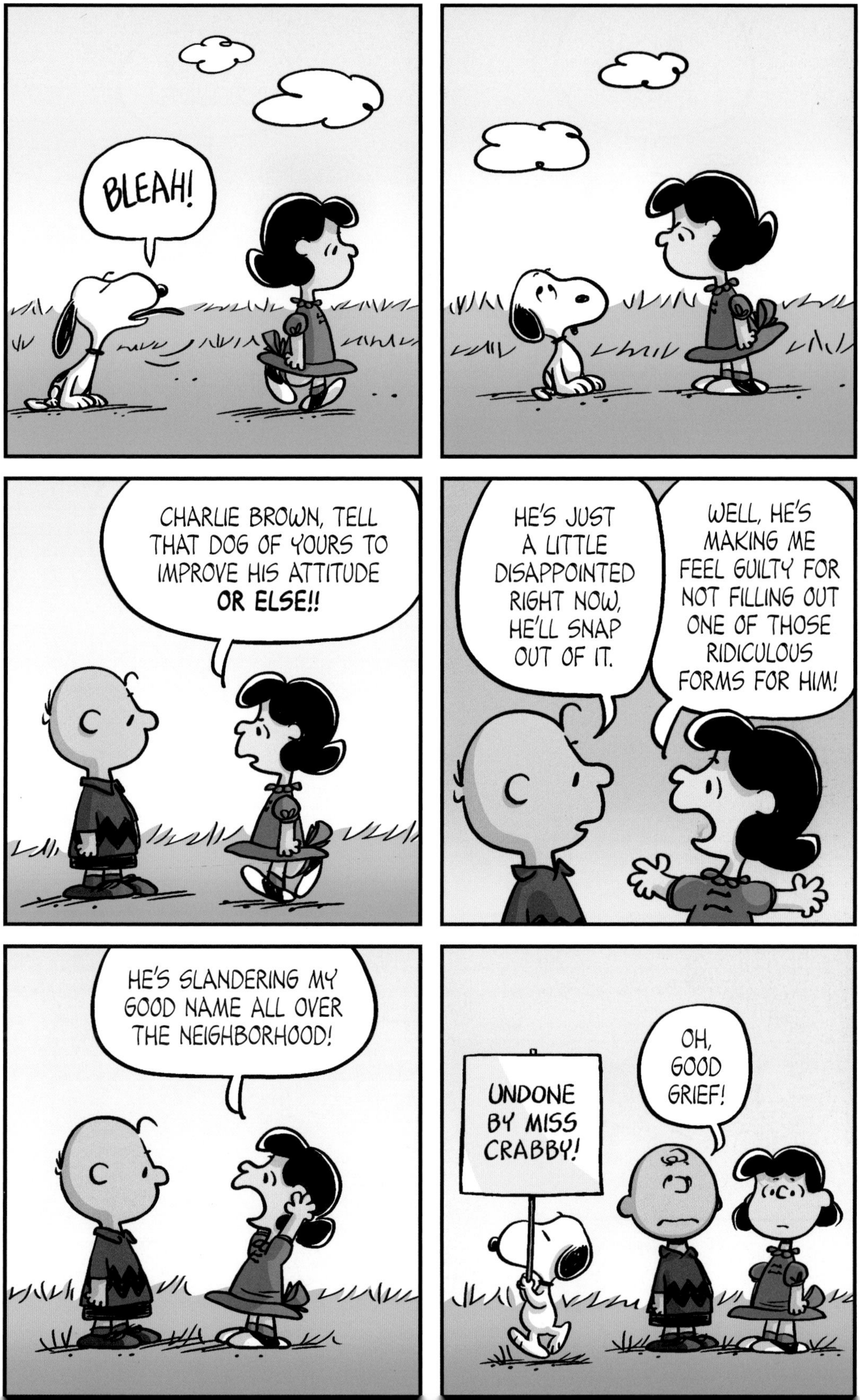
BLEAH!
CHARLIE BROWN, TELL THAT DOG OF YOURS TO IMPROVE HIS ATTITUDE **OR ELSE!!**
HE'S JUST A LITTLE DISAPPOINTED RIGHT NOW, HE'LL SNAP OUT OF IT.
WELL, HE'S MAKING ME FEEL GUILTY FOR NOT FILLING OUT ONE OF THOSE RIDICULOUS FORMS FOR HIM!
HE'S SLANDERING MY GOOD NAME ALL OVER THE NEIGHBORHOOD!
UNDONE BY MISS CRABBY!
OH, GOOD GRIEF!

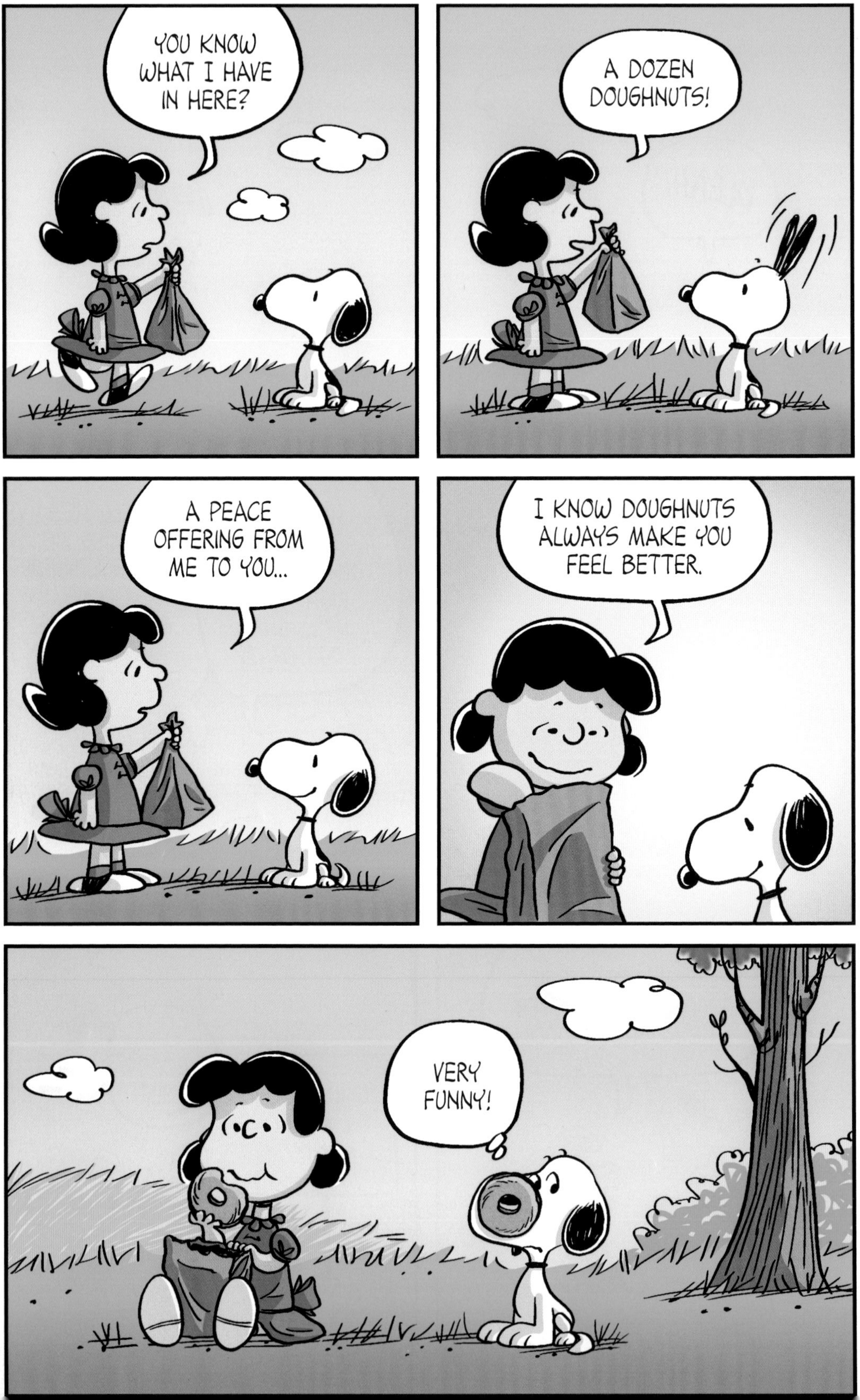
YOU KNOW WHAT I HAVE IN HERE?
A DOZEN DOUGHNUTS!
A PEACE OFFERING FROM ME TO YOU...
I KNOW DOUGHNUTS ALWAYS MAKE YOU FEEL BETTER.
VERY FUNNY!

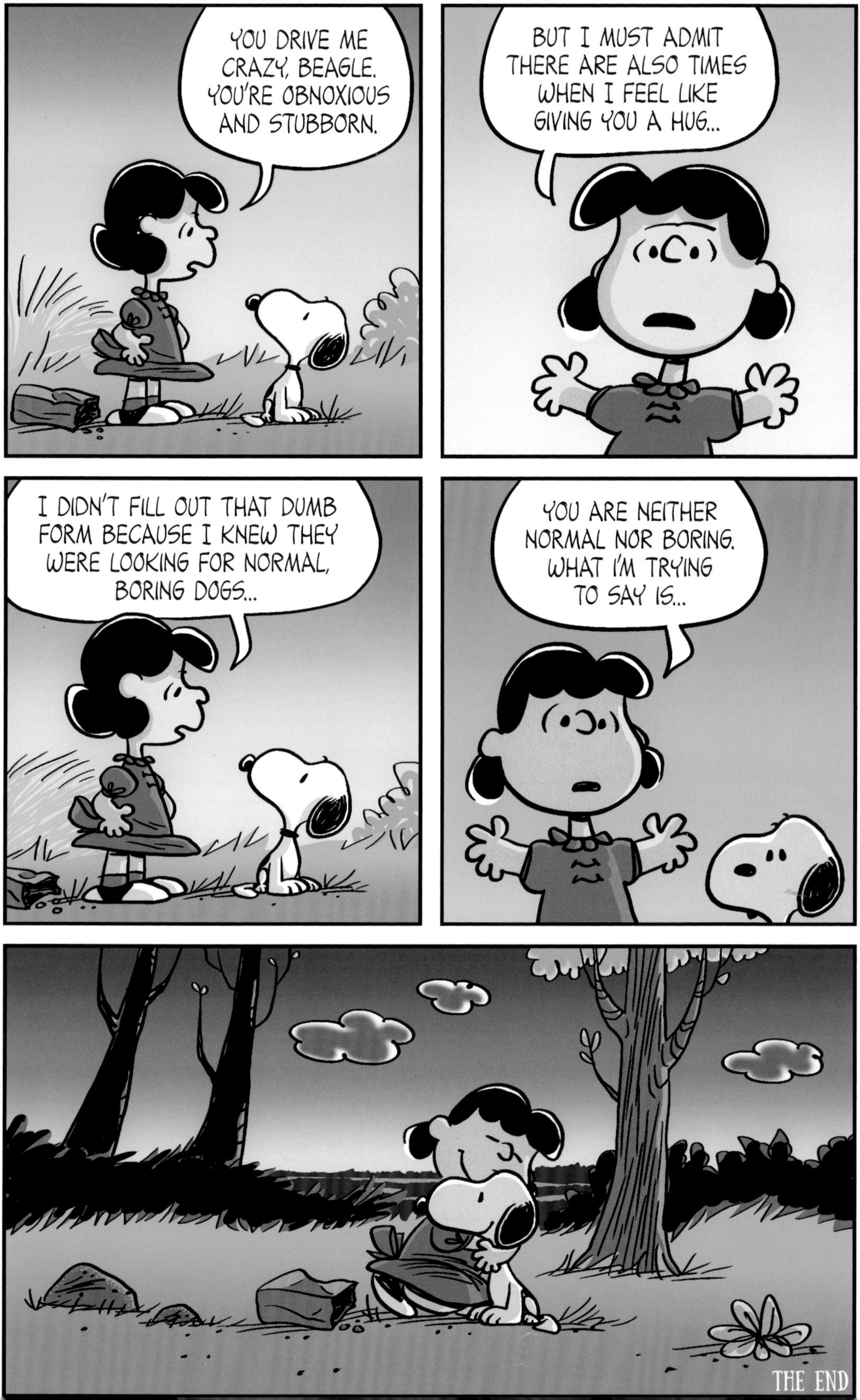
YOU DRIVE ME CRAZY, BEAGLE. YOU'RE OBNOXIOUS AND STUBBORN.
BUT I MUST ADMIT THERE ARE ALSO TIMES WHEN I FEEL LIKE GIVING YOU A HUG...
I DIDN'T FILL OUT THAT DUMB FORM BECAUSE I KNEW THEY WERE LOOKING FOR NORMAL, BORING DOGS...
YOU ARE NEITHER NORMAL NOR BORING. WHAT I'M TRYING TO SAY IS...
THE END

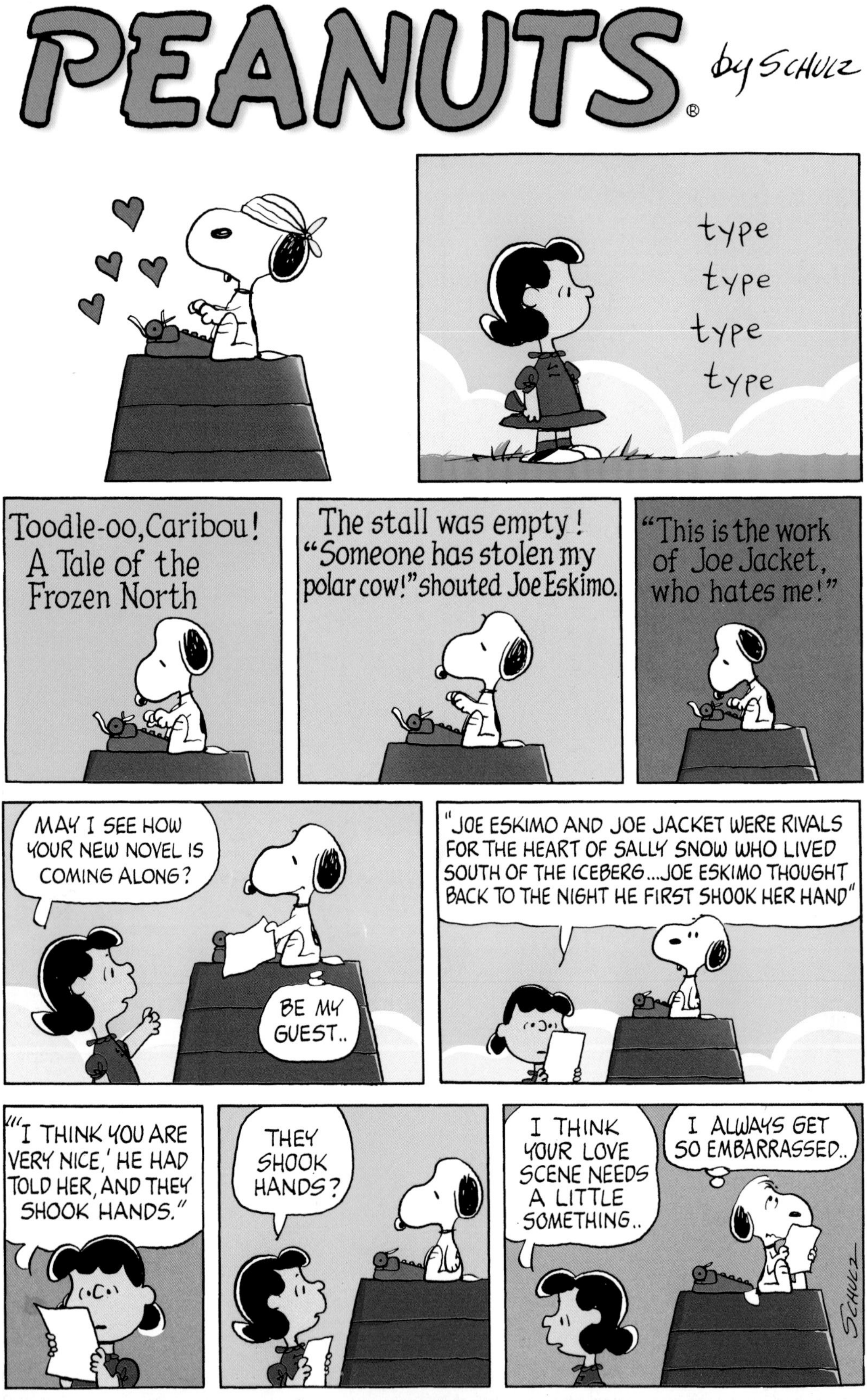
PEANUTS
by SCHULZ
type
type
type
type
Toodle-oo, Caribou! A Tale of the Frozen North
The stall was empty! "Someone has stolen my polar cow!" shouted Joe Eskimo.
"This is the work of Joe Jacket, who hates me!"
MAY I SEE HOW YOUR NEW NOVEL IS COMING ALONG?
BE MY GUEST..
"JOE ESKIMO AND JOE JACKET WERE RIVALS FOR THE HEART OF SALLY SNOW WHO LIVED SOUTH OF THE ICEBERG...JOE ESKIMO THOUGHT BACK TO THE NIGHT HE FIRST SHOOK HER HAND"
"'I THINK YOU ARE VERY NICE,' HE HAD TOLD HER, AND THEY SHOOK HANDS."
THEY SHOOK HANDS?
I THINK YOUR LOVE SCENE NEEDS A LITTLE SOMETHING..
I ALWAYS GET SO EMBARRASSED..
SCHULZ

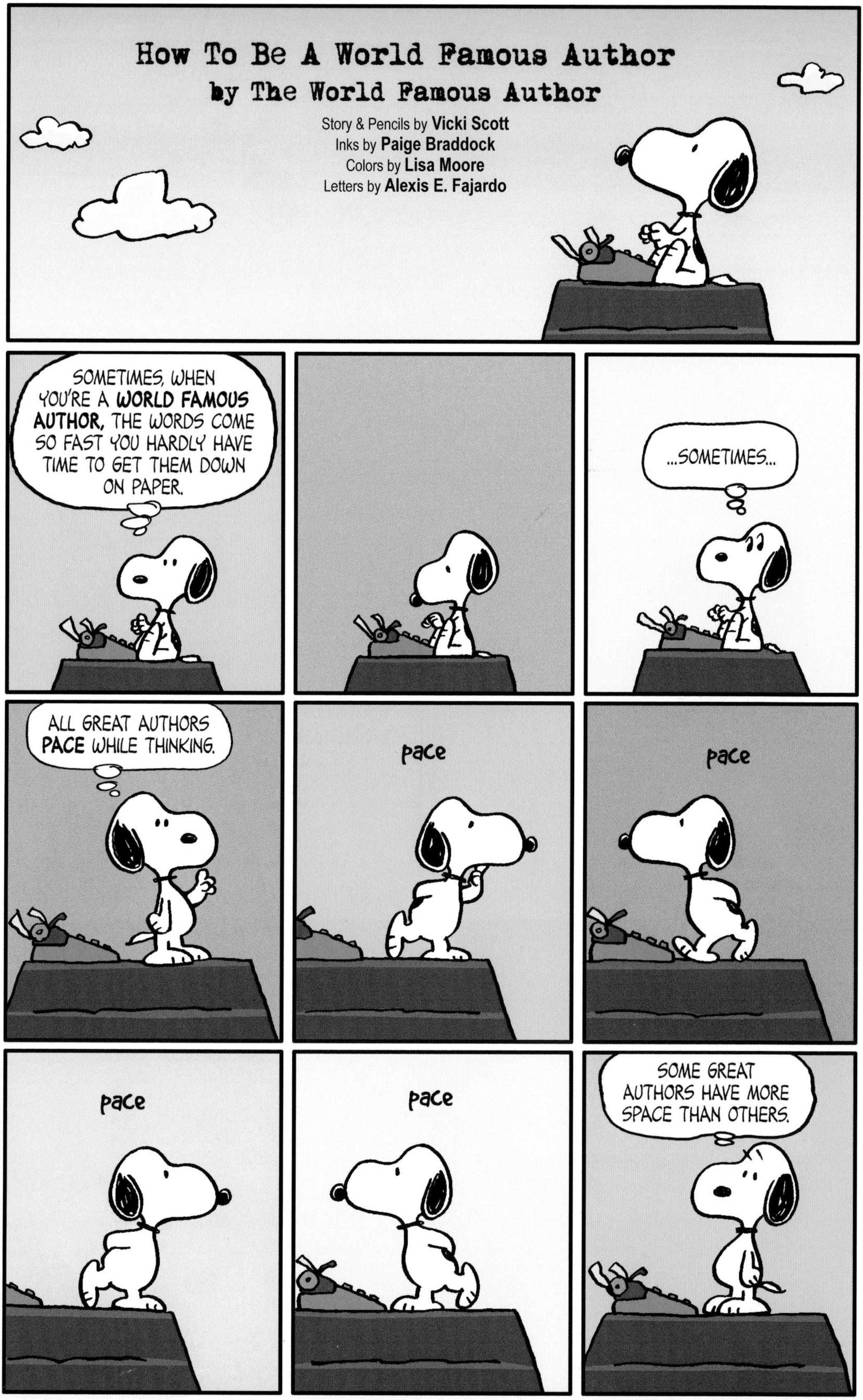
How To Be A World Famous Author
by The World Famous Author
Story & Pencils by Vicki Scott
Inks by Paige Braddock
Colors by Lisa Moore
Letters by Alexis E. Fajardo
SOMETIMES, WHEN YOU'RE A WORLD FAMOUS AUTHOR, THE WORDS COME SO FAST YOU HARDLY HAVE TIME TO GET THEM DOWN ON PAPER.
...SOMETIMES...
ALL GREAT AUTHORS PACE WHILE THINKING.
pace
pace
pace
pace
SOME GREAT AUTHORS HAVE MORE SPACE THAN OTHERS.

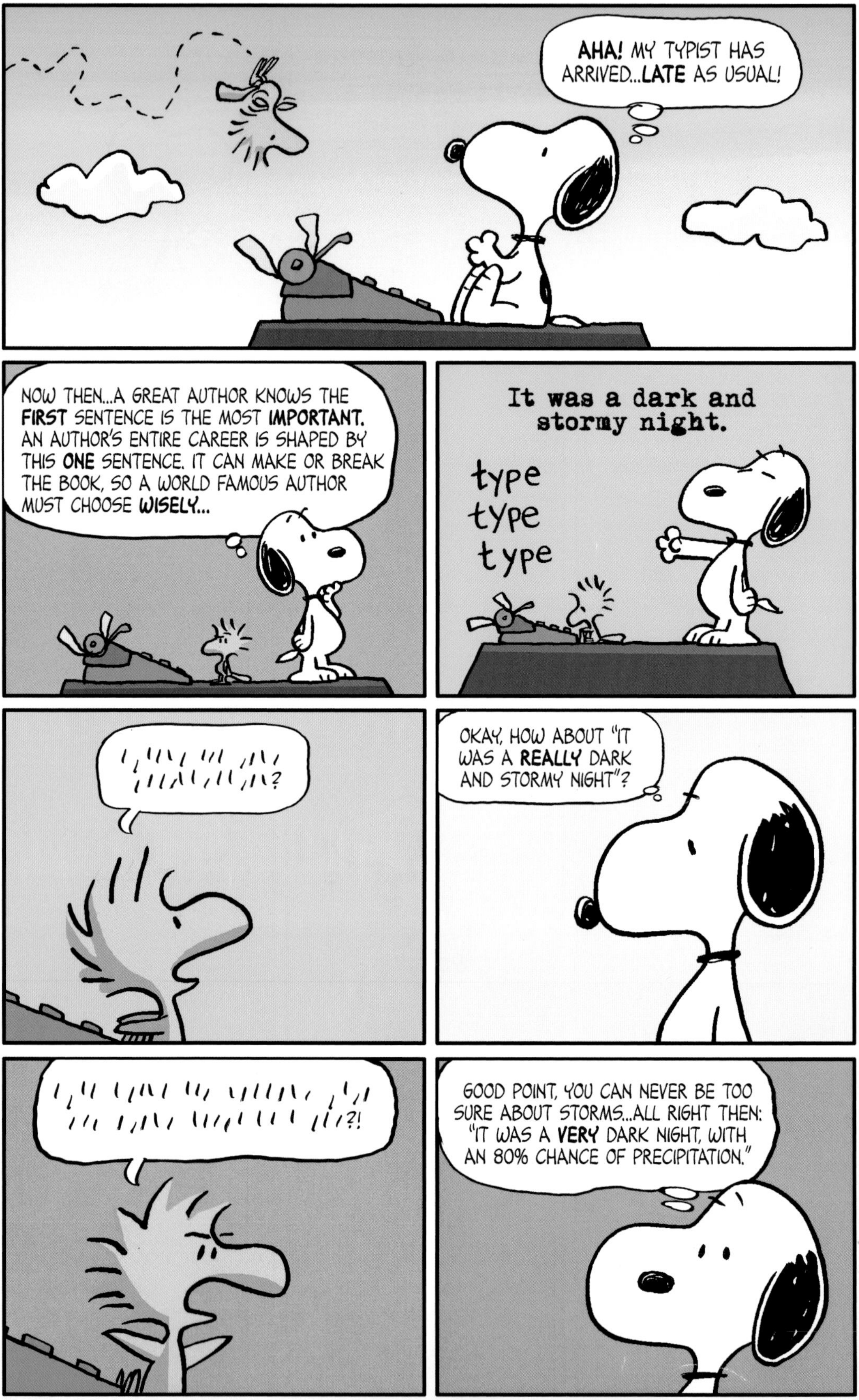
AHA! MY TYPIST HAS ARRIVED...LATE AS USUAL!
NOW THEN...A GREAT AUTHOR KNOWS THE FIRST SENTENCE IS THE MOST IMPORTANT. AN AUTHOR'S ENTIRE CAREER IS SHAPED BY THIS ONE SENTENCE. IT CAN MAKE OR BREAK THE BOOK, SO A WORLD FAMOUS AUTHOR MUST CHOOSE WISELY...
It was a dark and stormy night.
type
type
type
OKAY, HOW ABOUT "IT WAS A REALLY DARK AND STORMY NIGHT"?
GOOD POINT, YOU CAN NEVER BE TOO SURE ABOUT STORMS...ALL RIGHT THEN: "IT WAS A VERY DARK NIGHT, WITH AN 80% CHANCE OF PRECIPITATION."

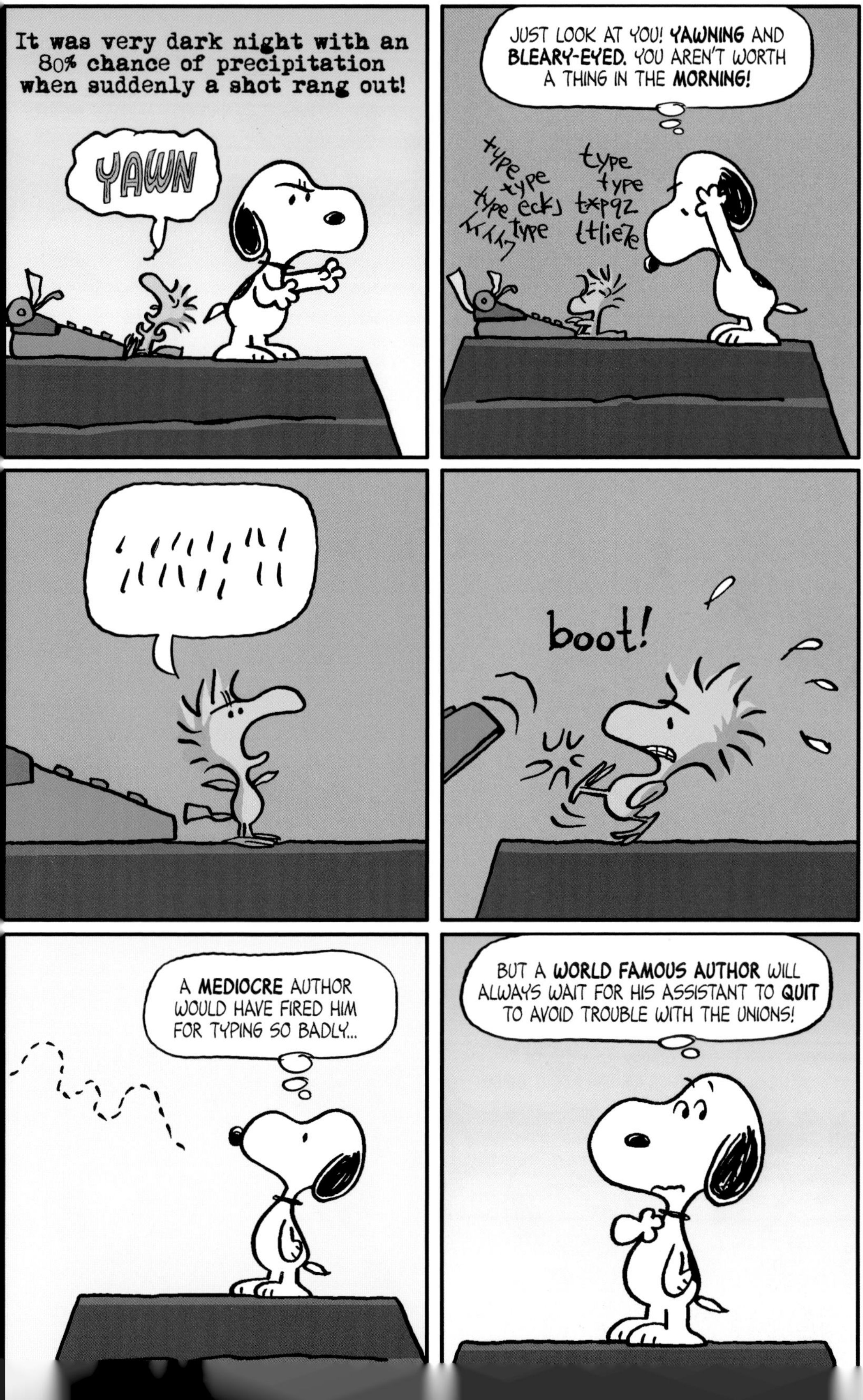
It was very dark night with an 80% chance of precipitation when suddenly a shot rang out!
YAWN
JUST LOOK AT YOU! YAWNING AND BLEARY-EYED. YOU AREN'T WORTH A THING IN THE MORNING!
boot!
A MEDIOCRE AUTHOR WOULD HAVE FIRED HIM FOR TYPING SO BADLY...
BUT A WORLD FAMOUS AUTHOR WILL ALWAYS WAIT FOR HIS ASSISTANT TO QUIT TO AVOID TROUBLE WITH THE UNIONS!

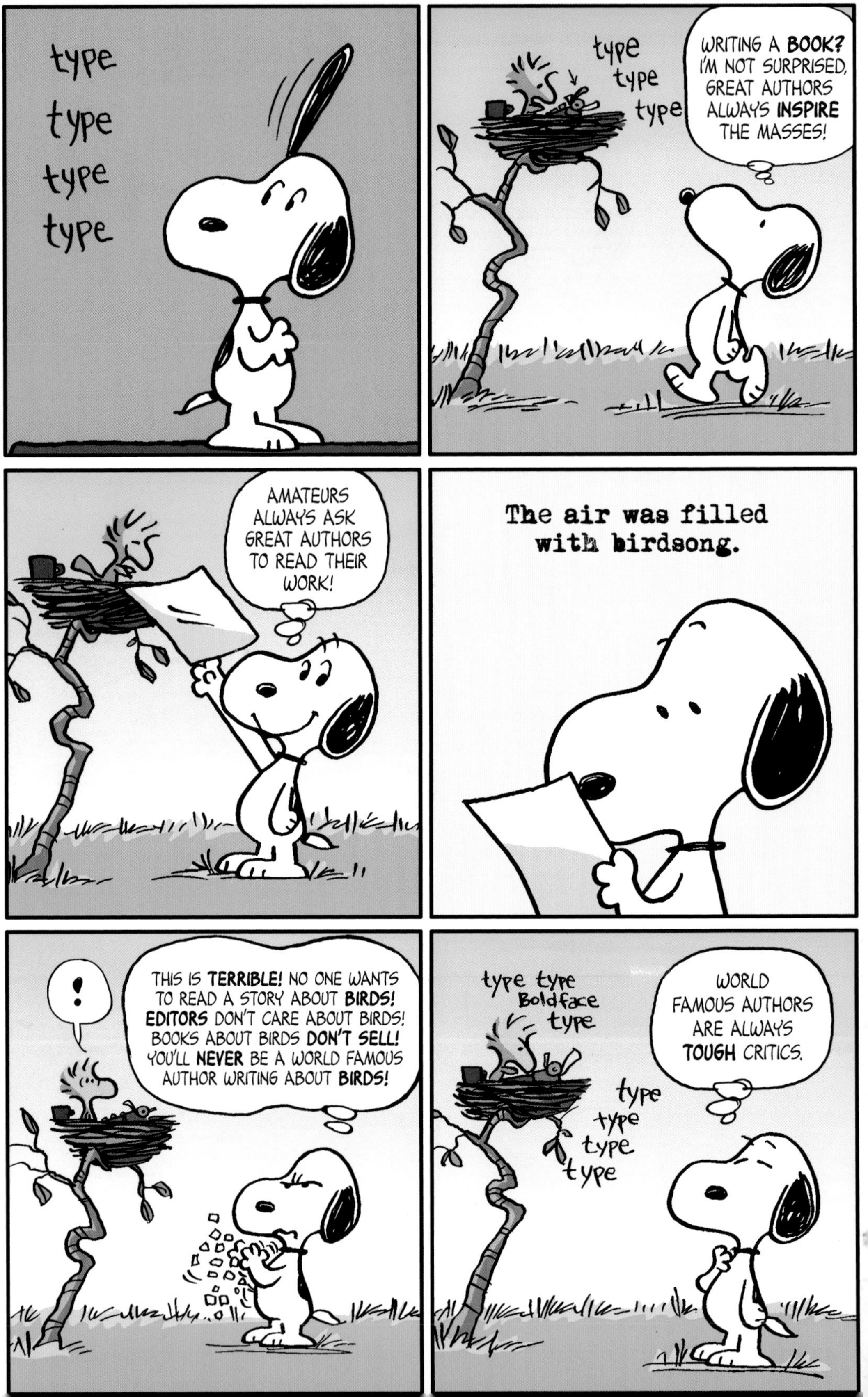
type
type
type
type
type
type
type
WRITING A BOOK? I'M NOT SURPRISED, GREAT AUTHORS ALWAYS INSPIRE THE MASSES!
AMATEURS ALWAYS ASK GREAT AUTHORS TO READ THEIR WORK!
The air was filled with birdsong.
!
THIS IS TERRIBLE! NO ONE WANTS TO READ A STORY ABOUT BIRDS! EDITORS DON'T CARE ABOUT BIRDS! BOOKS ABOUT BIRDS DON'T SELL! YOU'LL NEVER BE A WORLD FAMOUS AUTHOR WRITING ABOUT BIRDS!
type type
Boldface
type
WORLD FAMOUS AUTHORS ARE ALWAYS TOUGH CRITICS.
type
type
type
type

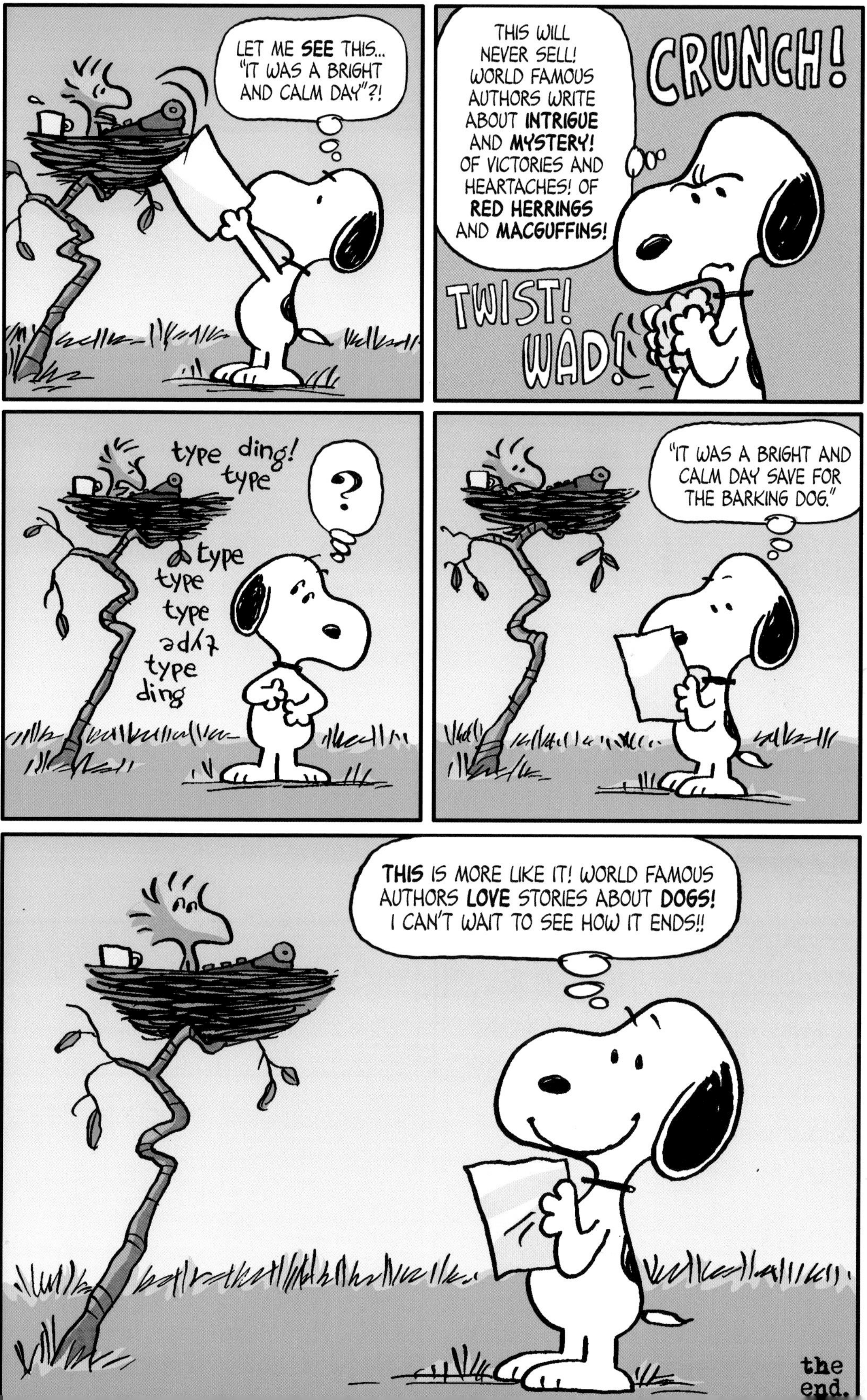
LET ME **SEE** THIS... "IT WAS A BRIGHT AND CALM DAY"?!
THIS WILL NEVER SELL! WORLD FAMOUS AUTHORS WRITE ABOUT **INTRIGUE** AND **MYSTERY!** OF VICTORIES AND HEARTACHES! OF **RED HERRINGS** AND **MACGUFFINS!**
CRUNCH!
TWIST!
WAD!
type ding! type
type
type
type
type
type
ding
?
"IT WAS A BRIGHT AND CALM DAY SAVE FOR THE BARKING DOG."
THIS IS MORE LIKE IT! WORLD FAMOUS AUTHORS **LOVE** STORIES ABOUT **DOGS!** I CAN'T WAIT TO SEE HOW IT ENDS!!
the end.

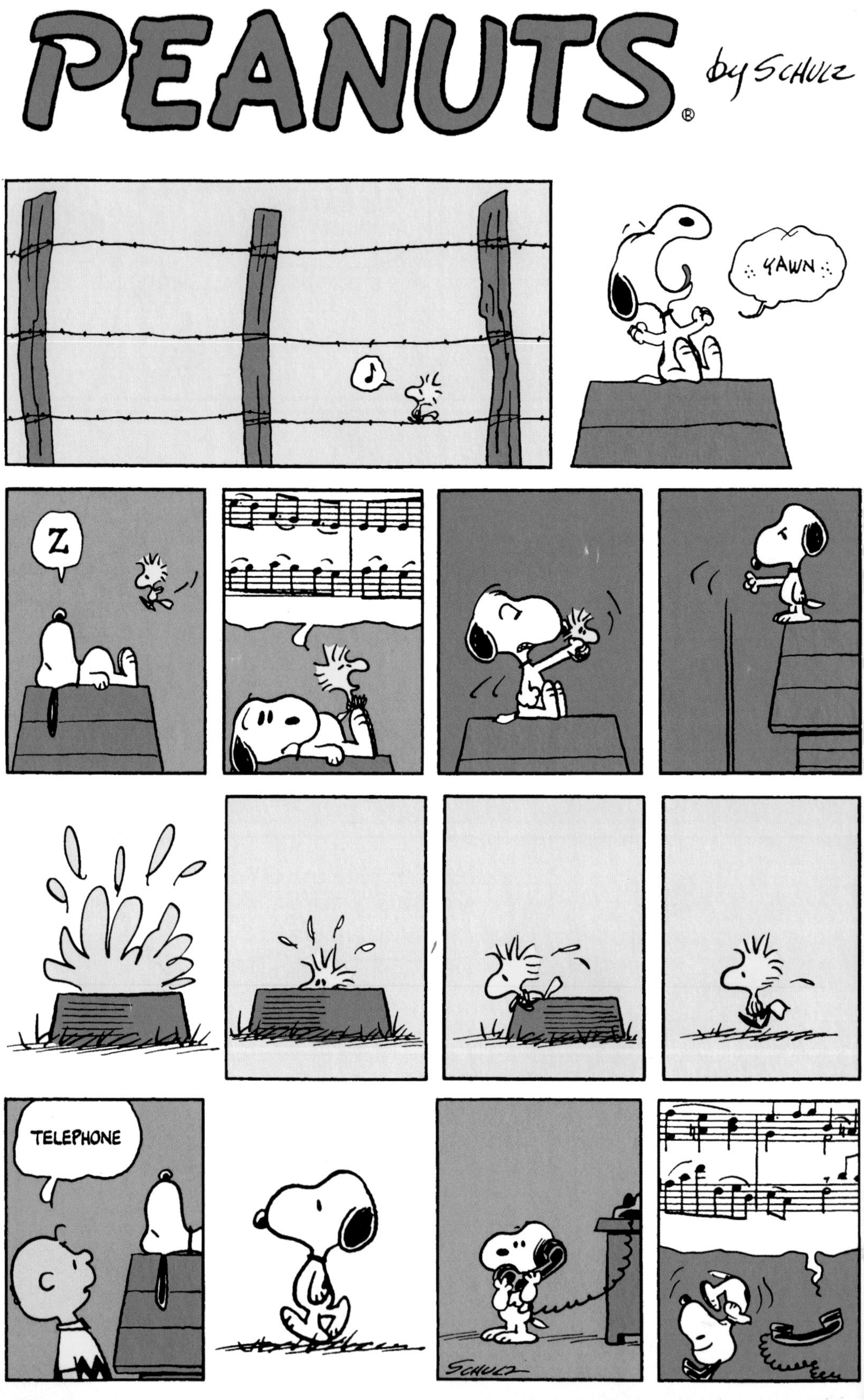
PEANUTS
by SCHULZ
YAWN
Z
TELEPHONE
SCHULZ

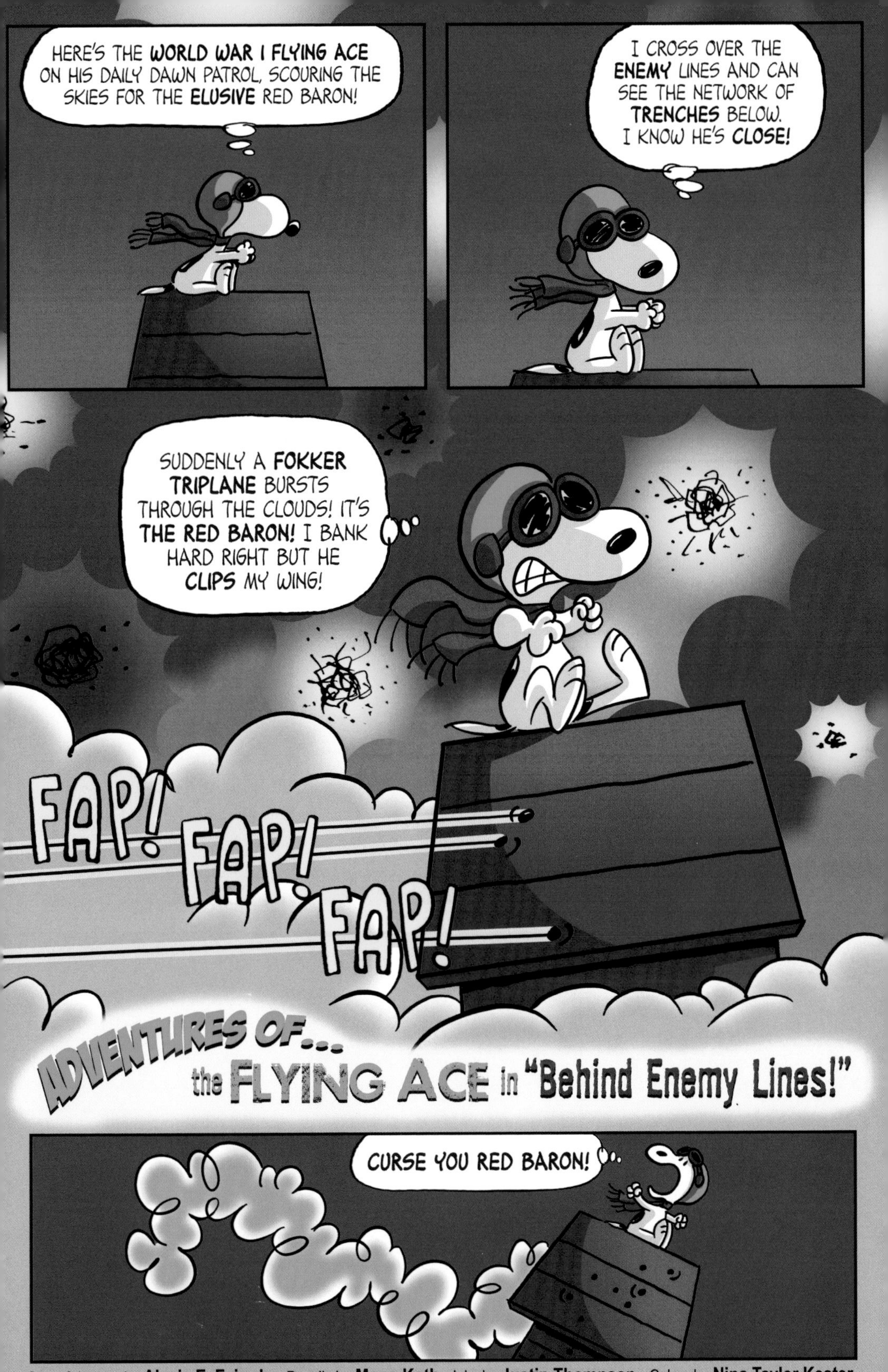
HERE'S THE WORLD WAR I FLYING ACE ON HIS DAILY DAWN PATROL, SCOURING THE SKIES FOR THE ELUSIVE RED BARON!
I CROSS OVER THE ENEMY LINES AND CAN SEE THE NETWORK OF TRENCHES BELOW. I KNOW HE'S CLOSE!
SUDDENLY A FOKKER TRIPLANE BURSTS THROUGH THE CLOUDS! IT'S THE RED BARON! I BANK HARD RIGHT BUT HE CLIPS MY WING!
FAP! FAP! FAP!
ADVENTURES OF... the FLYING ACE in "Behind Enemy Lines!"
CURSE YOU RED BARON!

Story & Letters by **Alexis E. Fajardo** Pencils by **Mona Koth** Inks by **Justin Thompson** Colors by **Nina Taylor Kester**

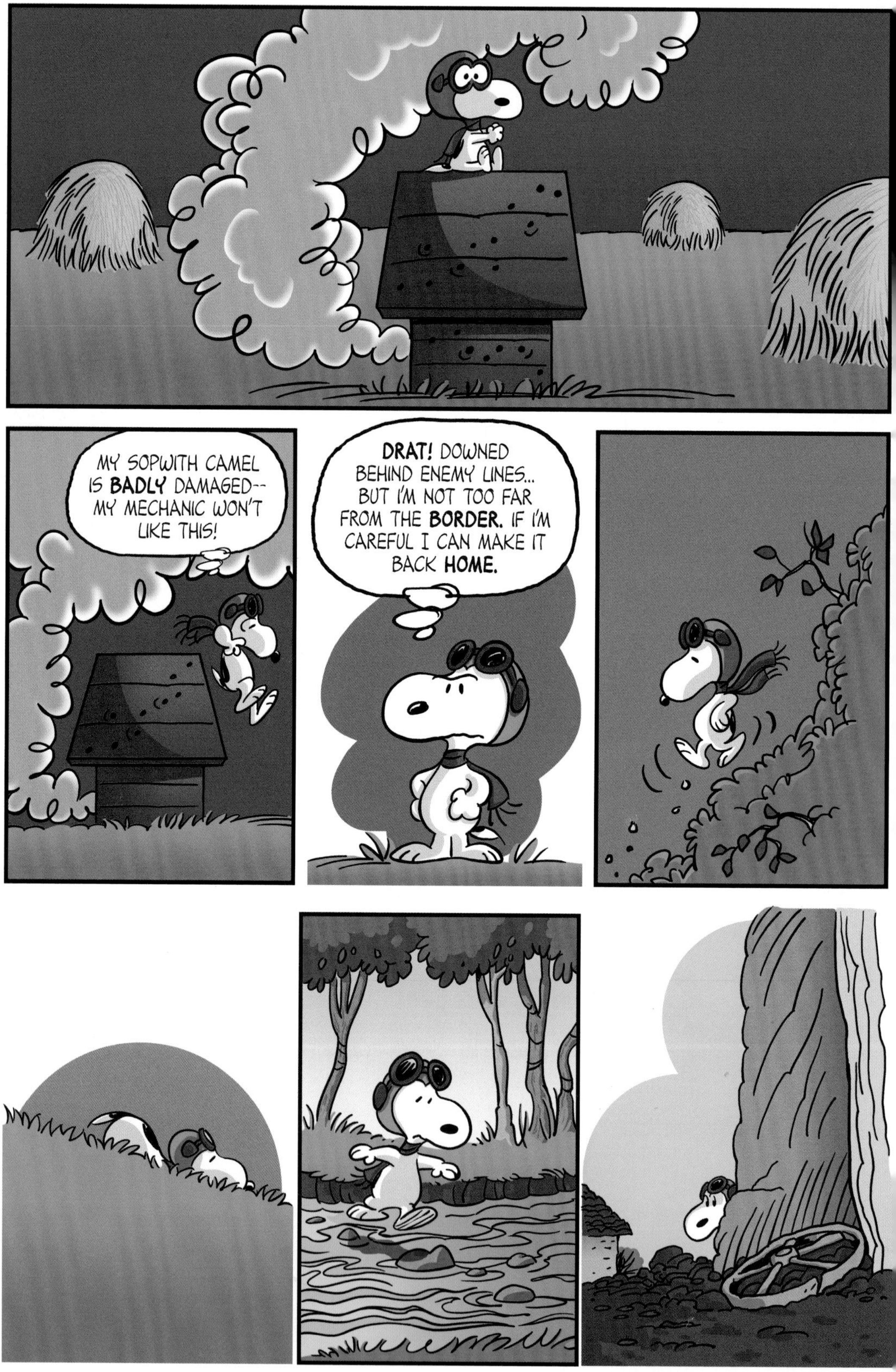
MY SOPWITH CAMEL IS **BADLY** DAMAGED-- MY MECHANIC WON'T LIKE THIS!
DRAT! DOWNED BEHIND ENEMY LINES... BUT I'M NOT TOO FAR FROM THE **BORDER.** IF I'M CAREFUL I CAN MAKE IT BACK **HOME.**

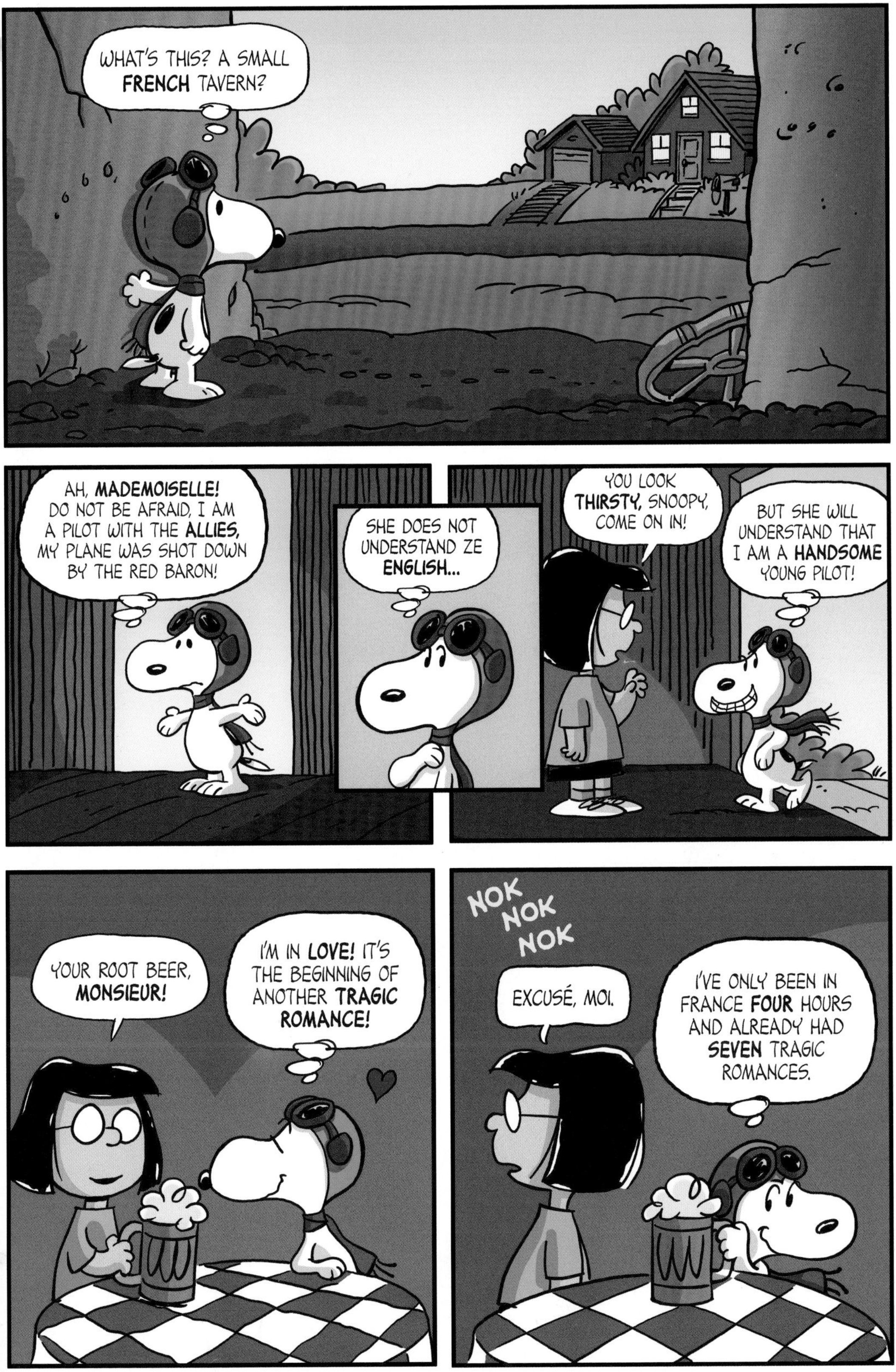
WHAT'S THIS? A SMALL FRENCH TAVERN?
AH, MADEMOISELLE! DO NOT BE AFRAID, I AM A PILOT WITH THE ALLIES, MY PLANE WAS SHOT DOWN BY THE RED BARON!
SHE DOES NOT UNDERSTAND ZE ENGLISH...
YOU LOOK THIRSTY, SNOOPY, COME ON IN!
BUT SHE WILL UNDERSTAND THAT I AM A HANDSOME YOUNG PILOT!
YOUR ROOT BEER, MONSIEUR!
I'M IN LOVE! IT'S THE BEGINNING OF ANOTHER TRAGIC ROMANCE!
NOK NOK NOK
EXCUSÉ, MOI.
I'VE ONLY BEEN IN FRANCE FOUR HOURS AND ALREADY HAD SEVEN TRAGIC ROMANCES.

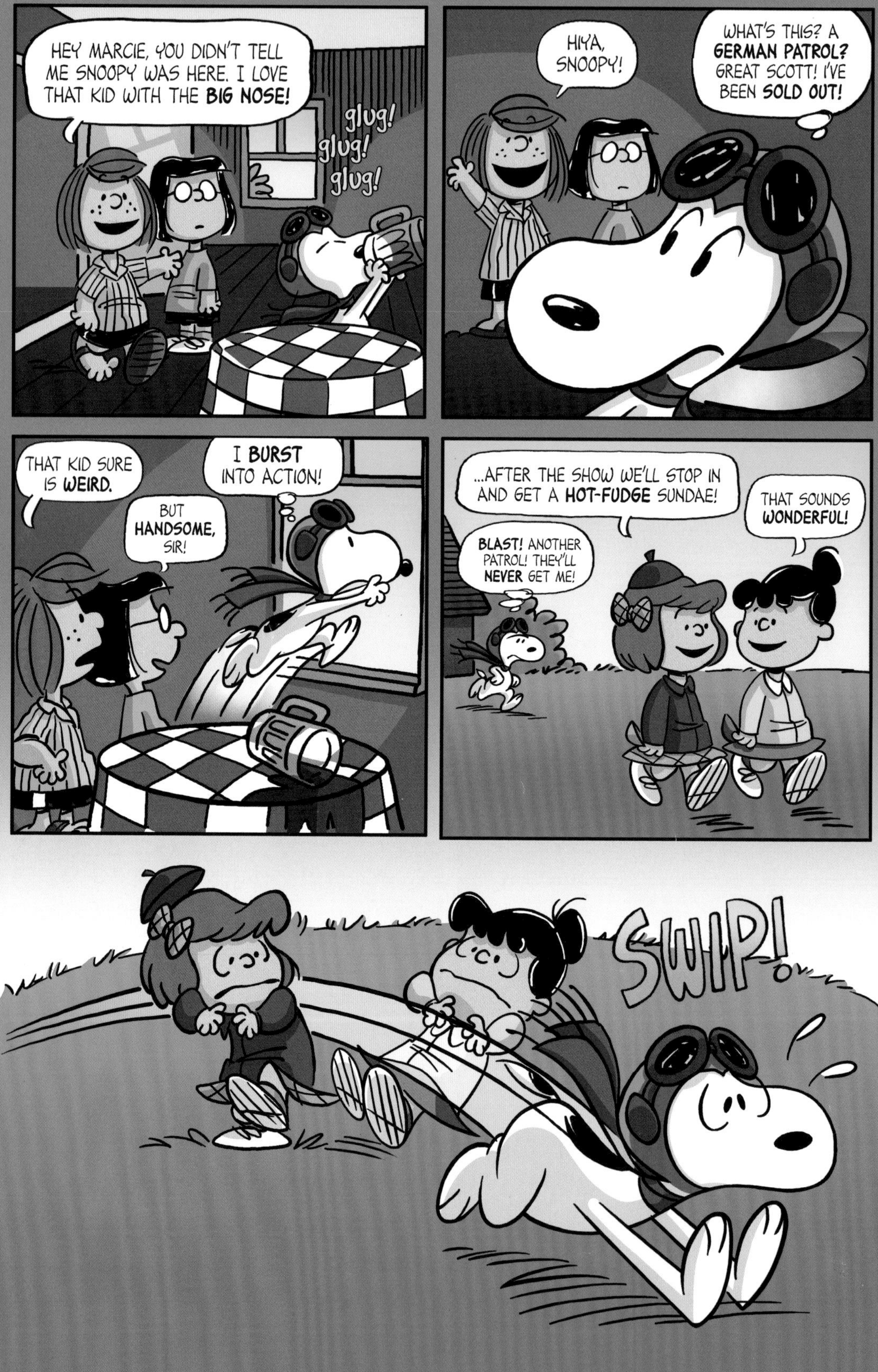
HEY MARCIE, YOU DIDN'T TELL ME SNOOPY WAS HERE. I LOVE THAT KID WITH THE **BIG NOSE!**
glug! glug! glug!
HIYA, SNOOPY!
WHAT'S THIS? A **GERMAN PATROL?** GREAT SCOTT! I'VE BEEN **SOLD OUT!**
THAT KID SURE IS **WEIRD.**
I **BURST** INTO ACTION!
BUT **HANDSOME,** SIR!
...AFTER THE SHOW WE'LL STOP IN AND GET A **HOT-FUDGE** SUNDAE!
THAT SOUNDS **WONDERFUL!**
BLAST! ANOTHER PATROL! THEY'LL **NEVER** GET ME!
SWIP!

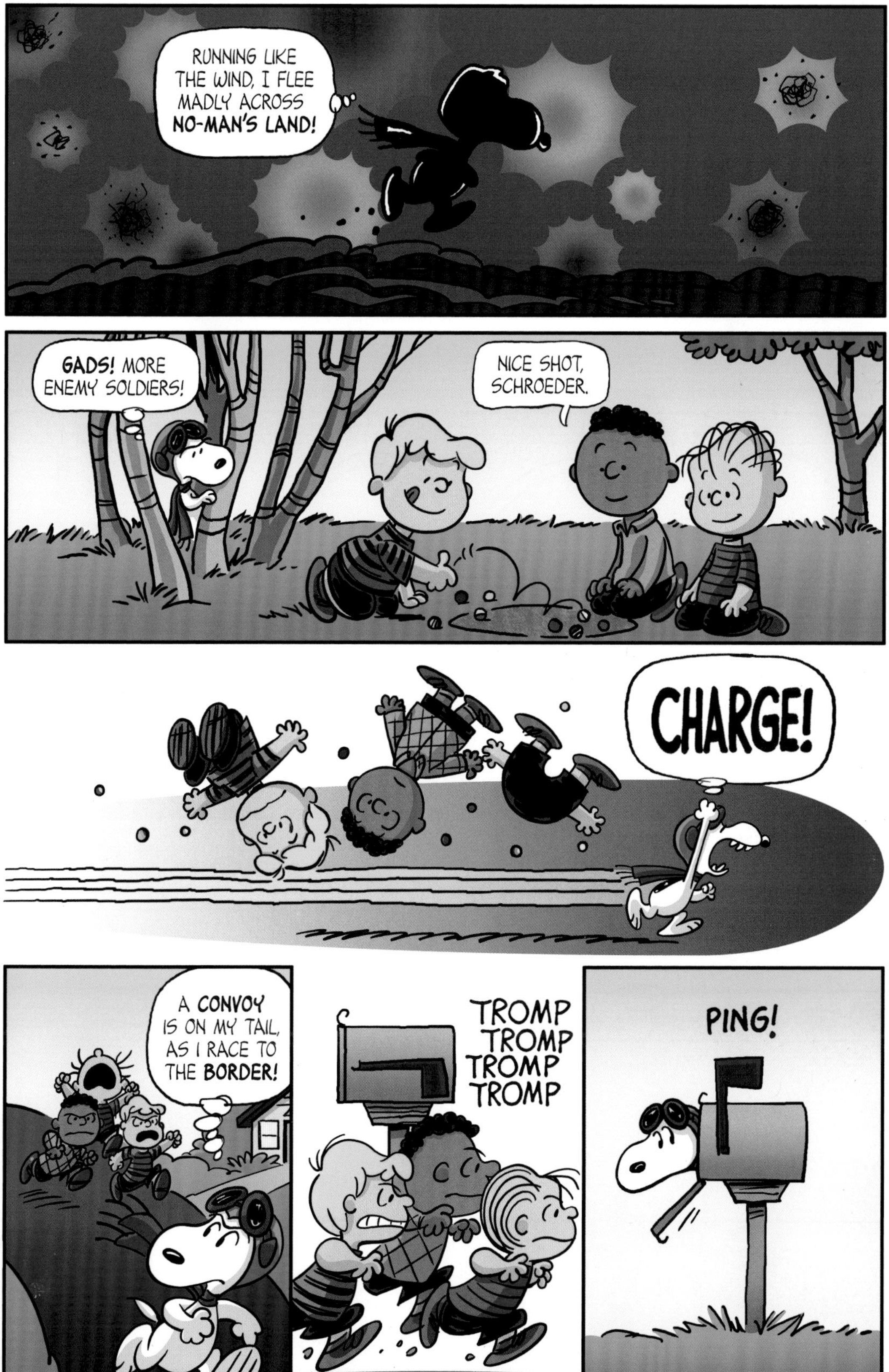
RUNNING LIKE THE WIND, I FLEE MADLY ACROSS NO-MAN'S LAND!
GADS! MORE ENEMY SOLDIERS!
NICE SHOT, SCHROEDER.
CHARGE!
A CONVOY IS ON MY TAIL, AS I RACE TO THE BORDER!
TROMP TROMP TROMP TROMP
PING!

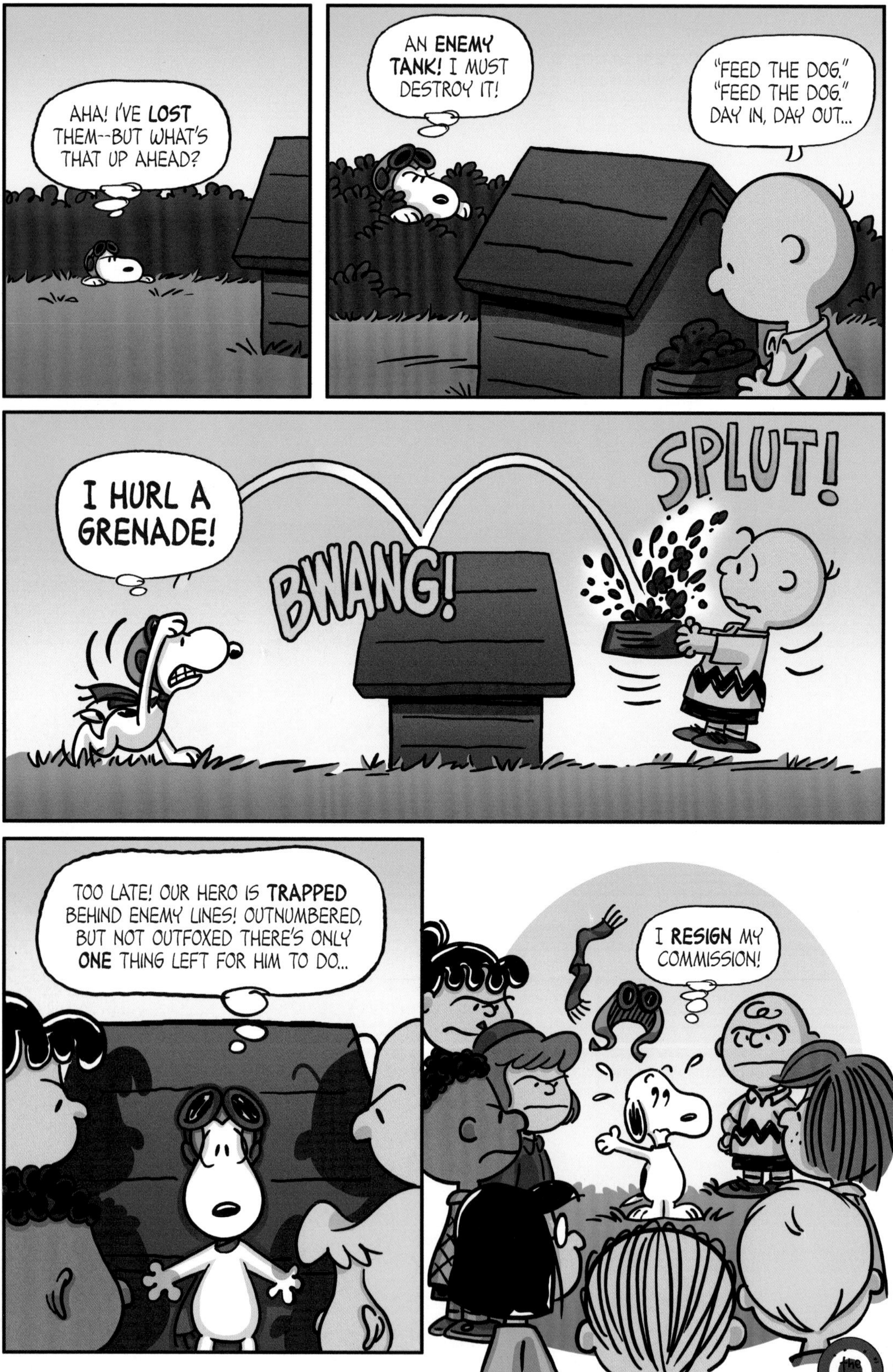
AHA! I'VE LOST THEM--BUT WHAT'S THAT UP AHEAD?
AN ENEMY TANK! I MUST DESTROY IT!
"FEED THE DOG." "FEED THE DOG." DAY IN, DAY OUT...
I HURL A GRENADE!
BWANG!
SPLUT!
TOO LATE! OUR HERO IS TRAPPED BEHIND ENEMY LINES! OUTNUMBERED, BUT NOT OUTFOXED THERE'S ONLY ONE THING LEFT FOR HIM TO DO...
I RESIGN MY COMMISSION!
the end

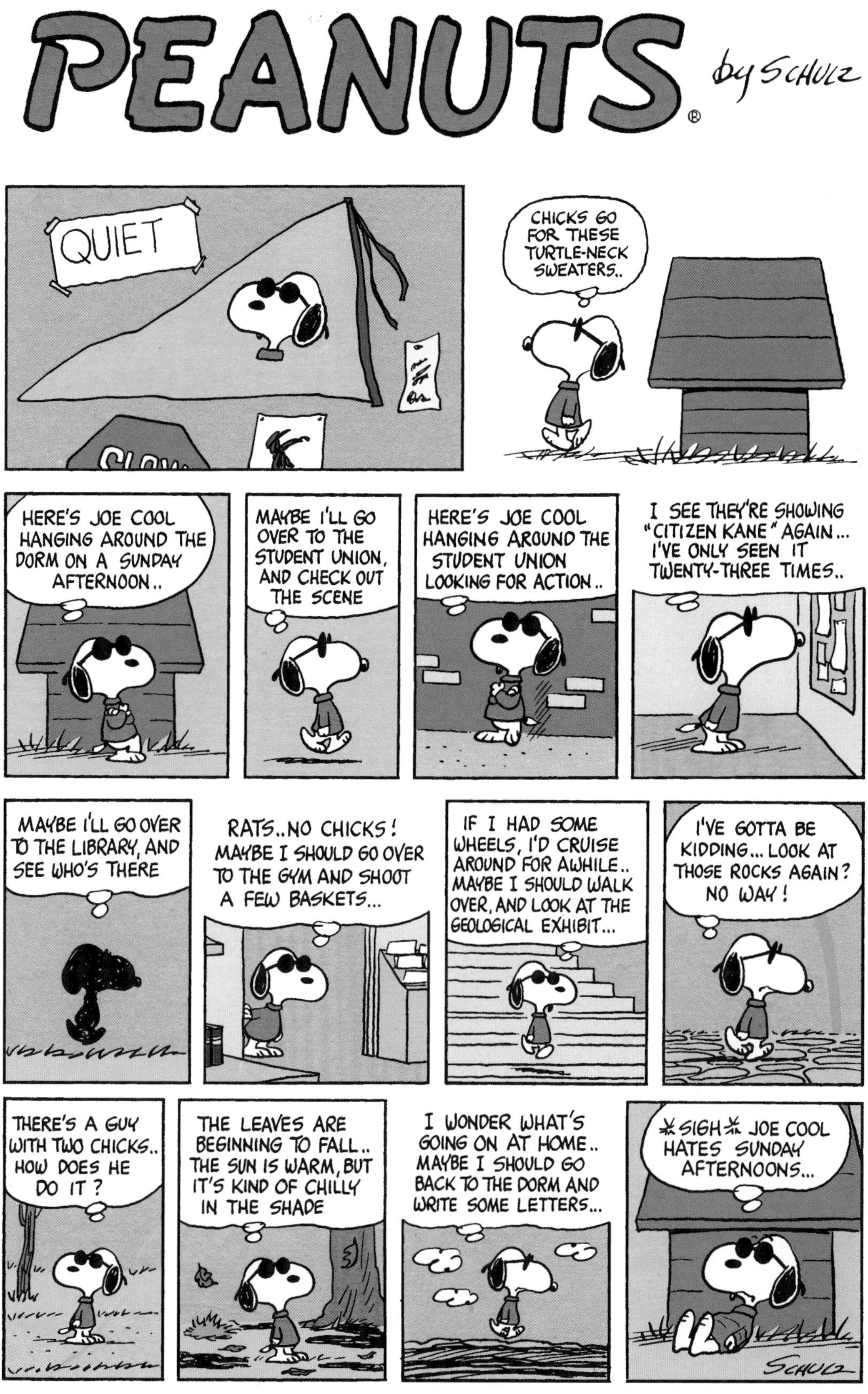
PEANUTS
by SCHULZ
QUIET
SLOW
CHICKS GO FOR THESE TURTLE-NECK SWEATERS..
HERE'S JOE COOL HANGING AROUND THE DORM ON A SUNDAY AFTERNOON..
MAYBE I'LL GO OVER TO THE STUDENT UNION, AND CHECK OUT THE SCENE
HERE'S JOE COOL HANGING AROUND THE STUDENT UNION LOOKING FOR ACTION..
I SEE THEY'RE SHOWING "CITIZEN KANE" AGAIN... I'VE ONLY SEEN IT TWENTY-THREE TIMES..
MAYBE I'LL GO OVER TO THE LIBRARY, AND SEE WHO'S THERE
RATS..NO CHICKS! MAYBE I SHOULD GO OVER TO THE GYM AND SHOOT A FEW BASKETS...
IF I HAD SOME WHEELS, I'D CRUISE AROUND FOR AWHILE.. MAYBE I SHOULD WALK OVER, AND LOOK AT THE GEOLOGICAL EXHIBIT...
I'VE GOTTA BE KIDDING... LOOK AT THOSE ROCKS AGAIN? NO WAY!
THERE'S A GUY WITH TWO CHICKS.. HOW DOES HE DO IT?
THE LEAVES ARE BEGINNING TO FALL.. THE SUN IS WARM, BUT IT'S KIND OF CHILLY IN THE SHADE
I WONDER WHAT'S GOING ON AT HOME.. MAYBE I SHOULD GO BACK TO THE DORM AND WRITE SOME LETTERS...
SIGH JOE COOL HATES SUNDAY AFTERNOONS...
SCHULZ

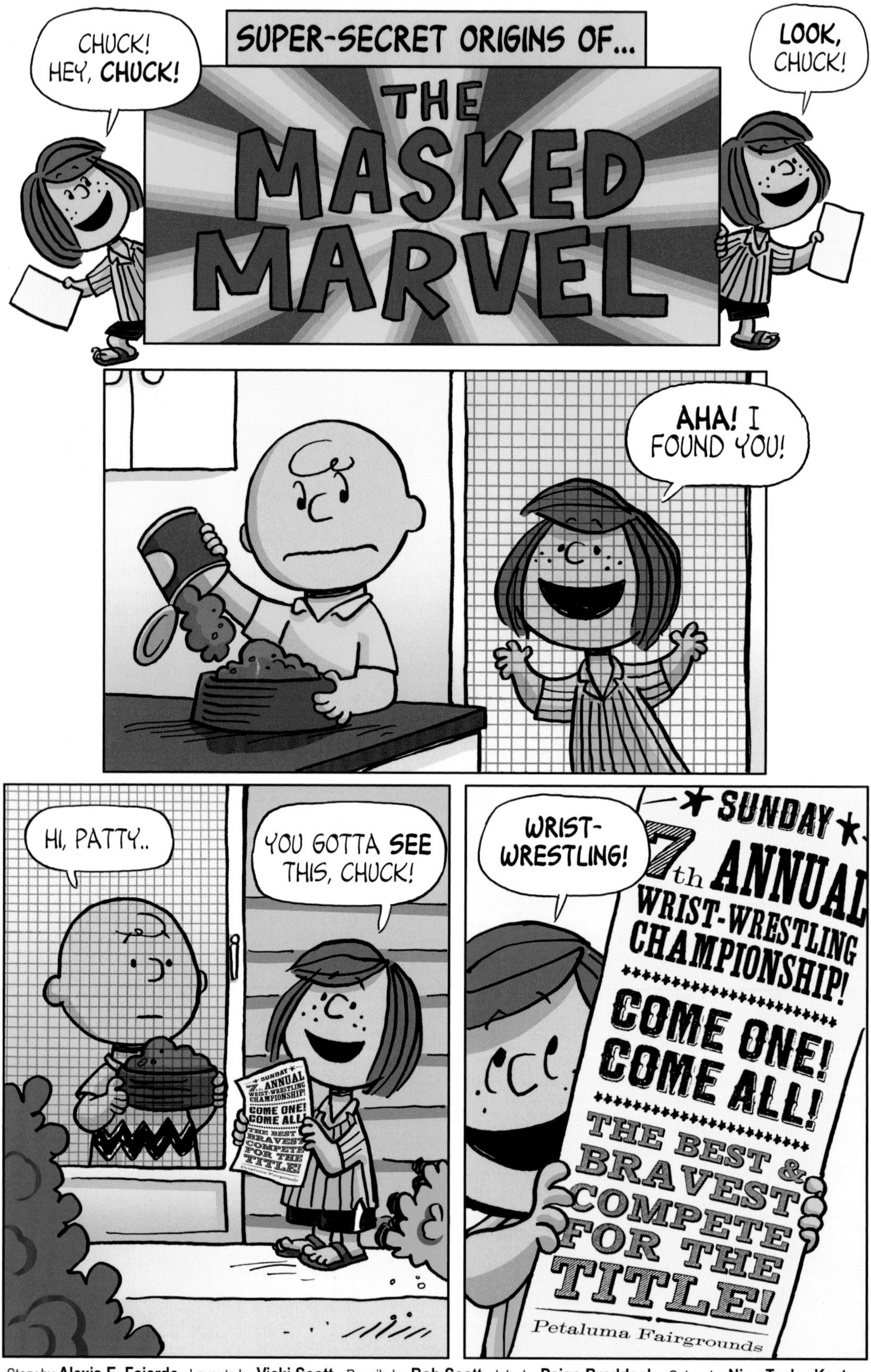
CHUCK! HEY, CHUCK!
SUPER-SECRET ORIGINS OF...
THE MASKED MARVEL
LOOK, CHUCK!
AHA! I FOUND YOU!
HI, PATTY..
YOU GOTTA SEE THIS, CHUCK!
WRIST-WRESTLING!
SUNDAY
7th ANNUAL WRIST-WRESTLING CHAMPIONSHIP!
COME ONE! COME ALL!
THE BEST & BRAVEST COMPETE FOR THE TITLE!
Petaluma Fairgrounds

Story by **Alexis E. Fajardo** Layouts by **Vicki Scott** Pencils by **Bob Scott** Inks by **Paige Braddock** Colors by **Nina Taylor Kester**

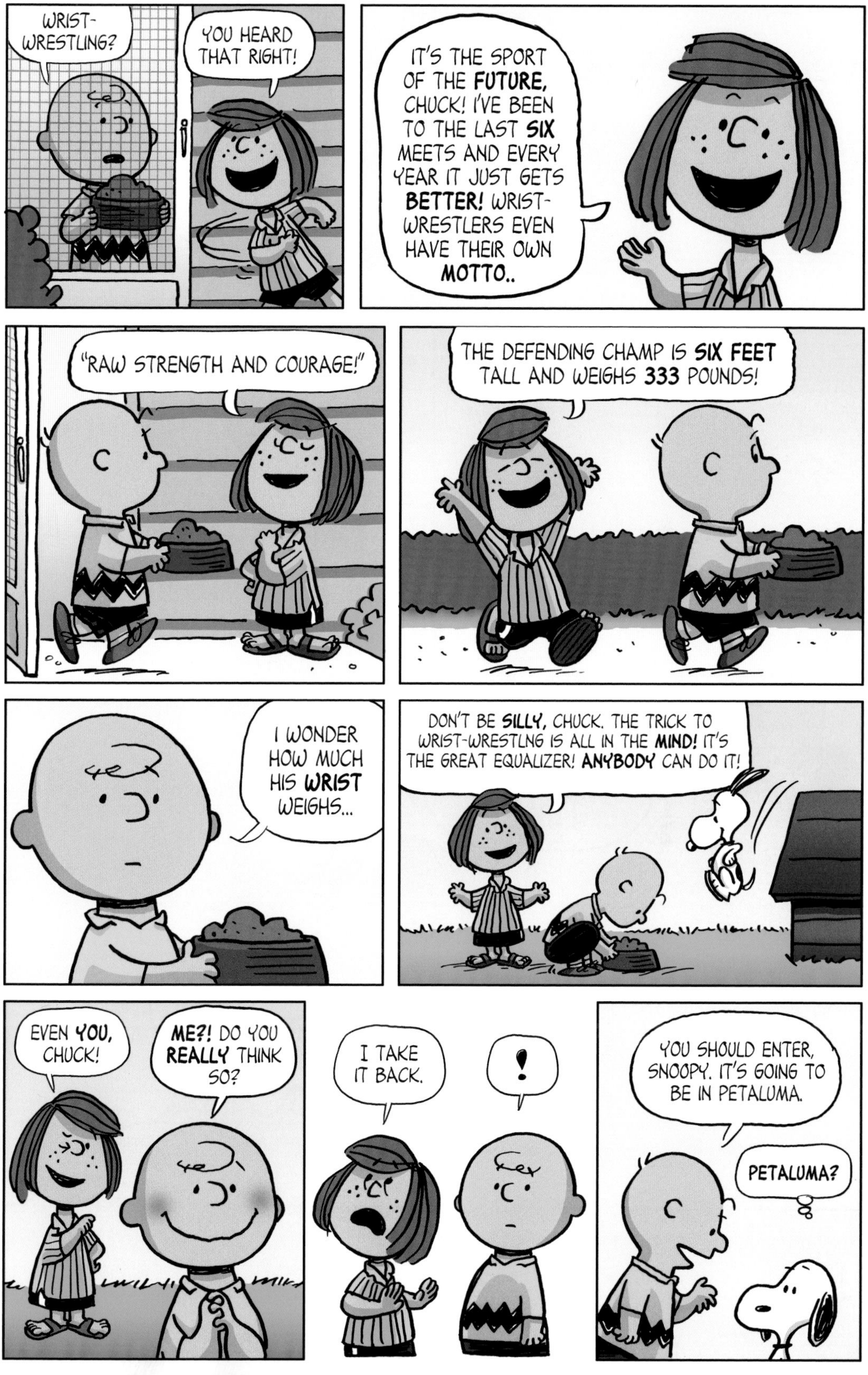
WRIST-WRESTLING?
YOU HEARD THAT RIGHT!
IT'S THE SPORT OF THE **FUTURE,** CHUCK! I'VE BEEN TO THE LAST **SIX** MEETS AND EVERY YEAR IT JUST GETS **BETTER!** WRIST-WRESTLERS EVEN HAVE THEIR OWN **MOTTO..**
"RAW STRENGTH AND COURAGE!"
THE DEFENDING CHAMP IS **SIX FEET** TALL AND WEIGHS **333** POUNDS!
I WONDER HOW MUCH HIS **WRIST** WEIGHS...
DON'T BE **SILLY,** CHUCK. THE TRICK TO WRIST-WRESTLNG IS ALL IN THE **MIND!** IT'S THE GREAT EQUALIZER! **ANYBODY** CAN DO IT!
EVEN **YOU,** CHUCK!
ME?! DO YOU **REALLY** THINK SO?
I TAKE IT BACK.
!
YOU SHOULD ENTER, SNOOPY. IT'S GOING TO BE IN PETALUMA.
PETALUMA?

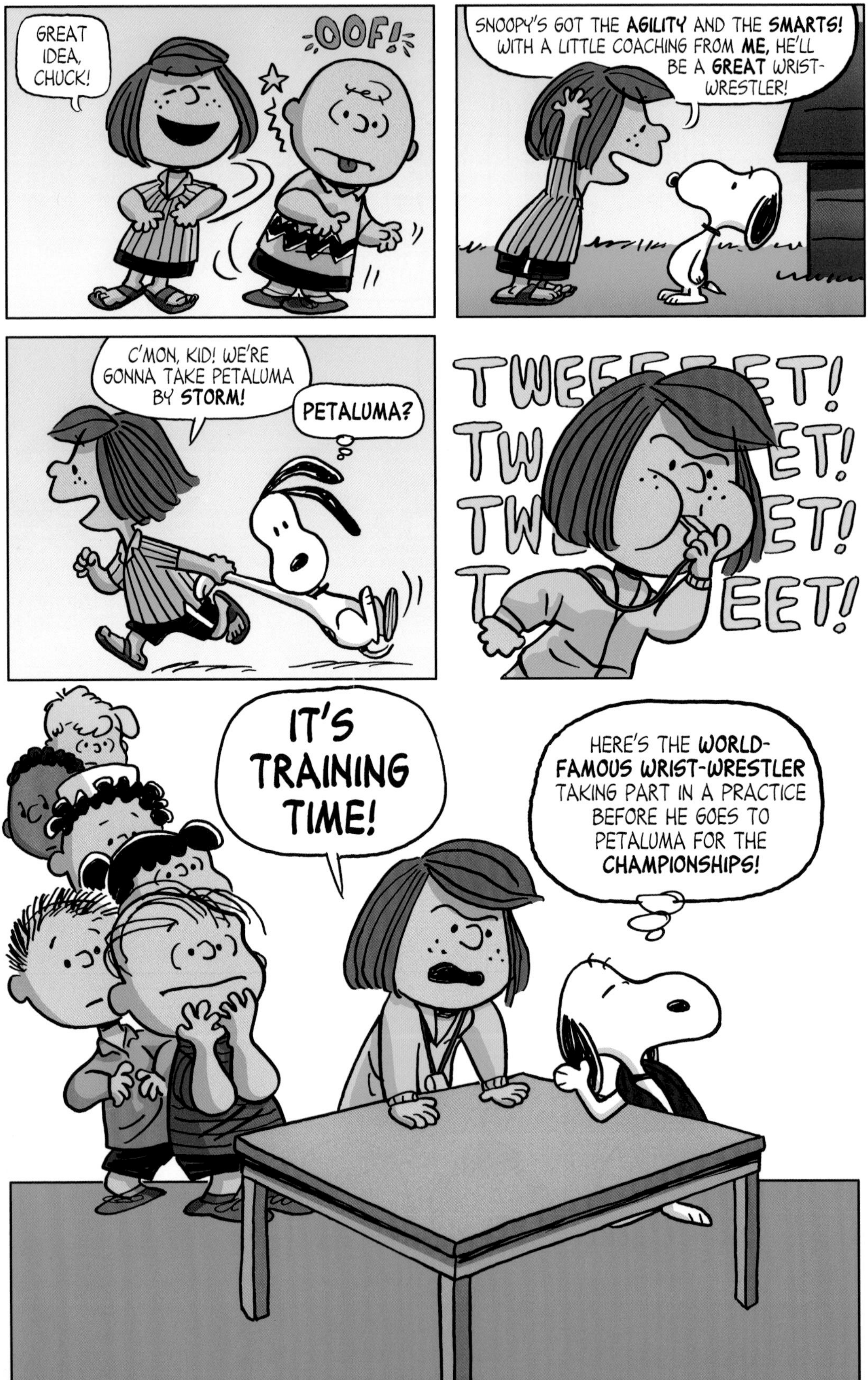
GREAT IDEA, CHUCK!
OOF!
SNOOPY'S GOT THE AGILITY AND THE SMARTS! WITH A LITTLE COACHING FROM ME, HE'LL BE A GREAT WRIST-WRESTLER!
C'MON, KID! WE'RE GONNA TAKE PETALUMA BY STORM!
PETALUMA?
TWEEEEET! TWEEEEET! TWEEEEET! TWEEEEET!
IT'S TRAINING TIME!
HERE'S THE WORLD-FAMOUS WRIST-WRESTLER TAKING PART IN A PRACTICE BEFORE HE GOES TO PETALUMA FOR THE CHAMPIONSHIPS!

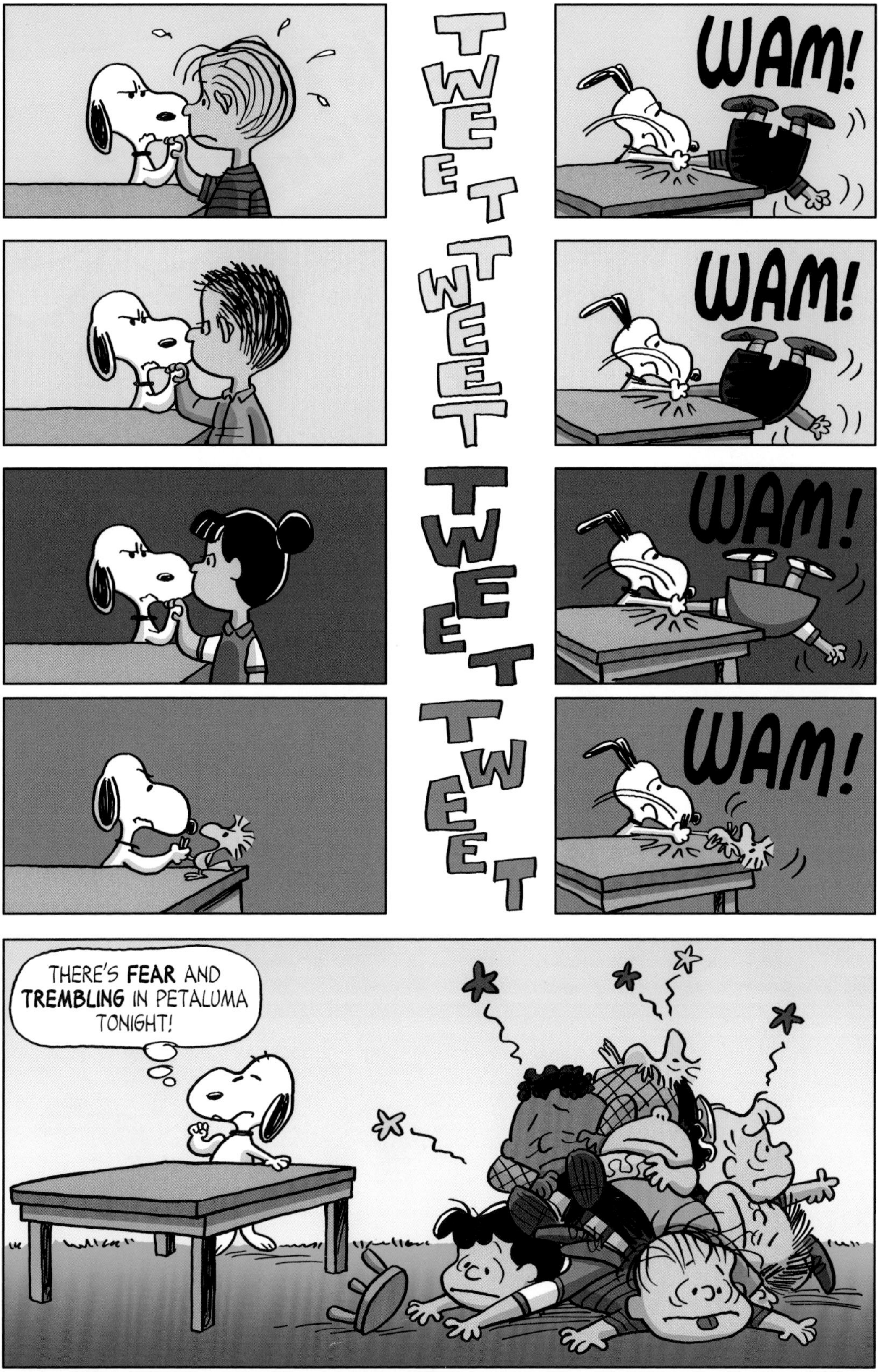
TWEET
WAM!
TWEET
WAM!
TWEET
WAM!
TWEET
WAM!
THERE'S **FEAR** AND **TREMBLING** IN PETALUMA TONIGHT!

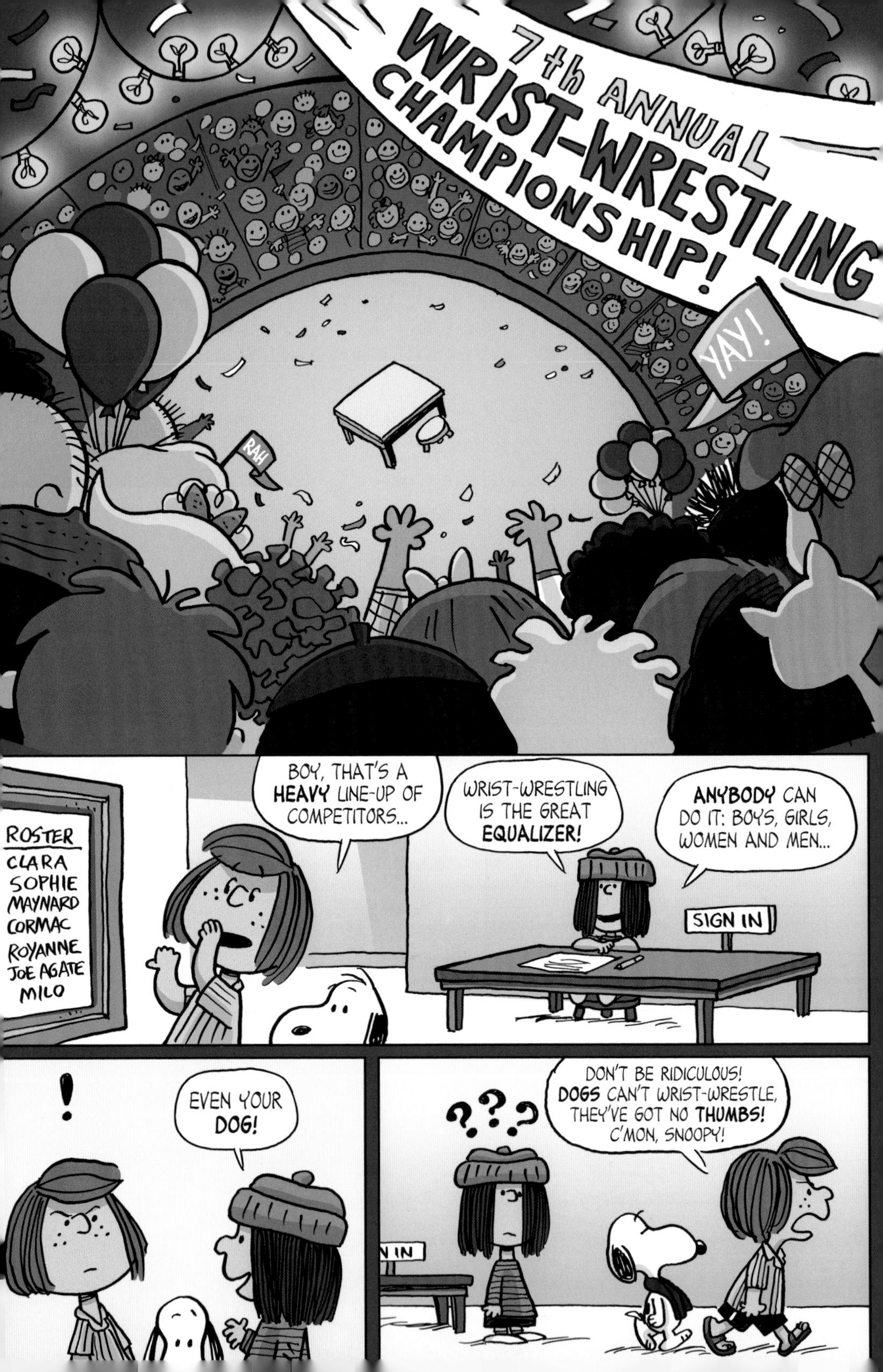

7th ANNUAL WRIST-WRESTLING CHAMPIONSHIP!
YAY!
RAH
ROSTER
CLARA
SOPHIE
MAYNARD
CORMAC
ROYANNE
JOE AGATE
MILO
BOY, THAT'S A HEAVY LINE-UP OF COMPETITORS...
WRIST-WRESTLING IS THE GREAT EQUALIZER!
ANYBODY CAN DO IT: BOYS, GIRLS, WOMEN AND MEN...
SIGN IN
!
EVEN YOUR DOG!
???
DON'T BE RIDICULOUS! DOGS CAN'T WRIST-WRESTLE, THEY'VE GOT NO THUMBS! C'MON, SNOOPY!

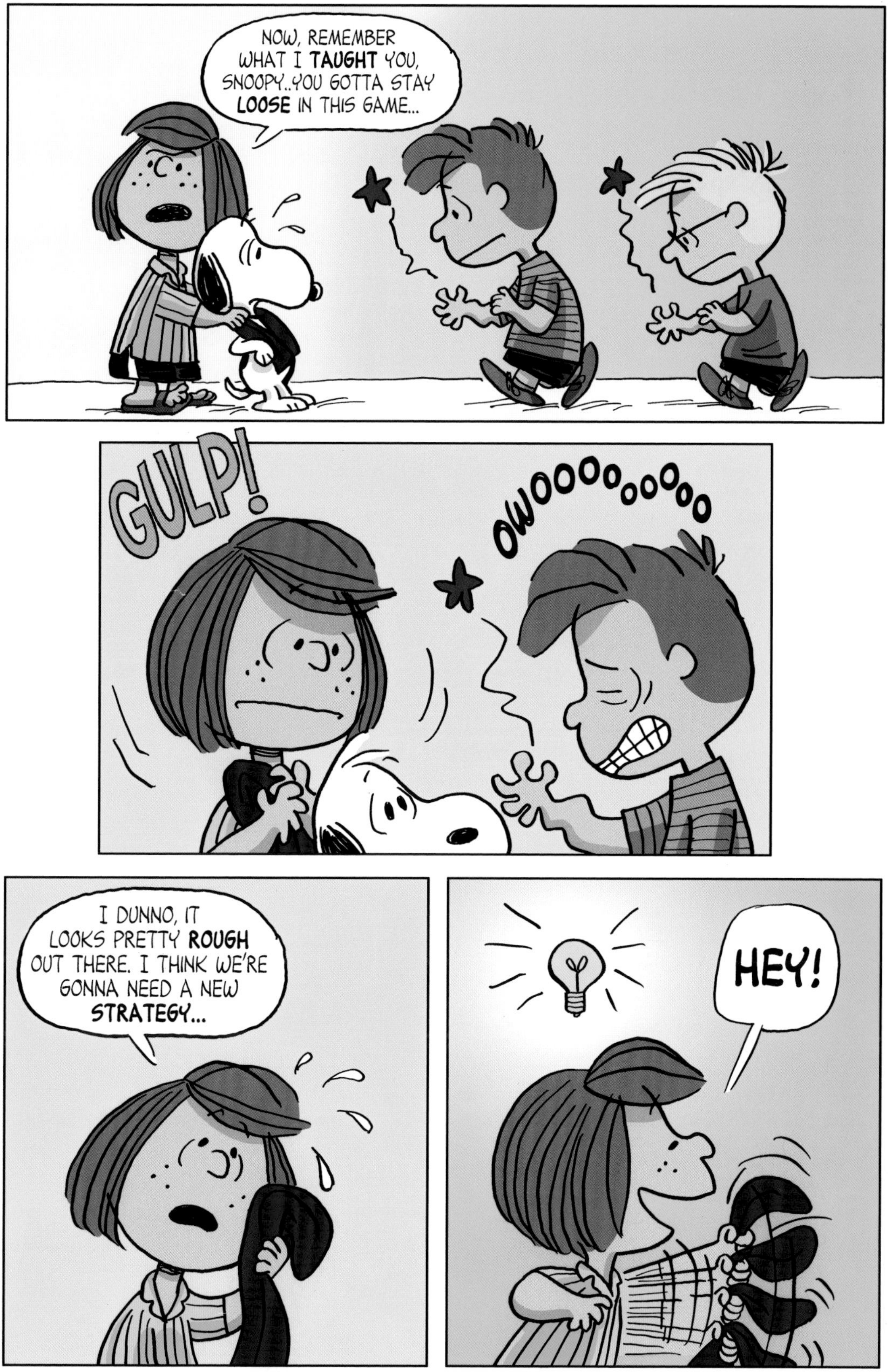
NOW, REMEMBER WHAT I **TAUGHT** YOU, SNOOPY..YOU GOTTA STAY **LOOSE** IN THIS GAME...
GULP!
OWOOOOOOOOO
I DUNNO, IT LOOKS PRETTY **ROUGH** OUT THERE. I THINK WE'RE GONNA NEED A NEW **STRATEGY**...
HEY!

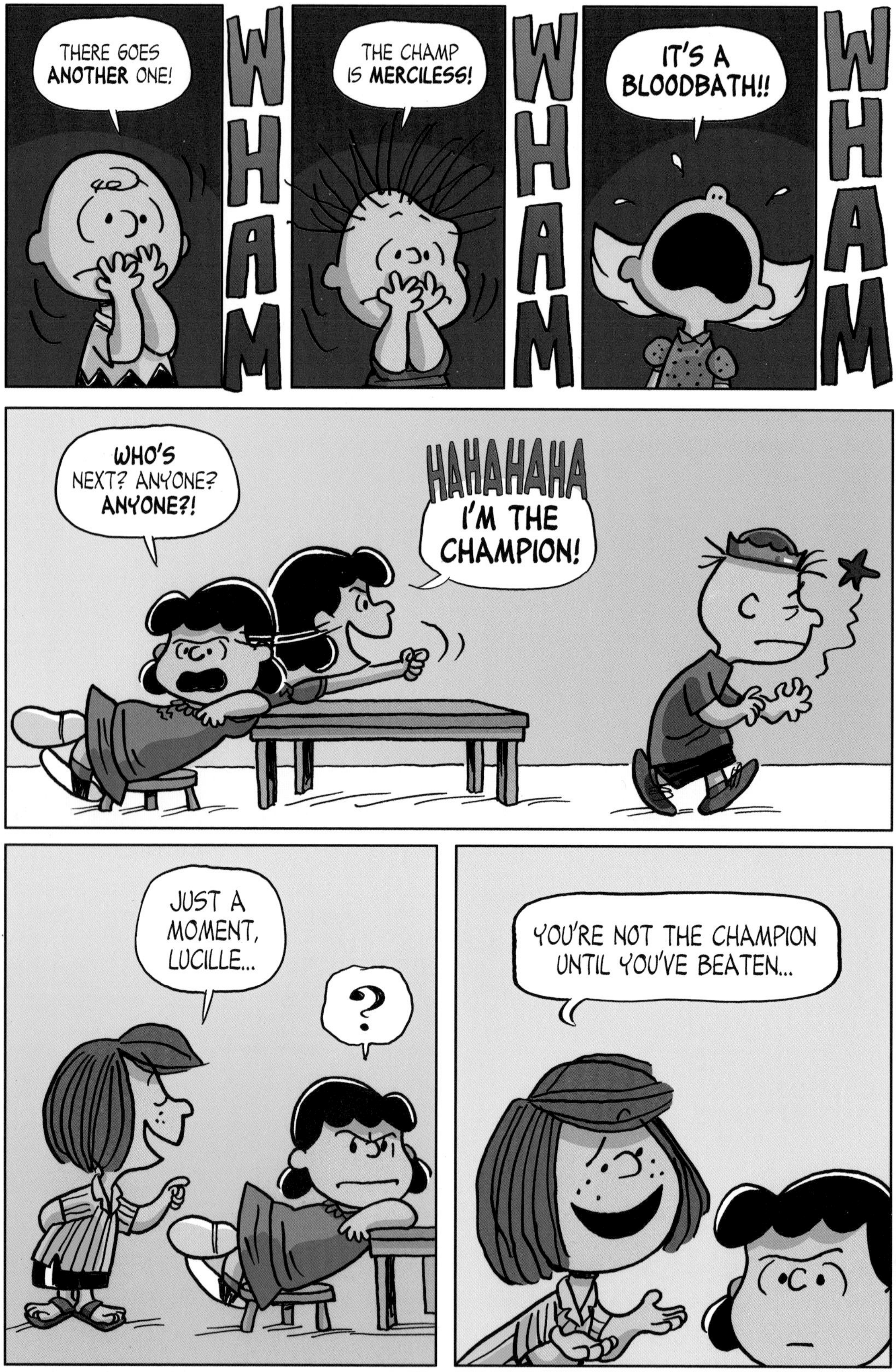
THERE GOES ANOTHER ONE!
WHAM
THE CHAMP IS MERCILESS!
WHAM
IT'S A BLOODBATH!!
WHAM
WHO'S NEXT? ANYONE? ANYONE?!
HAHAHAHA
I'M THE CHAMPION!
JUST A MOMENT, LUCILLE...
?
YOU'RE NOT THE CHAMPION UNTIL YOU'VE BEATEN...

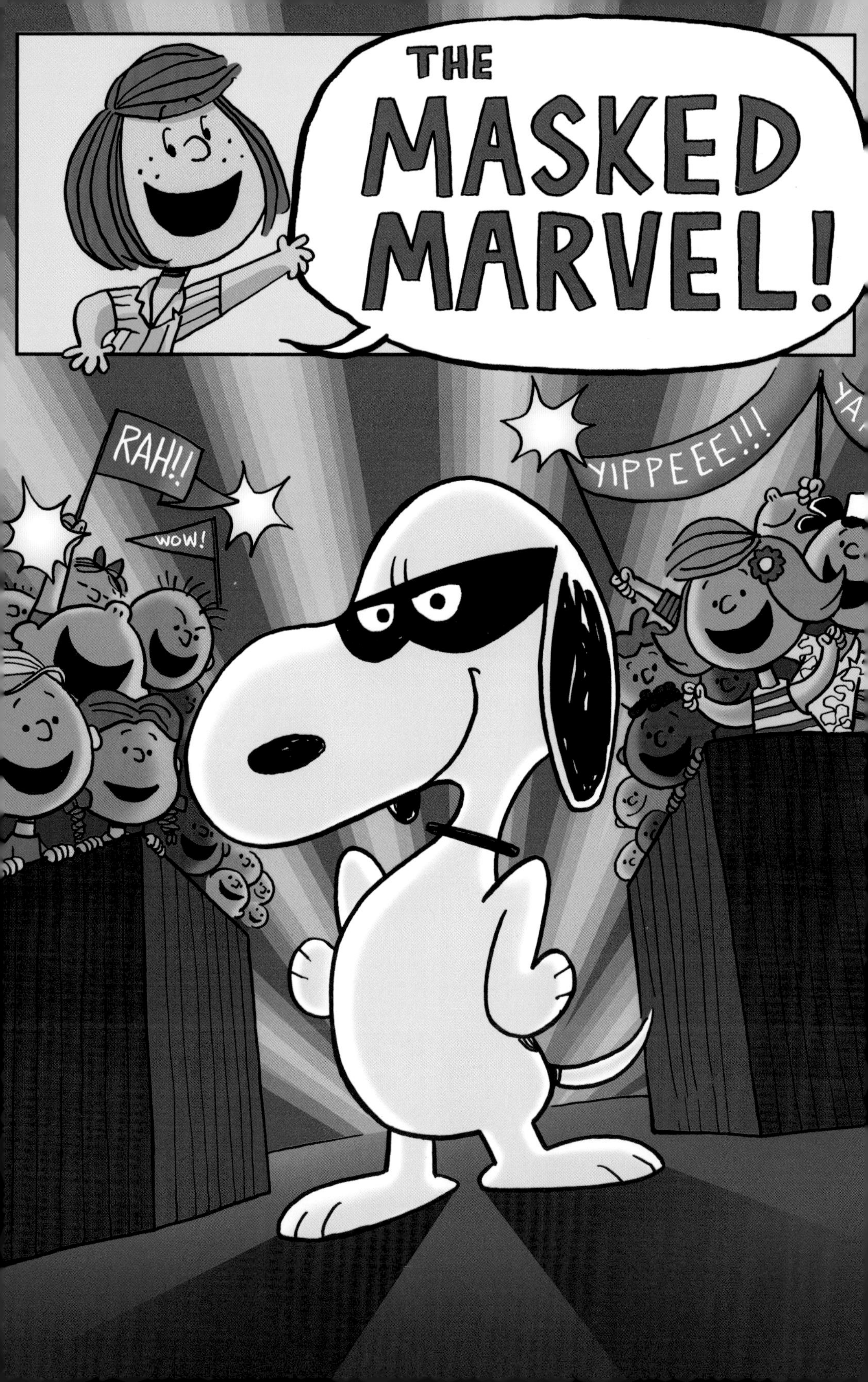
THE MASKED MARVEL!
RAH!!
WOW!
YIPPEEE!!!

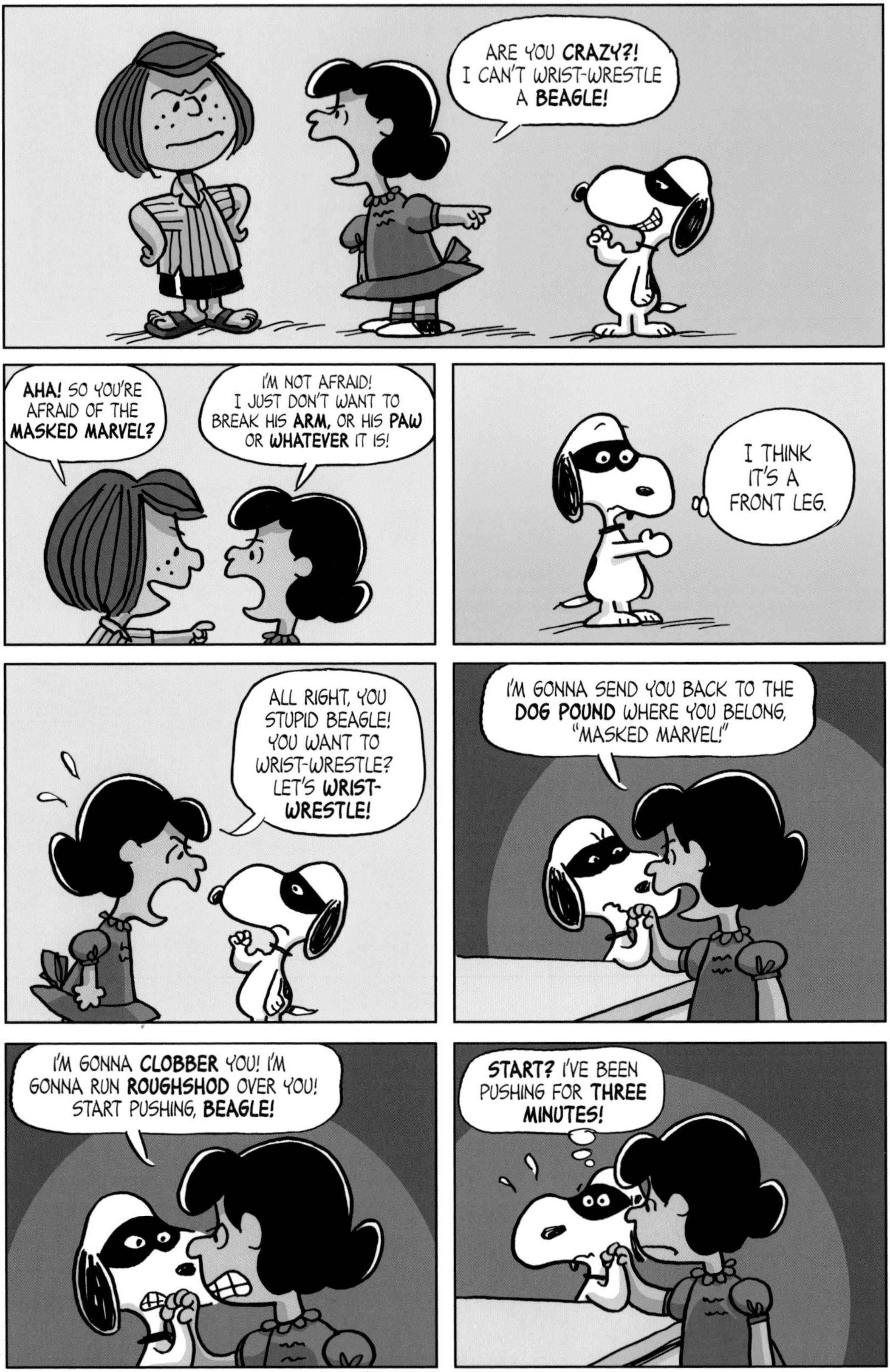
ARE YOU **CRAZY?!** I CAN'T WRIST-WRESTLE A **BEAGLE!**
AHA! SO YOU'RE AFRAID OF THE **MASKED MARVEL?**
I'M NOT AFRAID! I JUST DON'T WANT TO BREAK HIS **ARM,** OR HIS **PAW** OR **WHATEVER** IT IS!
I THINK IT'S A FRONT LEG.
ALL RIGHT, YOU STUPID BEAGLE! YOU WANT TO WRIST-WRESTLE? LET'S **WRIST-WRESTLE!**
I'M GONNA SEND YOU BACK TO THE **DOG POUND** WHERE YOU BELONG, "MASKED MARVEL!"
I'M GONNA **CLOBBER** YOU! I'M GONNA RUN **ROUGHSHOD** OVER YOU! START PUSHING, **BEAGLE!**
START? I'VE BEEN PUSHING FOR **THREE MINUTES!**

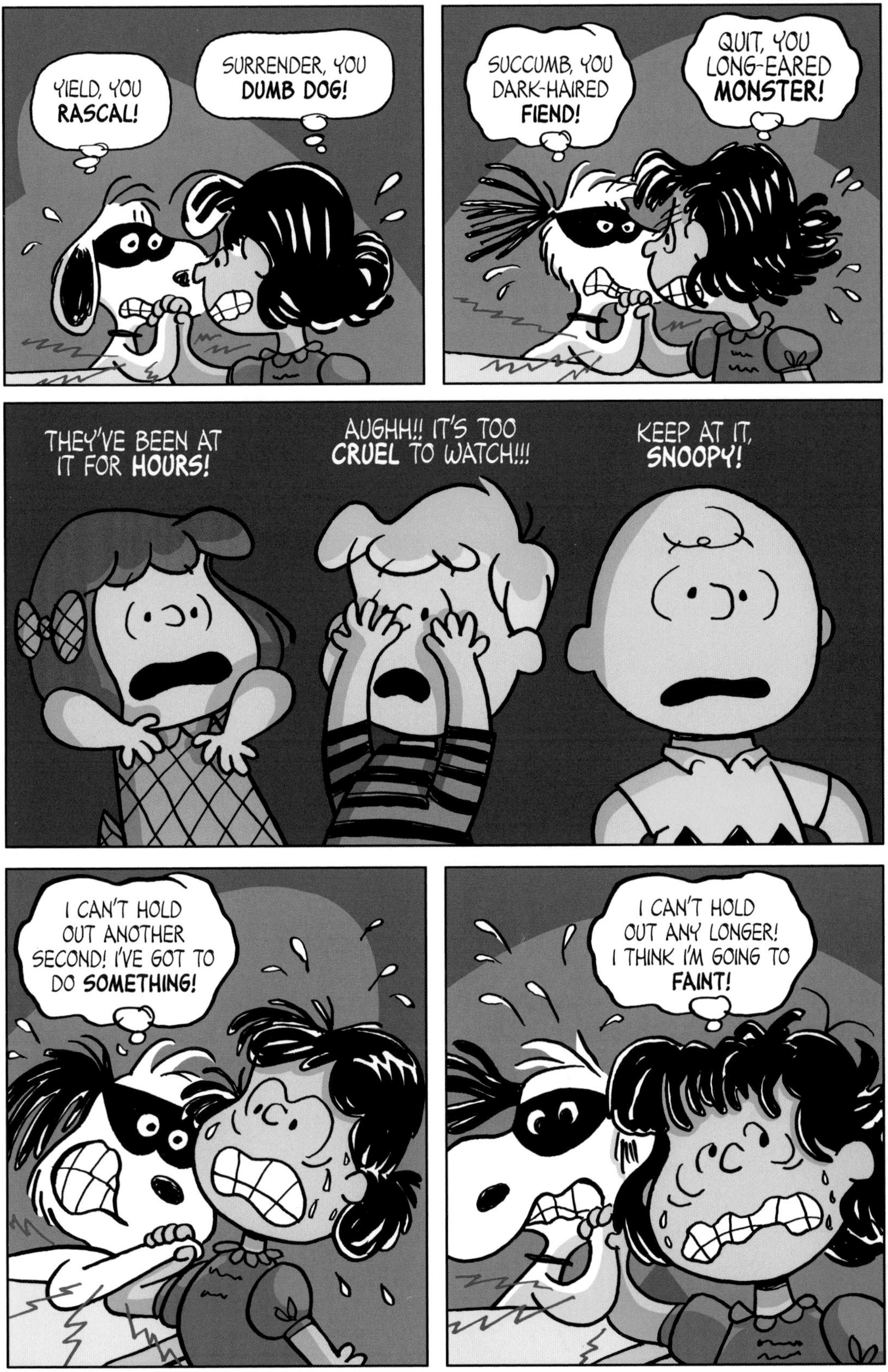
YIELD, YOU RASCAL!
SURRENDER, YOU DUMB DOG!
SUCCUMB, YOU DARK-HAIRED FIEND!
QUIT, YOU LONG-EARED MONSTER!
THEY'VE BEEN AT IT FOR HOURS!
AUGHH!! IT'S TOO CRUEL TO WATCH!!!
KEEP AT IT, SNOOPY!
I CAN'T HOLD OUT ANOTHER SECOND! I'VE GOT TO DO SOMETHING!
I CAN'T HOLD OUT ANY LONGER! I THINK I'M GOING TO FAINT!

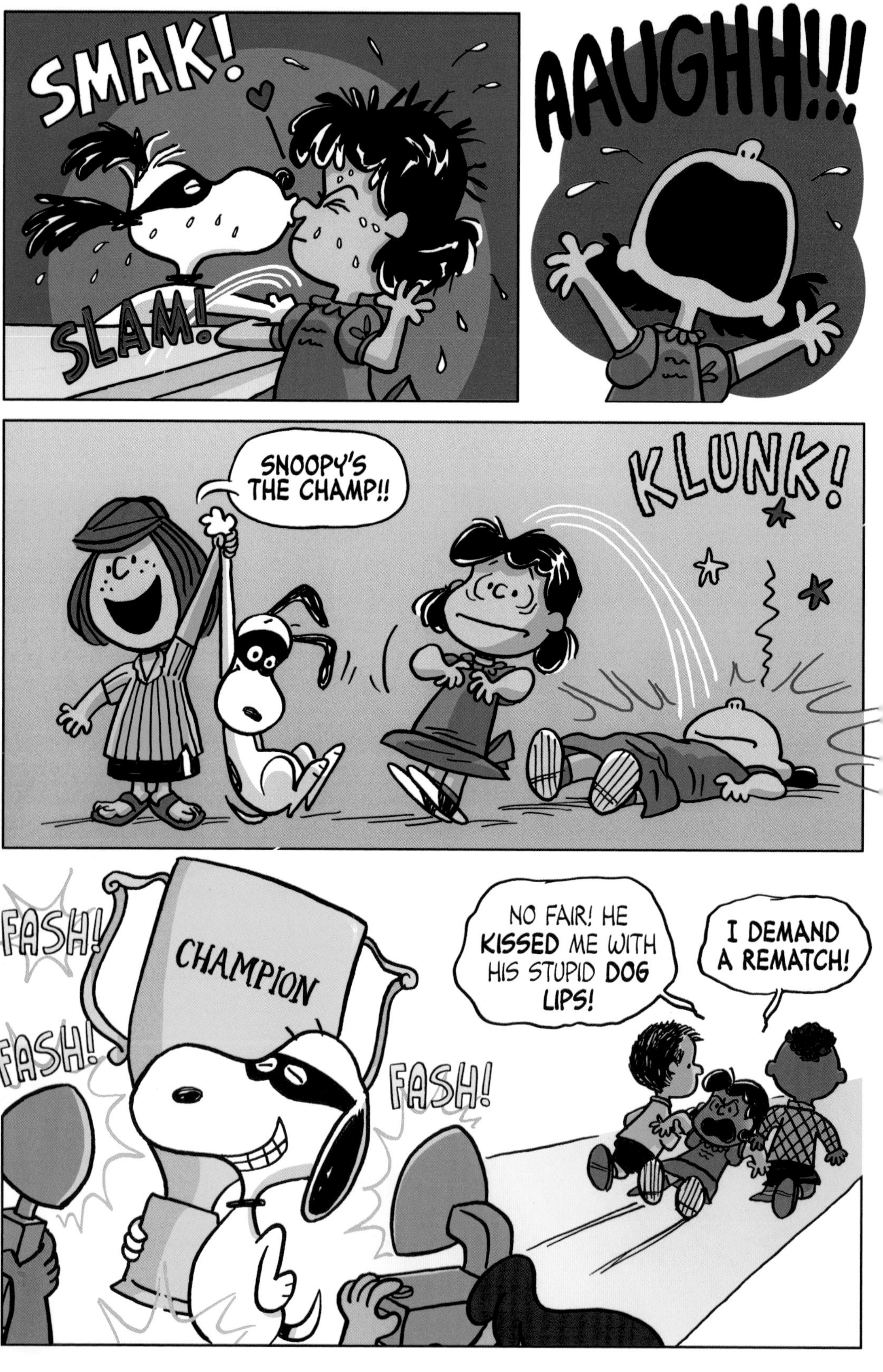
SMAK!
SLAM!
AAUGHH!!!
SNOOPY'S THE CHAMP!!
KLUNK!
FASH!
FASH!
CHAMPION
FASH!
NO FAIR! HE KISSED ME WITH HIS STUPID DOG LIPS!
I DEMAND A REMATCH!

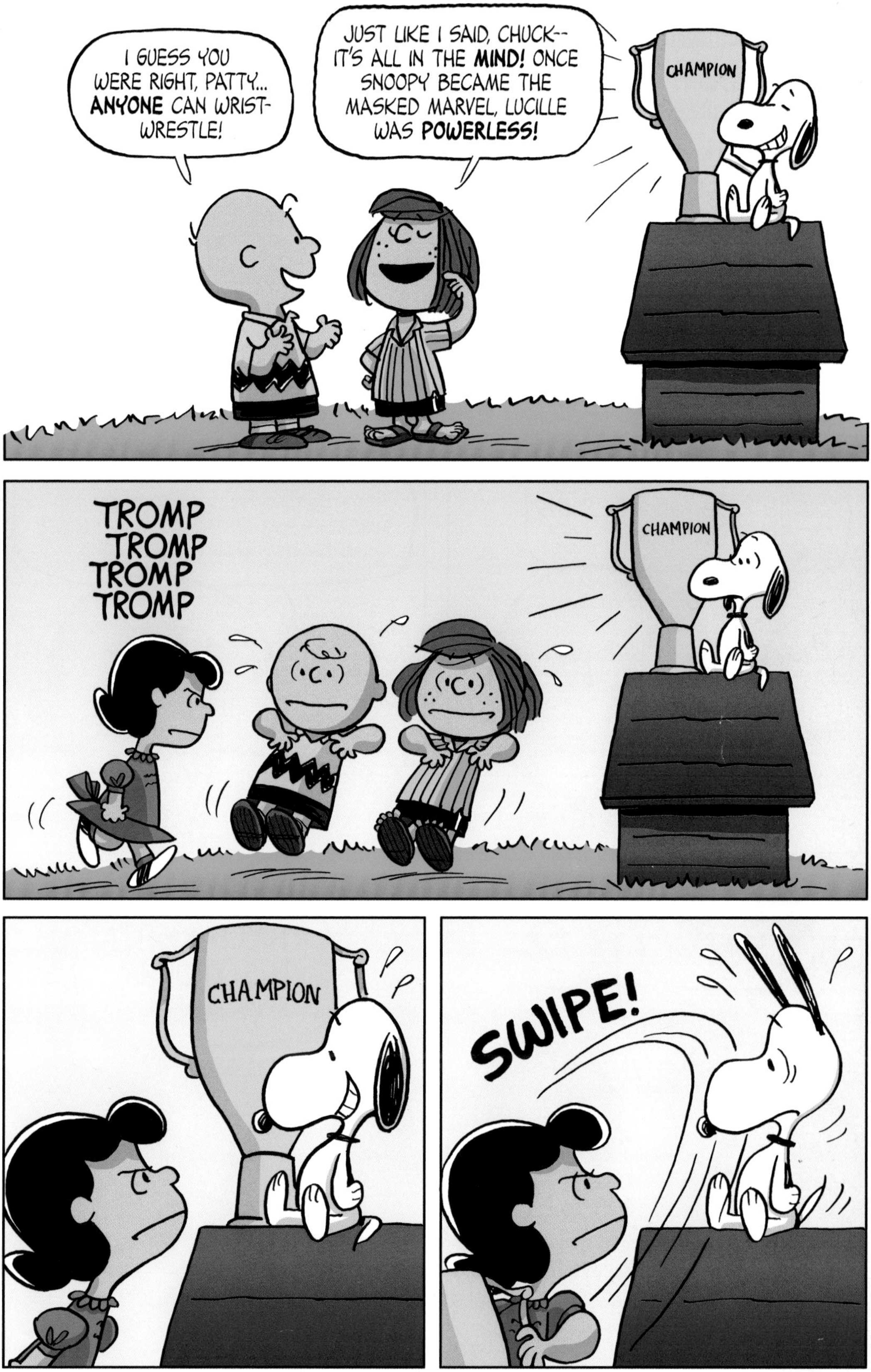
I GUESS YOU WERE RIGHT, PATTY... **ANYONE** CAN WRIST-WRESTLE!
JUST LIKE I SAID, CHUCK-- IT'S ALL IN THE **MIND!** ONCE SNOOPY BECAME THE MASKED MARVEL, LUCILLE WAS **POWERLESS!**
CHAMPION
TROMP TROMP TROMP TROMP
CHAMPION
CHAMPION
SWIPE!

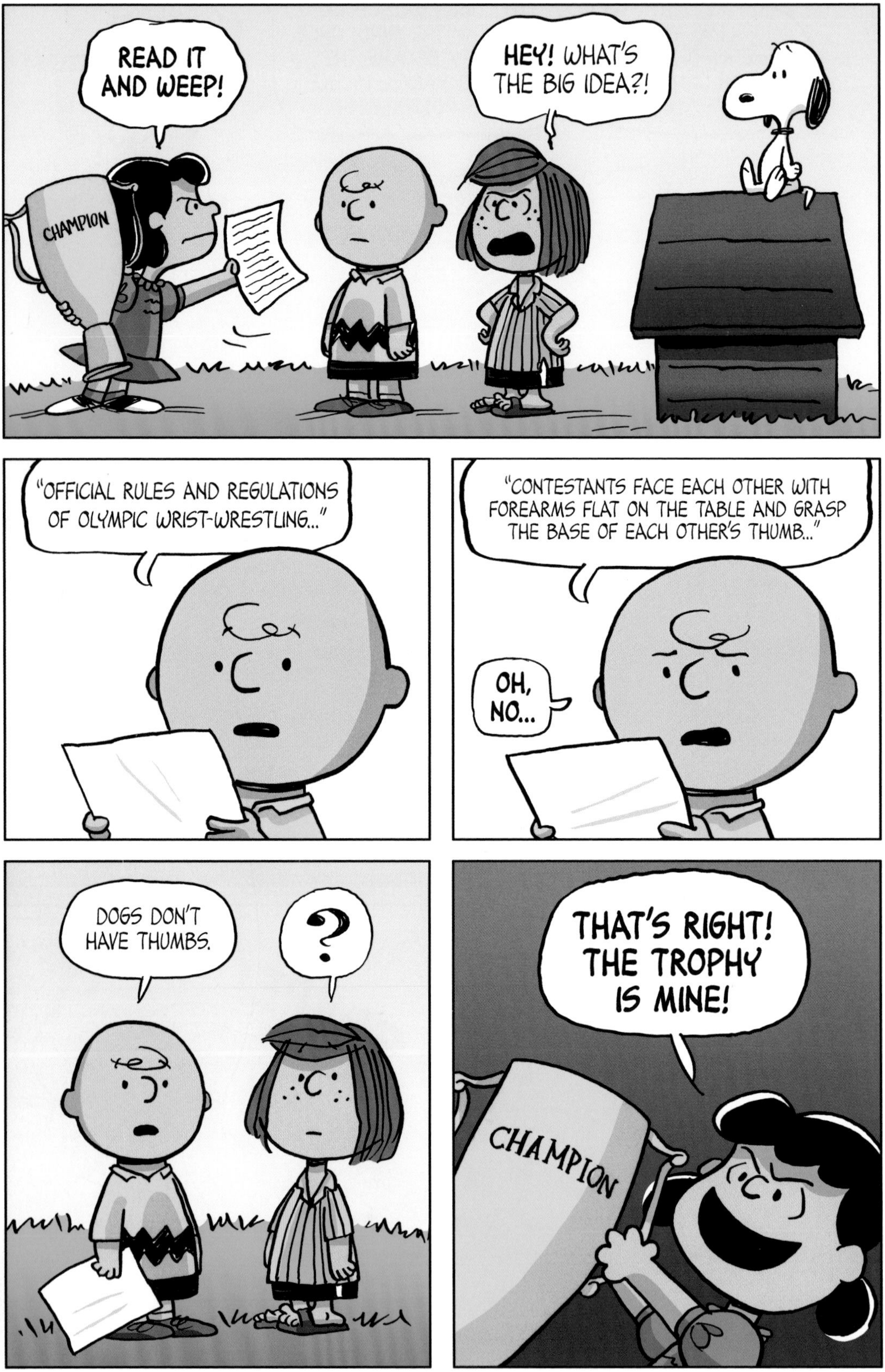
READ IT AND WEEP!
HEY! WHAT'S THE BIG IDEA?!
CHAMPION
"OFFICIAL RULES AND REGULATIONS OF OLYMPIC WRIST-WRESTLING..."
"CONTESTANTS FACE EACH OTHER WITH FOREARMS FLAT ON THE TABLE AND GRASP THE BASE OF EACH OTHER'S THUMB..."
OH, NO...
DOGS DON'T HAVE THUMBS.
?
THAT'S RIGHT! THE TROPHY IS MINE!
CHAMPION

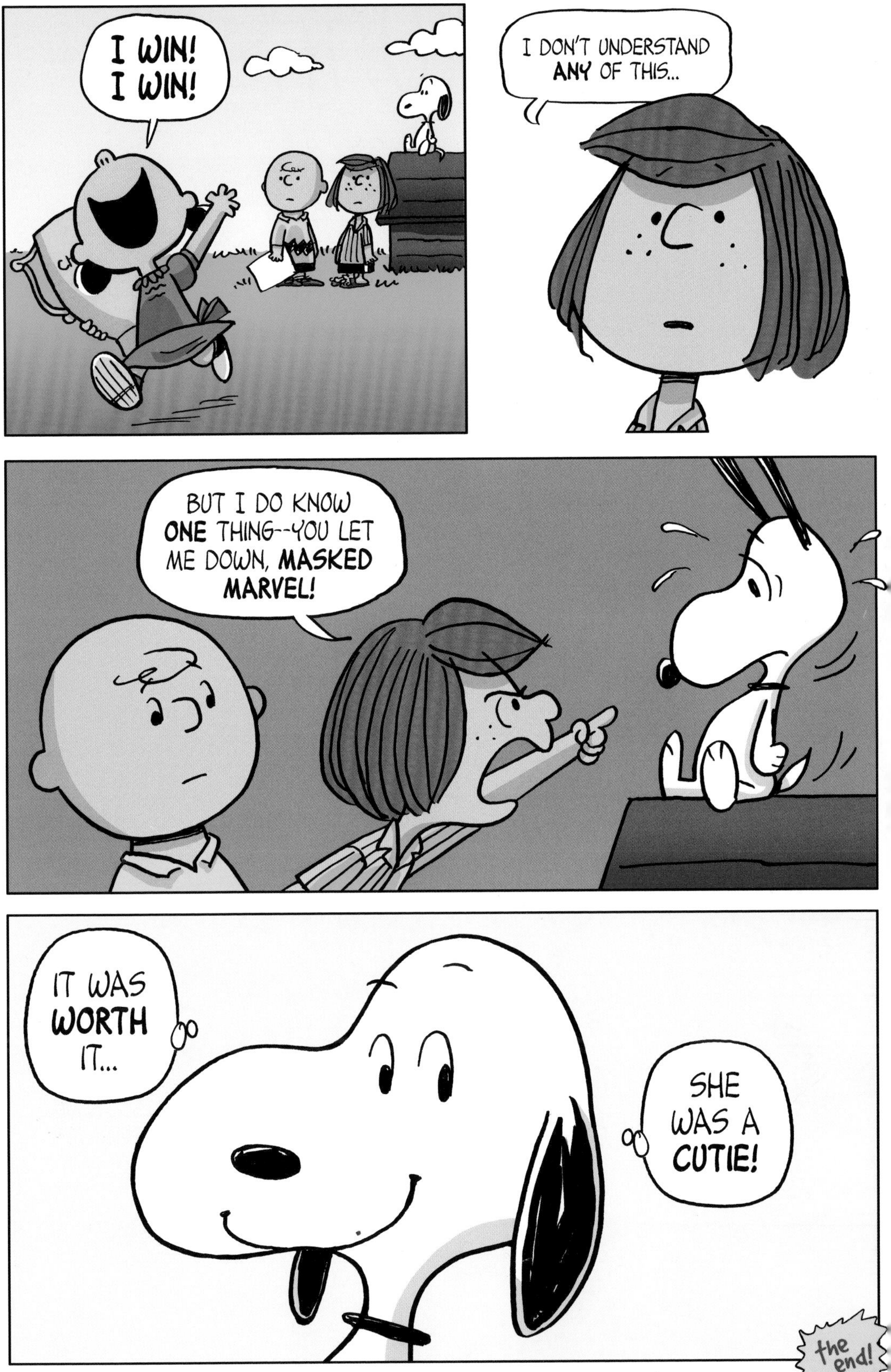
I WIN! I WIN!
I DON'T UNDERSTAND ANY OF THIS...
BUT I DO KNOW ONE THING--YOU LET ME DOWN, MASKED MARVEL!
IT WAS WORTH IT...
SHE WAS A CUTIE!
the end!

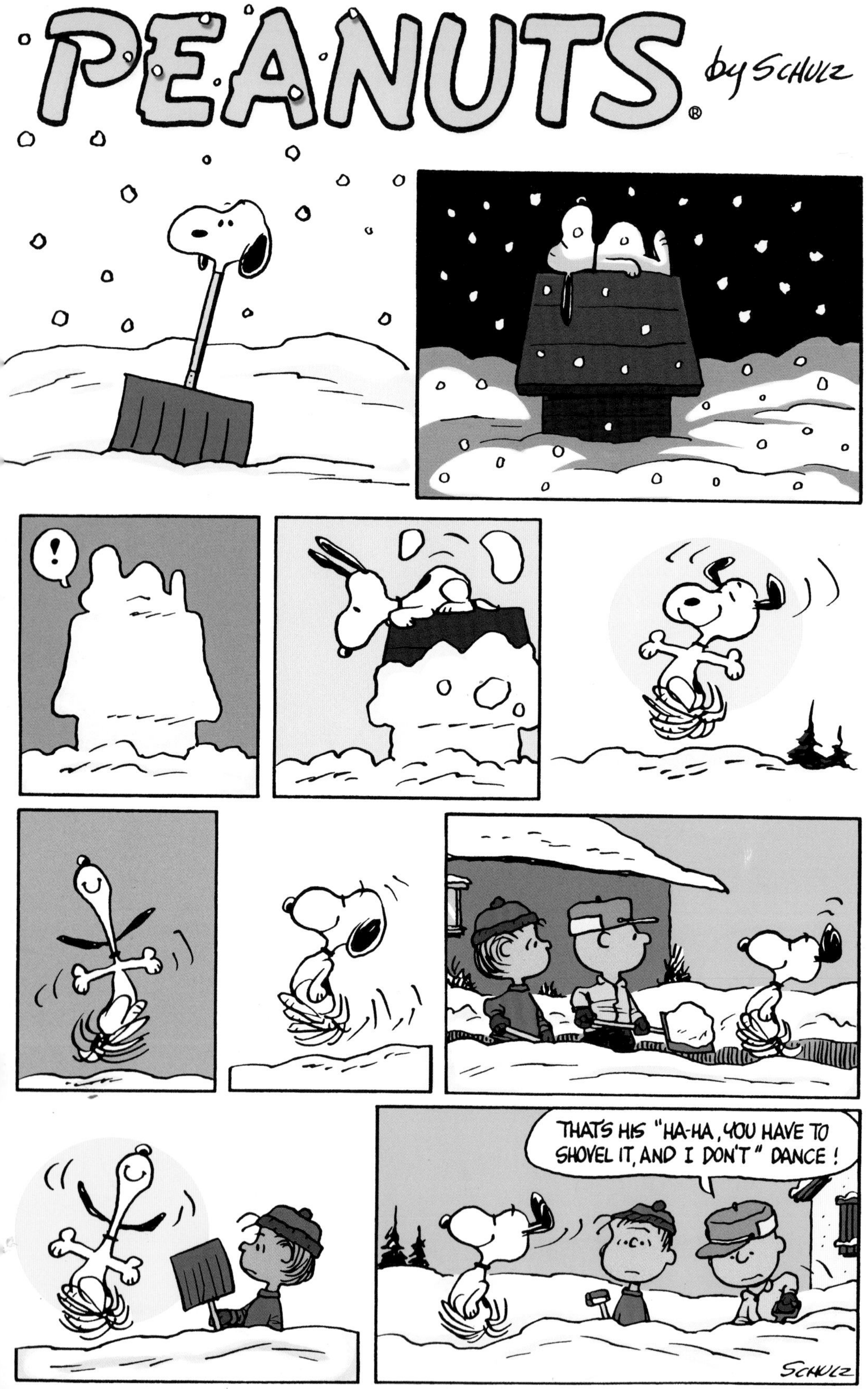
PEANUTS
by SCHULZ
!
THAT'S HIS "HA-HA, YOU HAVE TO SHOVEL IT, AND I DON'T" DANCE!
SCHULZ

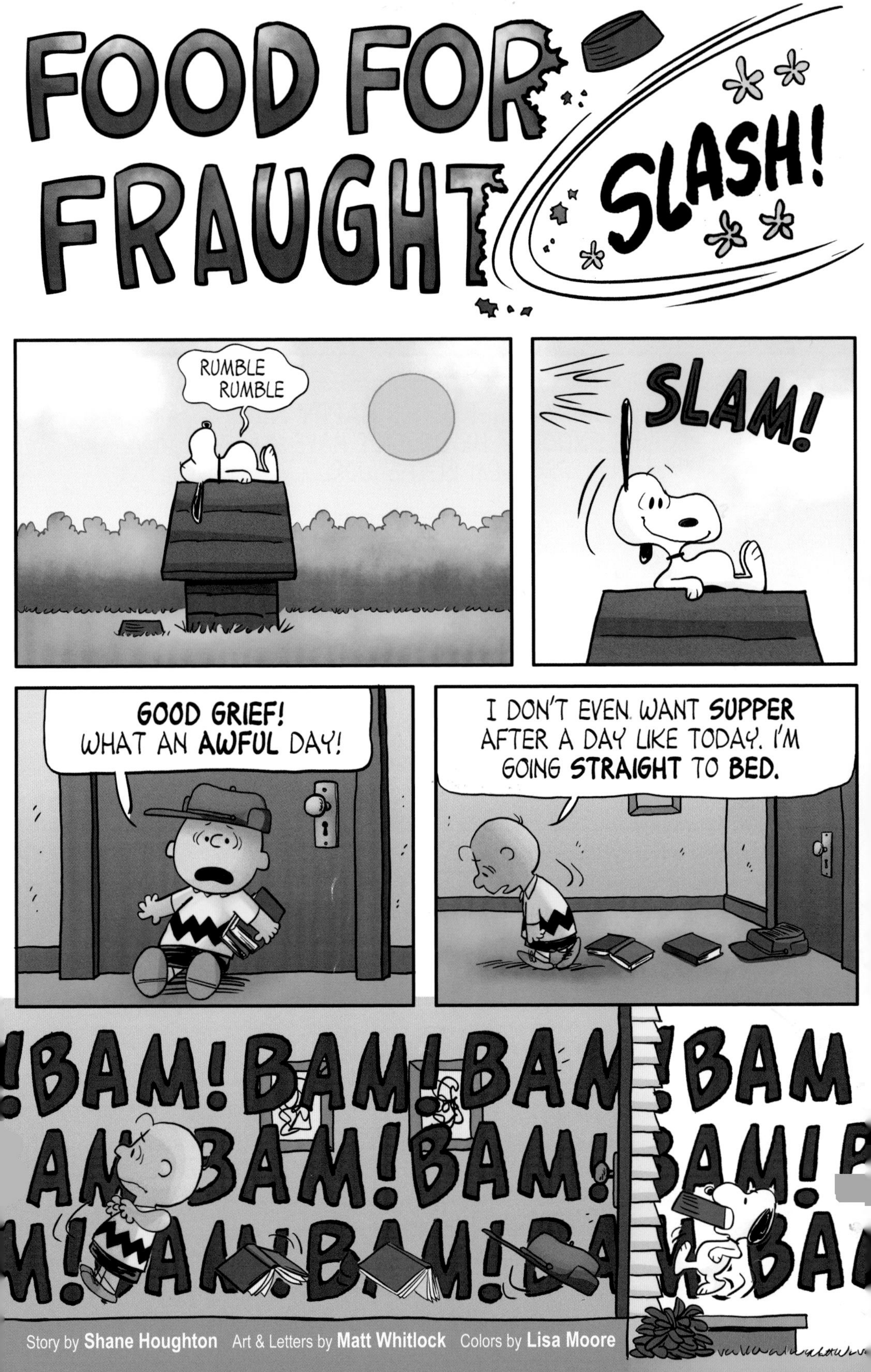
FOOD FOR FRAUGHT
SLASH!
RUMBLE RUMBLE
SLAM!
GOOD GRIEF! WHAT AN AWFUL DAY!
I DON'T EVEN WANT SUPPER AFTER A DAY LIKE TODAY. I'M GOING STRAIGHT TO BED.
BAM! BAM! BAM! BAM
BAM! BAM! BAM!
Story by Shane Houghton Art & Letters by Matt Whitlock Colors by Lisa Moore

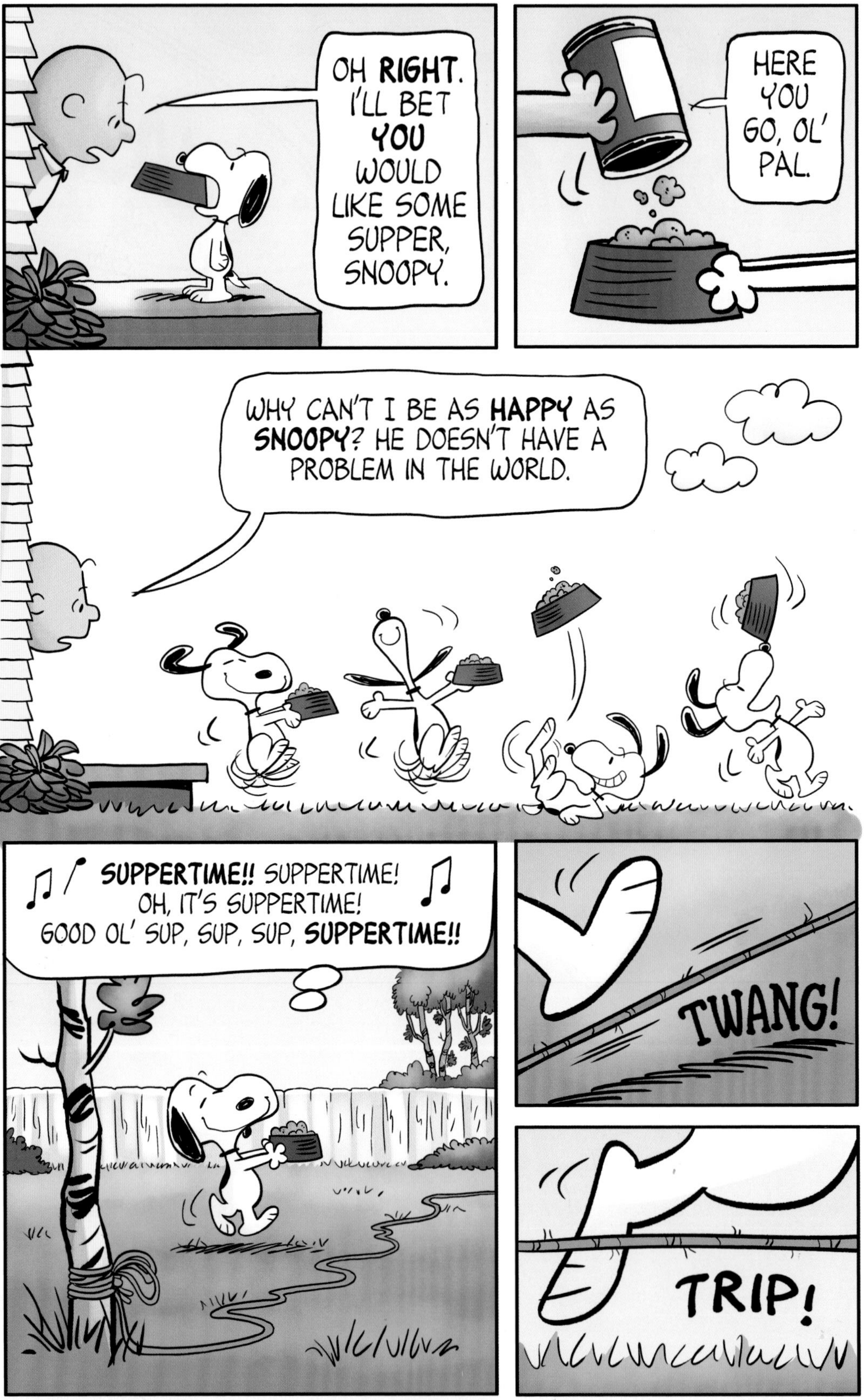
OH RIGHT. I'LL BET YOU WOULD LIKE SOME SUPPER, SNOOPY.
HERE YOU GO, OL' PAL.
WHY CAN'T I BE AS HAPPY AS SNOOPY? HE DOESN'T HAVE A PROBLEM IN THE WORLD.
SUPPERTIME!! SUPPERTIME! OH, IT'S SUPPERTIME! GOOD OL' SUP, SUP, SUP, SUPPERTIME!!
TWANG!
TRIP!

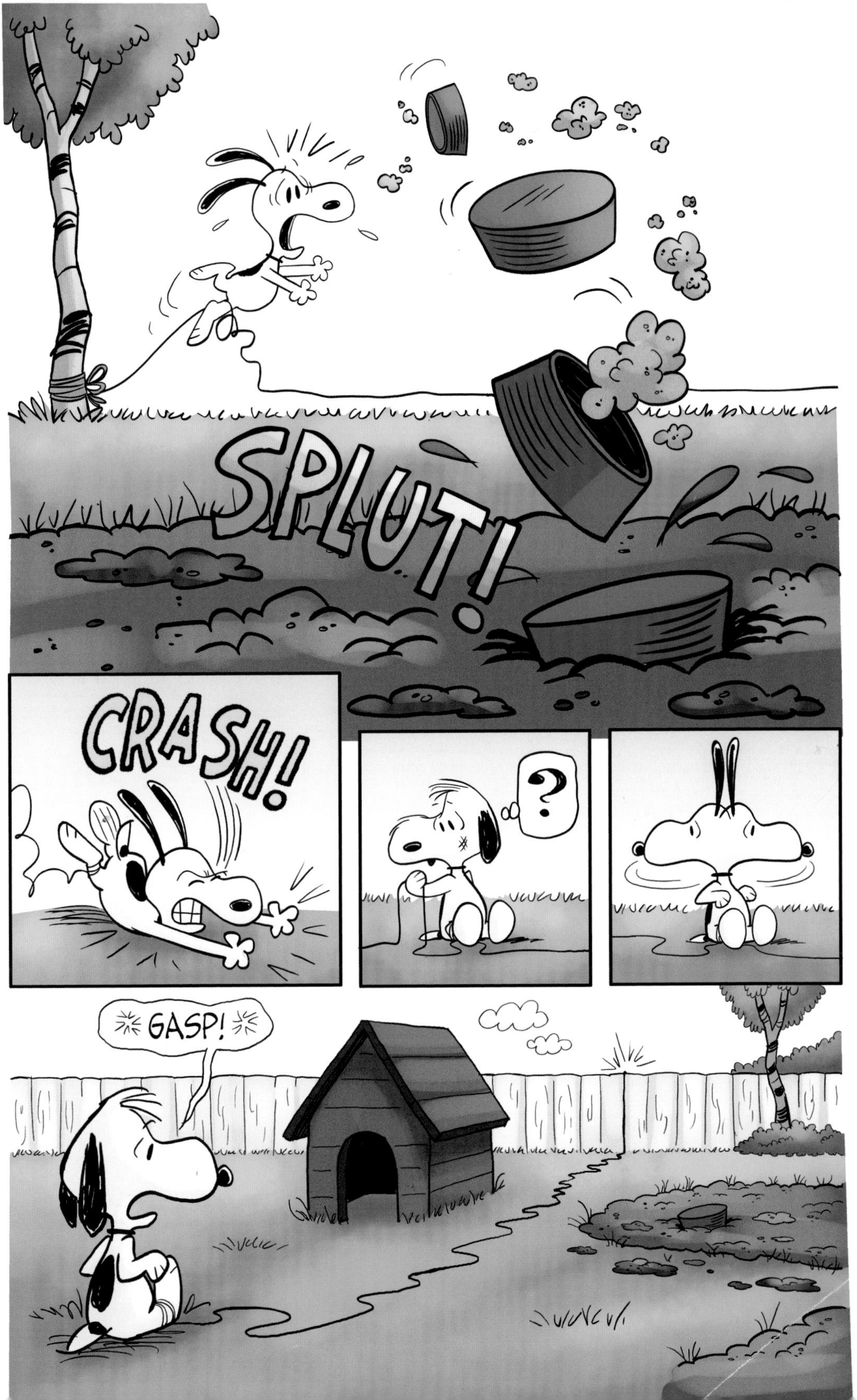
SPLUT!
CRASH!
?
GASP!

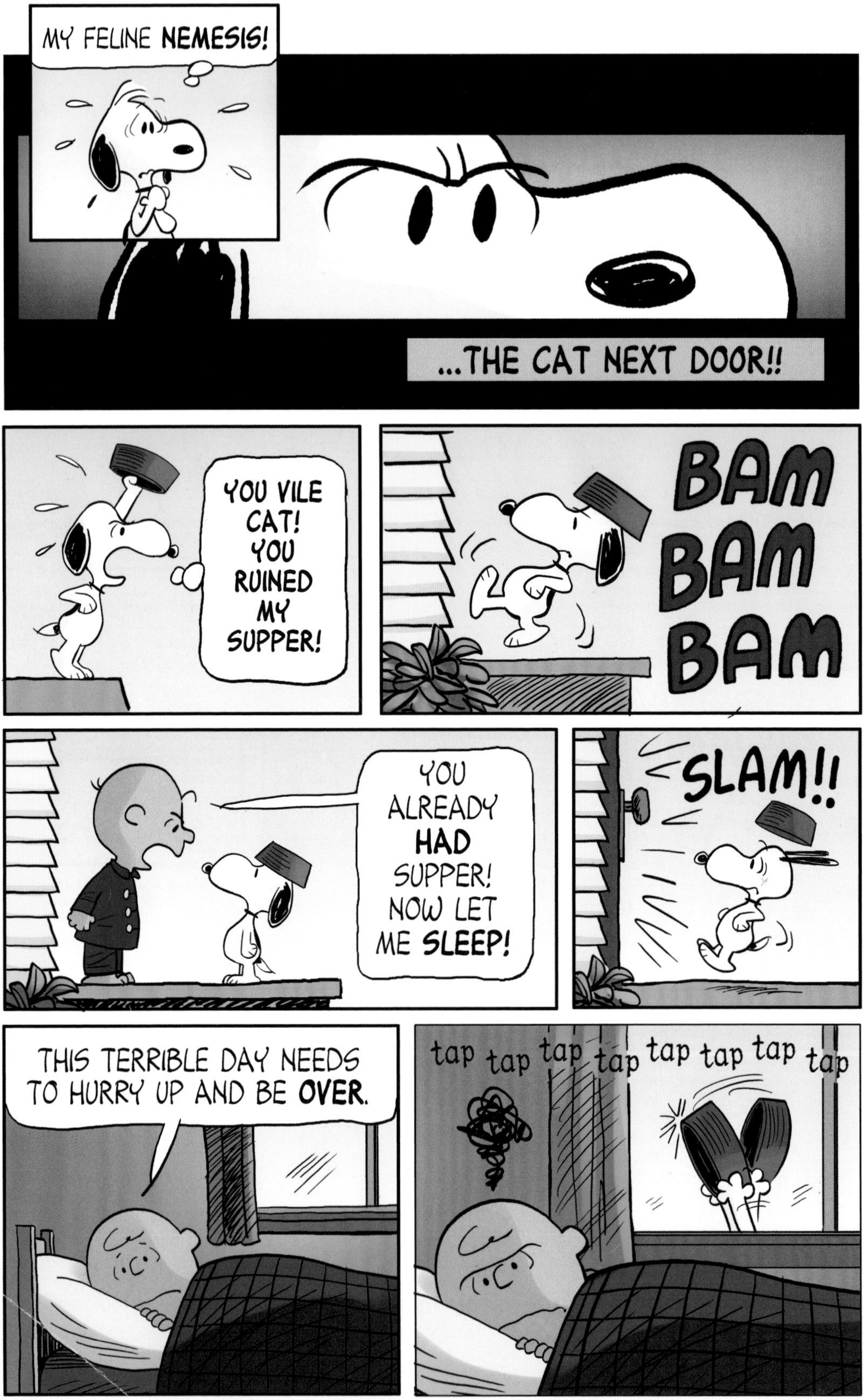
MY FELINE **NEMESIS!**
...THE CAT NEXT DOOR!!
YOU VILE CAT! YOU RUINED MY SUPPER!
BAM BAM BAM
YOU ALREADY **HAD** SUPPER! NOW LET ME **SLEEP!**
SLAM!!
THIS TERRIBLE DAY NEEDS TO HURRY UP AND BE **OVER**.
tap tap tap tap tap tap tap tap

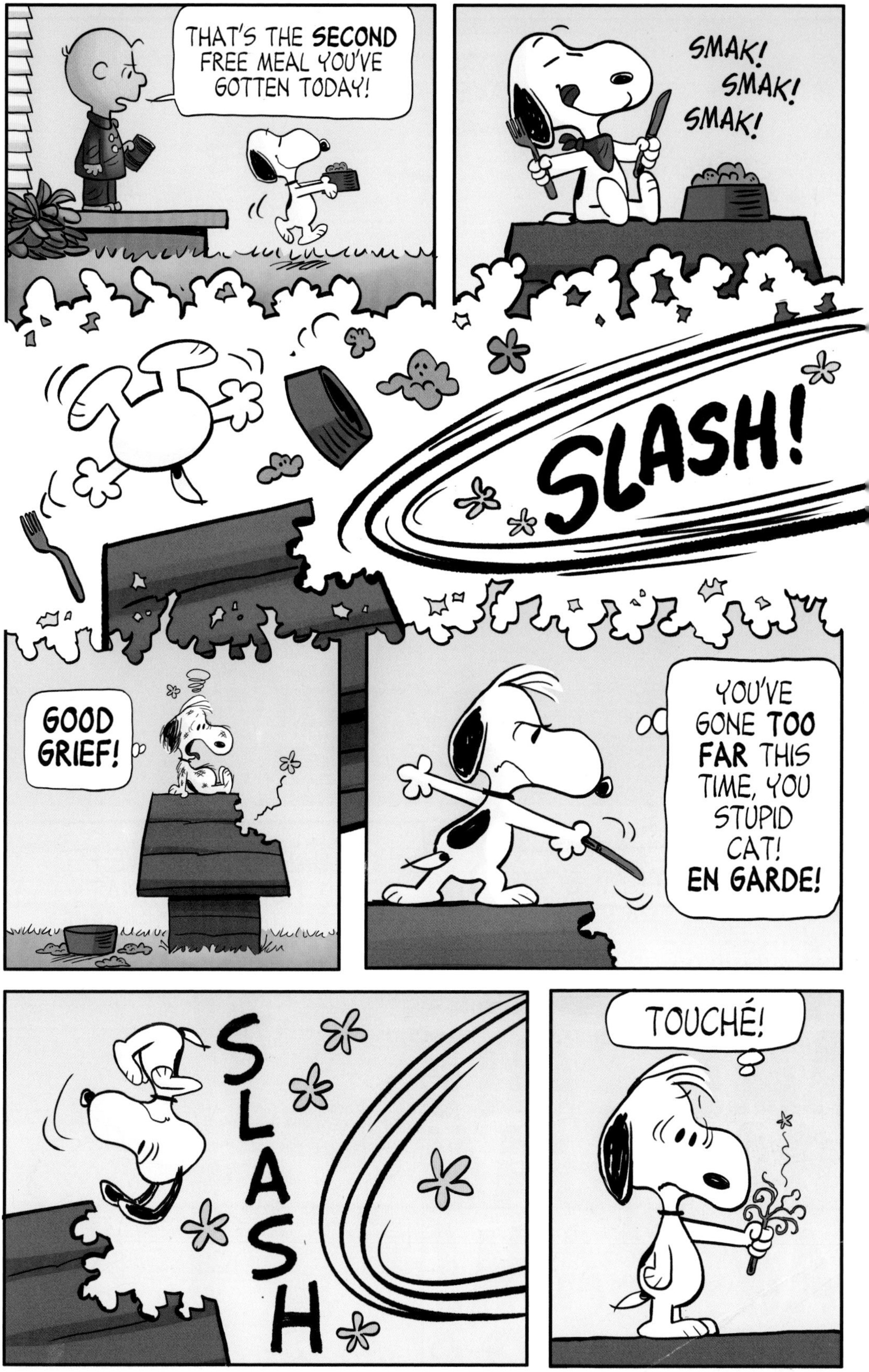
THAT'S THE SECOND FREE MEAL YOU'VE GOTTEN TODAY!
SMAK! SMAK! SMAK!
SLASH!
GOOD GRIEF!
YOU'VE GONE TOO FAR THIS TIME, YOU STUPID CAT! EN GARDE!
SLASH
TOUCHÉ!

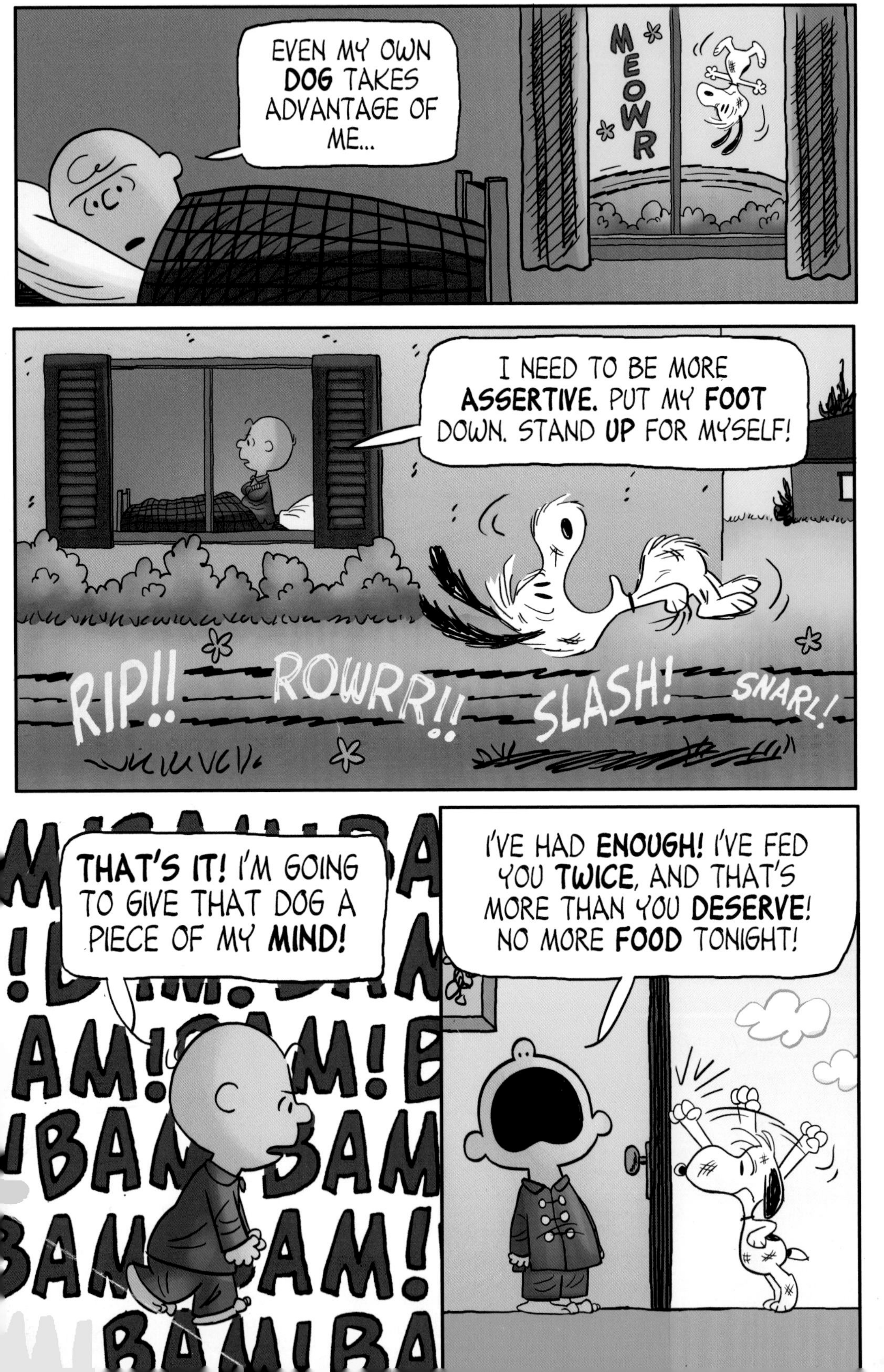
EVEN MY OWN DOG TAKES ADVANTAGE OF ME...
MEOWR
I NEED TO BE MORE ASSERTIVE. PUT MY FOOT DOWN. STAND UP FOR MYSELF!
RIP!! ROWRR!! SLASH! SNARL!
THAT'S IT! I'M GOING TO GIVE THAT DOG A PIECE OF MY MIND!
I'VE HAD ENOUGH! I'VE FED YOU TWICE, AND THAT'S MORE THAN YOU DESERVE! NO MORE FOOD TONIGHT!

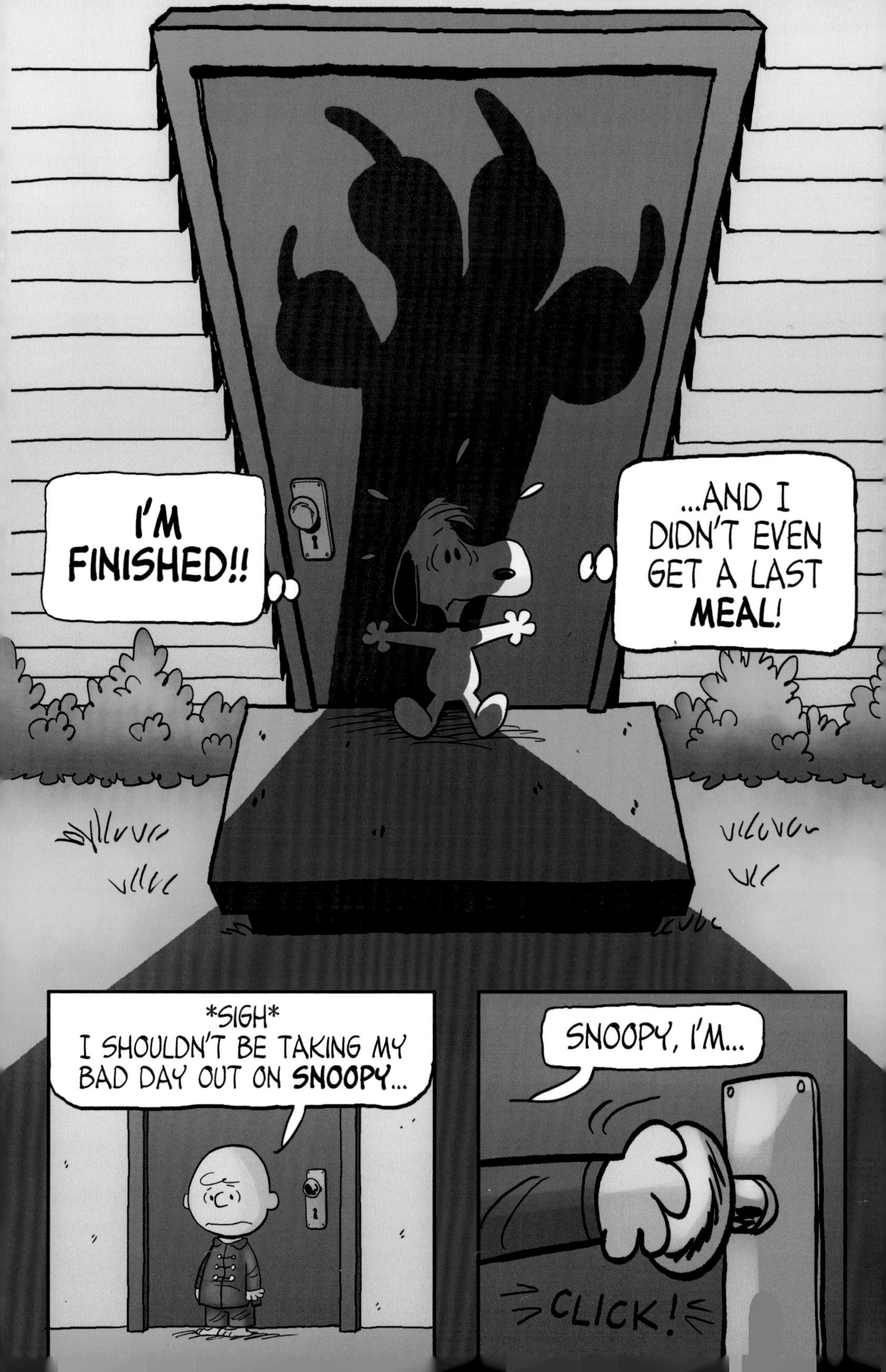
I'M FINISHED!!
...AND I DIDN'T EVEN GET A LAST MEAL!
SIGH I SHOULDN'T BE TAKING MY BAD DAY OUT ON SNOOPY...
SNOOPY, I'M...
CLICK!

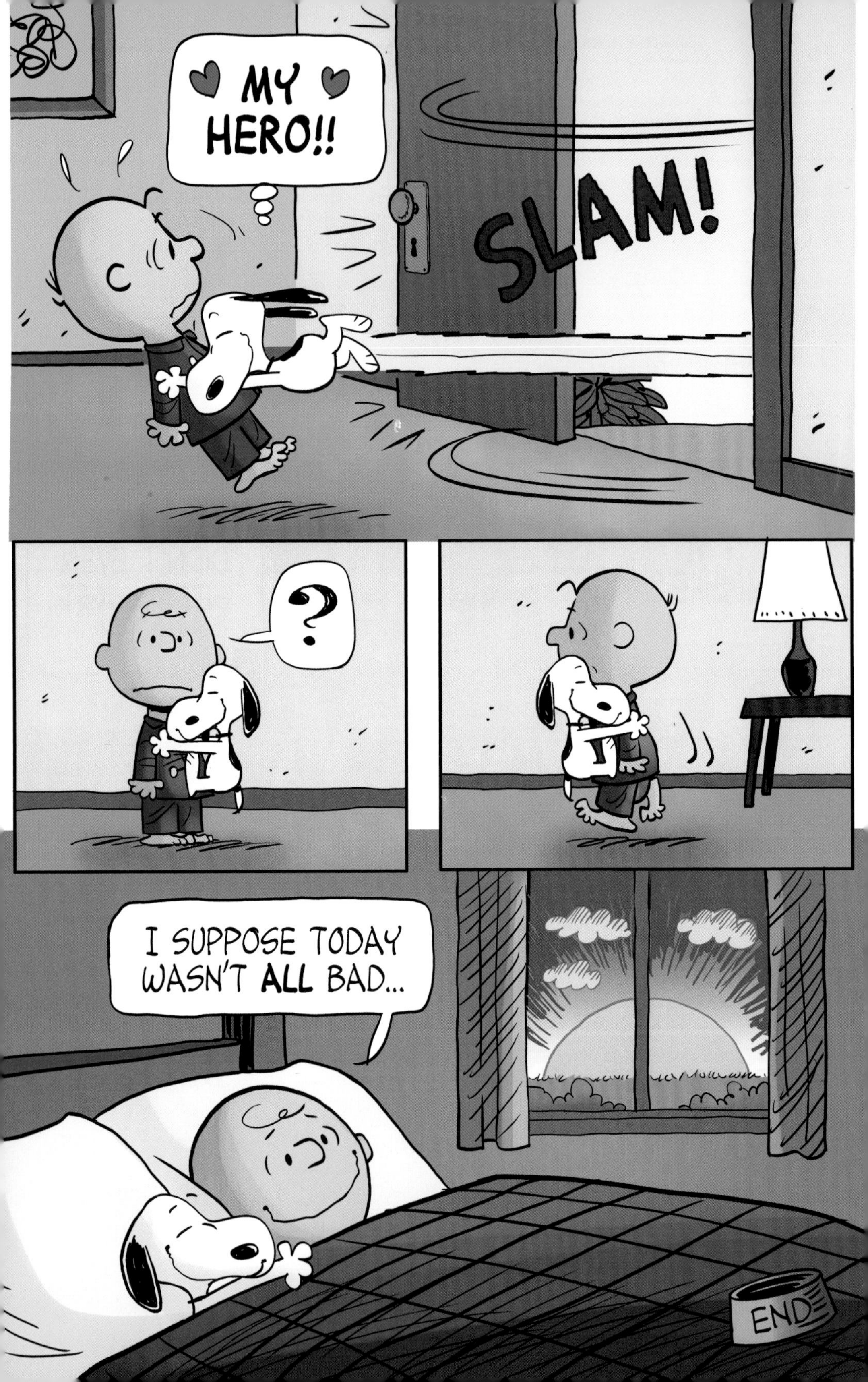
MY HERO!!
SLAM!
?
I SUPPOSE TODAY WASN'T ALL BAD...
END

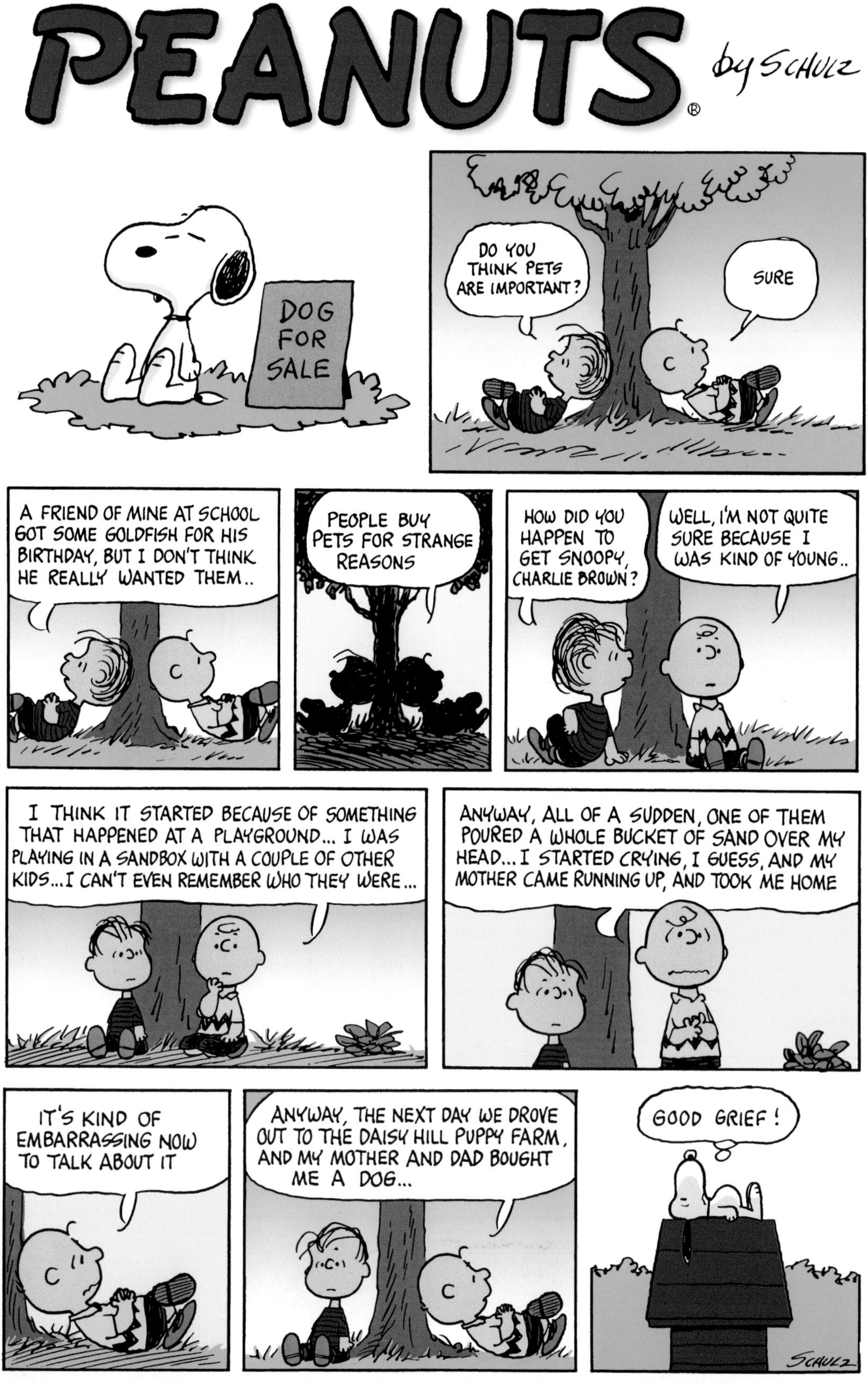
PEANUTS
by SCHULZ
DOG FOR SALE
DO YOU THINK PETS ARE IMPORTANT?
SURE
A FRIEND OF MINE AT SCHOOL GOT SOME GOLDFISH FOR HIS BIRTHDAY, BUT I DON'T THINK HE REALLY WANTED THEM..
PEOPLE BUY PETS FOR STRANGE REASONS
HOW DID YOU HAPPEN TO GET SNOOPY, CHARLIE BROWN?
WELL, I'M NOT QUITE SURE BECAUSE I WAS KIND OF YOUNG..
I THINK IT STARTED BECAUSE OF SOMETHING THAT HAPPENED AT A PLAYGROUND... I WAS PLAYING IN A SANDBOX WITH A COUPLE OF OTHER KIDS...I CAN'T EVEN REMEMBER WHO THEY WERE...
ANYWAY, ALL OF A SUDDEN, ONE OF THEM POURED A WHOLE BUCKET OF SAND OVER MY HEAD... I STARTED CRYING, I GUESS, AND MY MOTHER CAME RUNNING UP, AND TOOK ME HOME
IT'S KIND OF EMBARRASSING NOW TO TALK ABOUT IT
ANYWAY, THE NEXT DAY WE DROVE OUT TO THE DAISY HILL PUPPY FARM, AND MY MOTHER AND DAD BOUGHT ME A DOG...
GOOD GRIEF!
SCHULZ

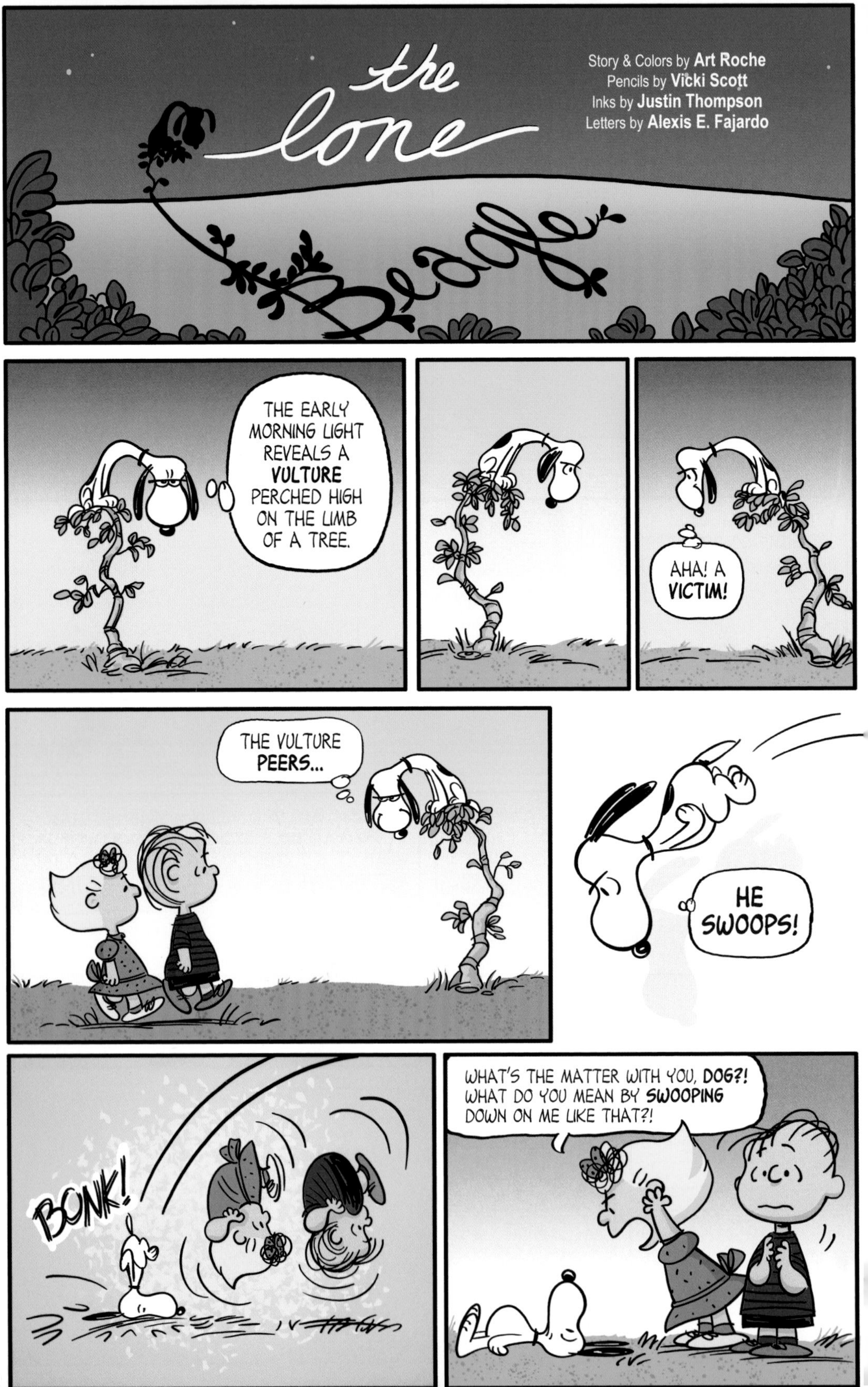
the lone Beagle
Story & Colors by Art Roche
Pencils by Vicki Scott
Inks by Justin Thompson
Letters by Alexis E. Fajardo
THE EARLY MORNING LIGHT REVEALS A VULTURE PERCHED HIGH ON THE LIMB OF A TREE.
AHA! A VICTIM!
THE VULTURE PEERS...
HE SWOOPS!
BONK!
WHAT'S THE MATTER WITH YOU, DOG?! WHAT DO YOU MEAN BY SWOOPING DOWN ON ME LIKE THAT?!

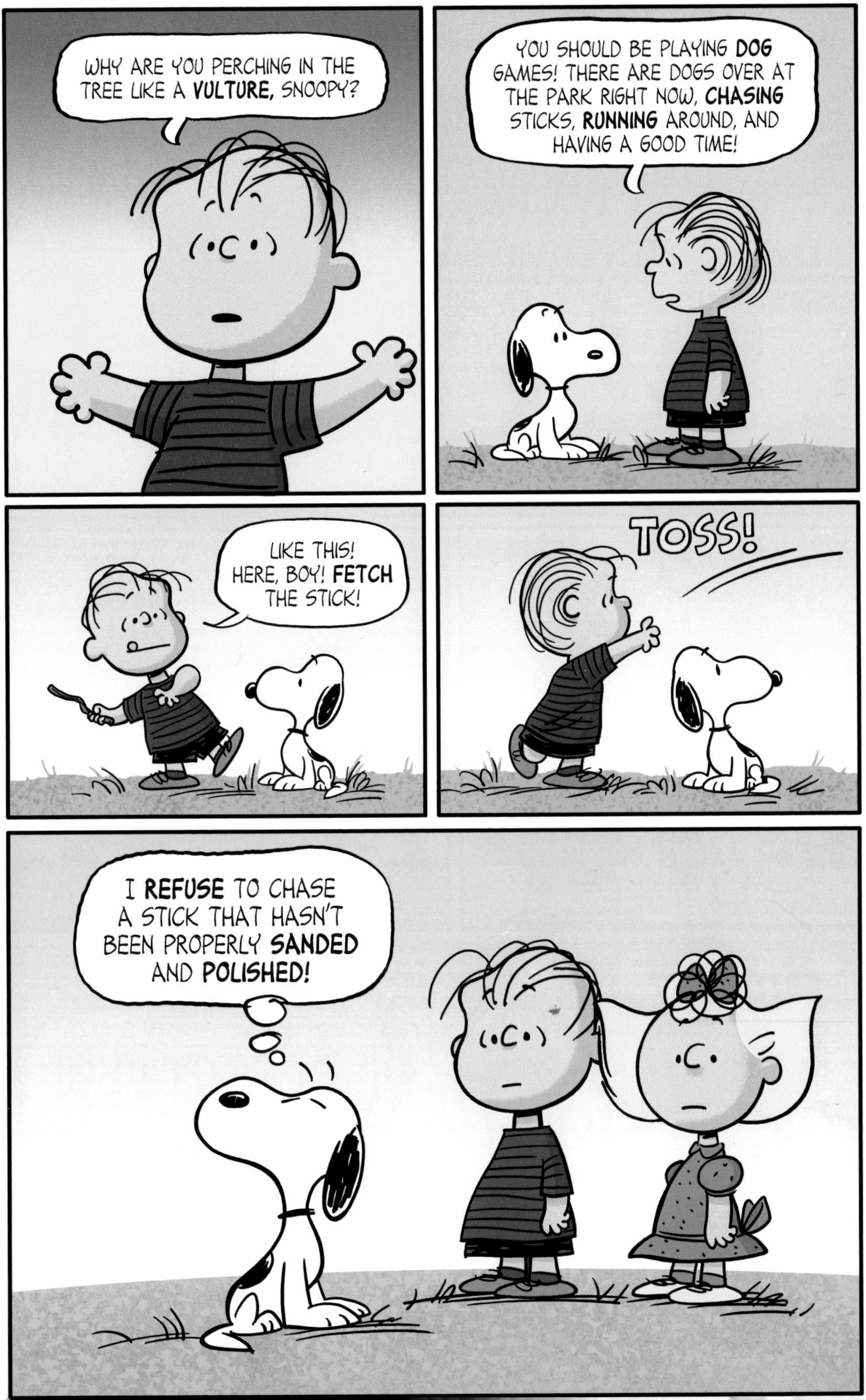
WHY ARE YOU PERCHING IN THE TREE LIKE A **VULTURE,** SNOOPY?
YOU SHOULD BE PLAYING **DOG** GAMES! THERE ARE DOGS OVER AT THE PARK RIGHT NOW, **CHASING** STICKS, **RUNNING** AROUND, AND HAVING A GOOD TIME!
LIKE THIS! HERE, BOY! **FETCH** THE STICK!
TOSS!
I **REFUSE** TO CHASE A STICK THAT HASN'T BEEN PROPERLY **SANDED** AND **POLISHED!**

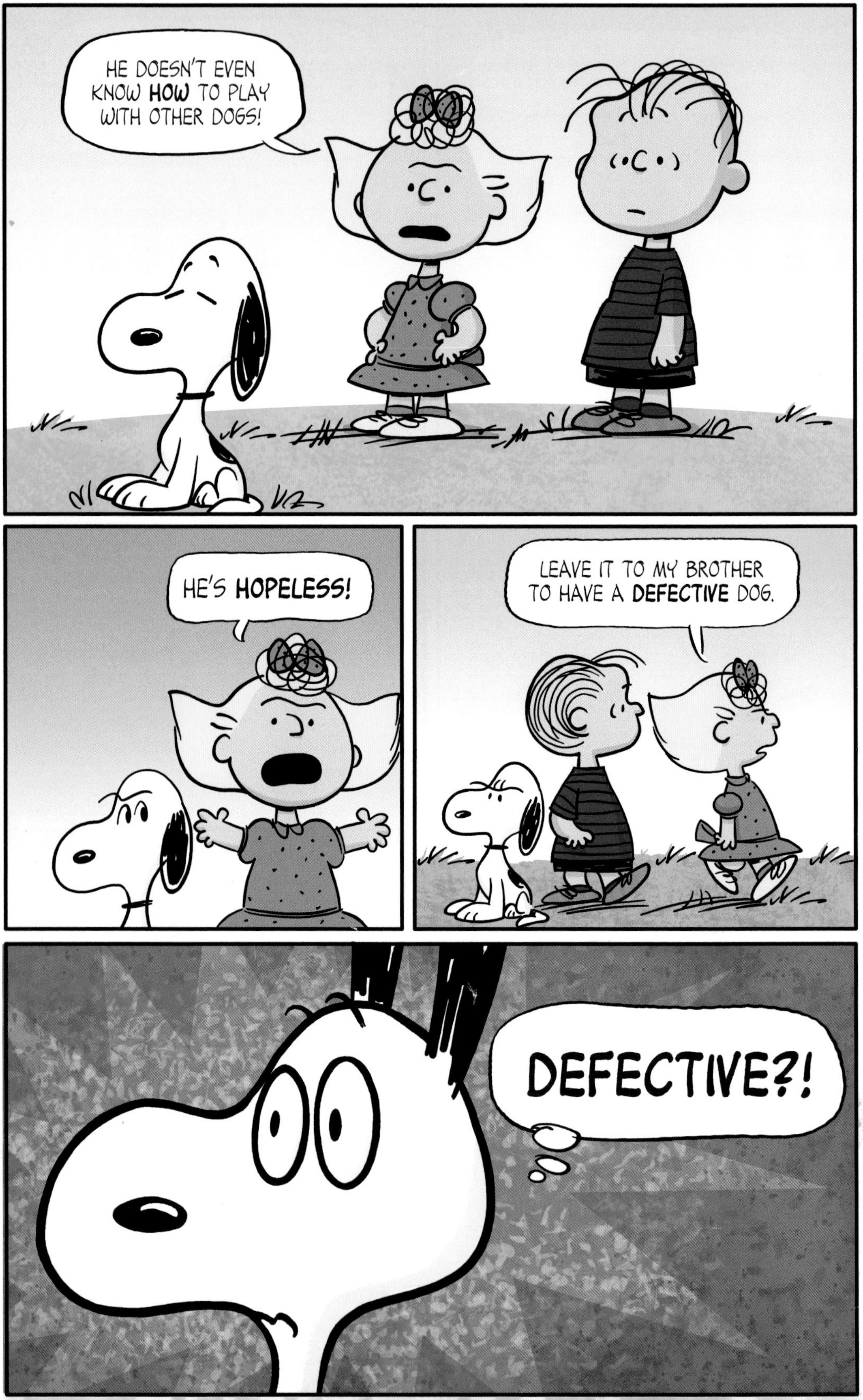
HE DOESN'T EVEN KNOW **HOW** TO PLAY WITH OTHER DOGS!
HE'S **HOPELESS!**
LEAVE IT TO MY BROTHER TO HAVE A **DEFECTIVE** DOG.
DEFECTIVE?!

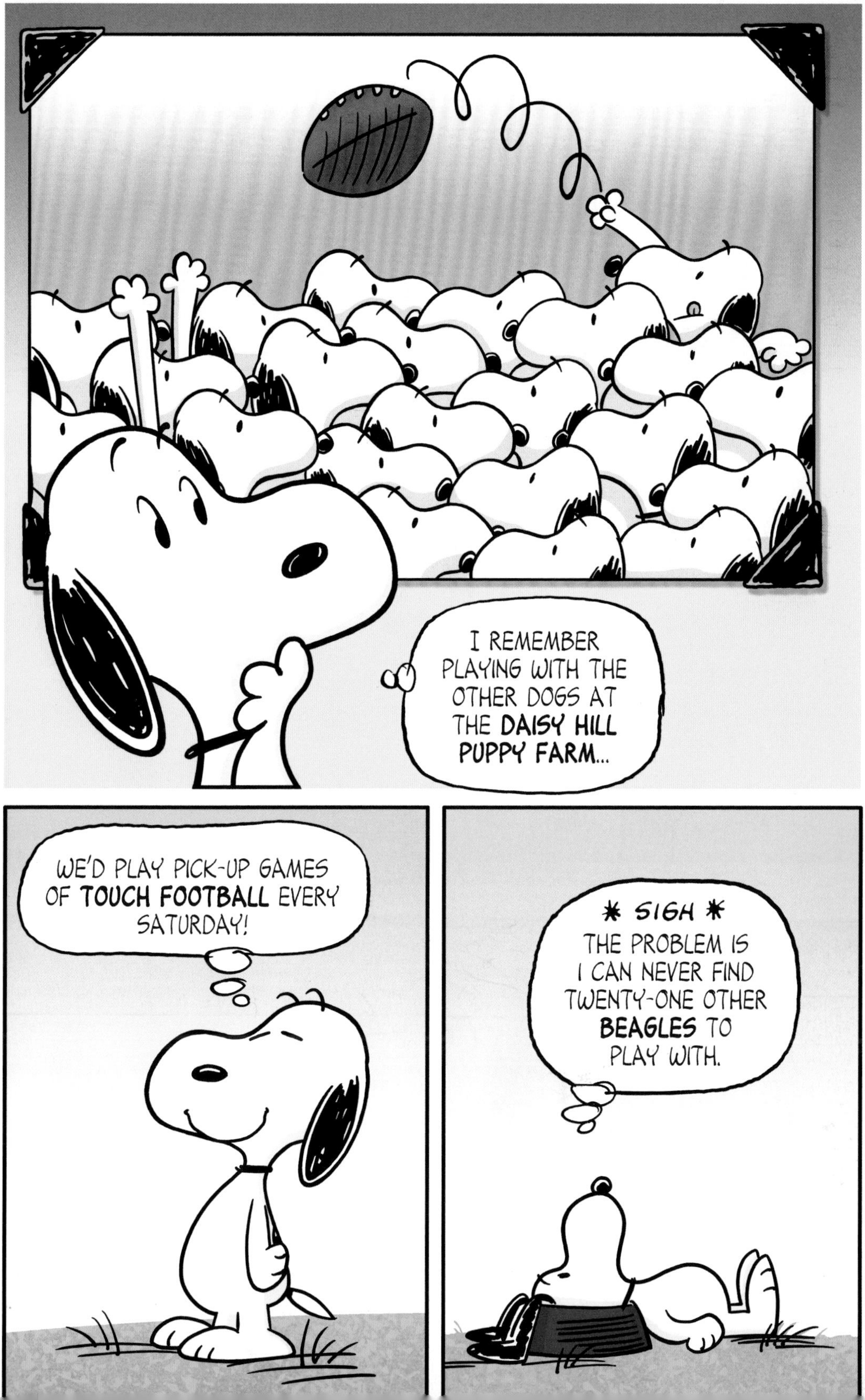
I REMEMBER PLAYING WITH THE OTHER DOGS AT THE **DAISY HILL PUPPY FARM**...
WE'D PLAY PICK-UP GAMES OF **TOUCH FOOTBALL** EVERY SATURDAY!
* SIGH *
THE PROBLEM IS I CAN NEVER FIND TWENTY-ONE OTHER **BEAGLES** TO PLAY WITH.

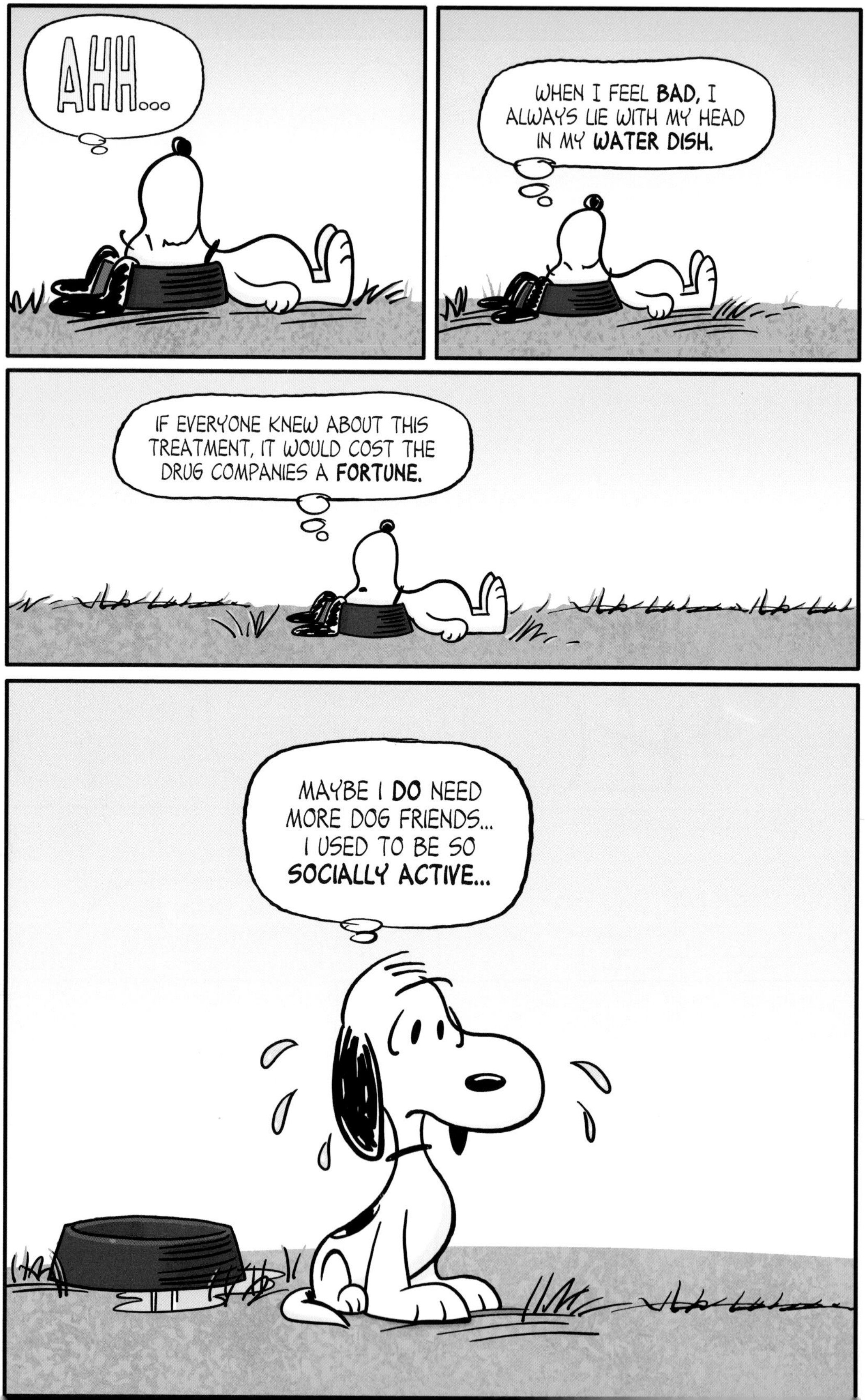
AHH...
WHEN I FEEL BAD, I ALWAYS LIE WITH MY HEAD IN MY WATER DISH.
IF EVERYONE KNEW ABOUT THIS TREATMENT, IT WOULD COST THE DRUG COMPANIES A FORTUNE.
MAYBE I DO NEED MORE DOG FRIENDS... I USED TO BE SO SOCIALLY ACTIVE...

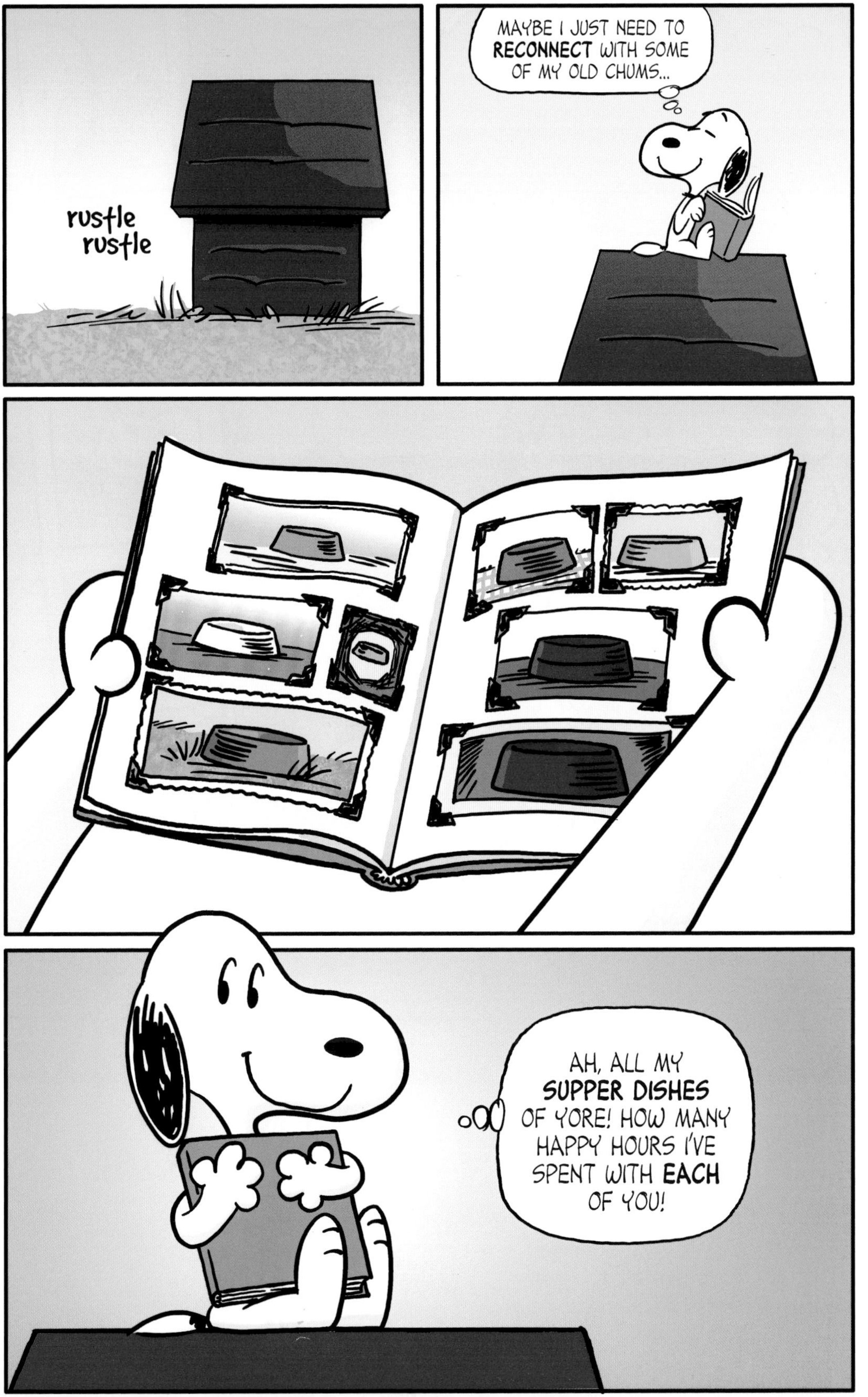
rustle rustle
MAYBE I JUST NEED TO **RECONNECT** WITH SOME OF MY OLD CHUMS...
AH, ALL MY **SUPPER DISHES** OF YORE! HOW MANY HAPPY HOURS I'VE SPENT WITH **EACH** OF YOU!

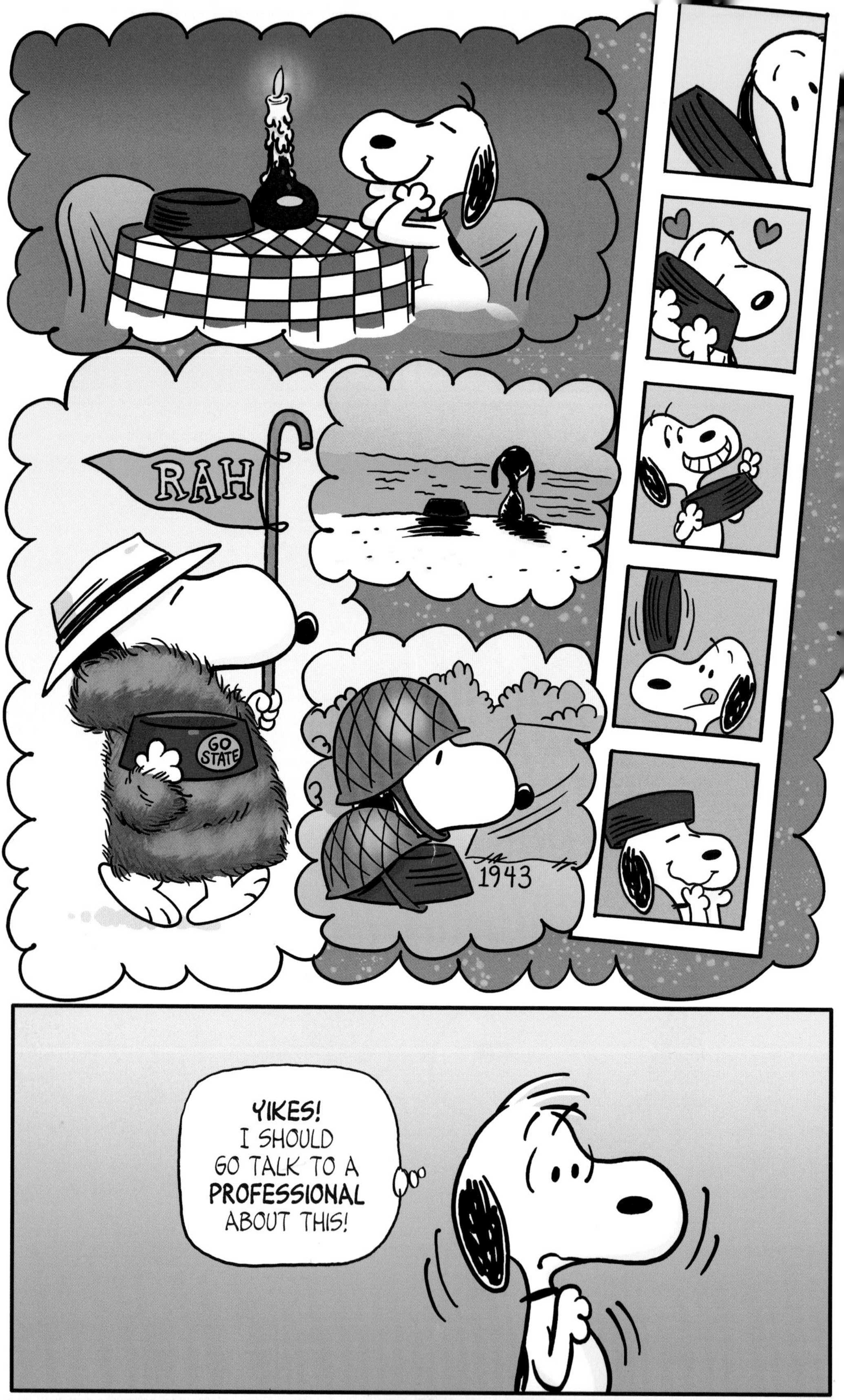
RAH
GO STATE
1943
YIKES! I SHOULD GO TALK TO A PROFESSIONAL ABOUT THIS!

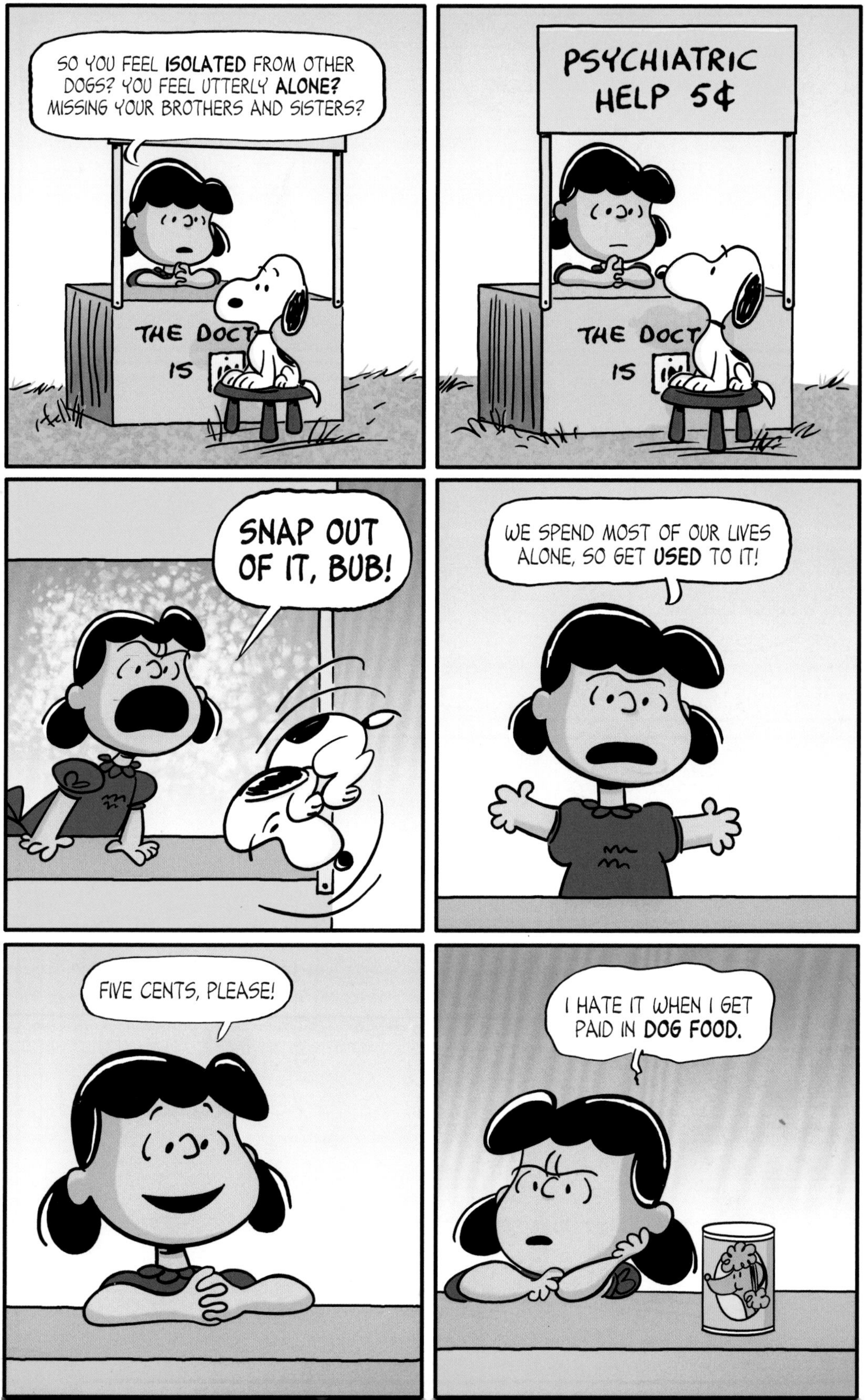
SO YOU FEEL ISOLATED FROM OTHER DOGS? YOU FEEL UTTERLY ALONE? MISSING YOUR BROTHERS AND SISTERS?
THE DOCT
IS
PSYCHIATRIC HELP 5¢
THE DOCT
IS
SNAP OUT OF IT, BUB!
WE SPEND MOST OF OUR LIVES ALONE, SO GET USED TO IT!
FIVE CENTS, PLEASE!
I HATE IT WHEN I GET PAID IN DOG FOOD.

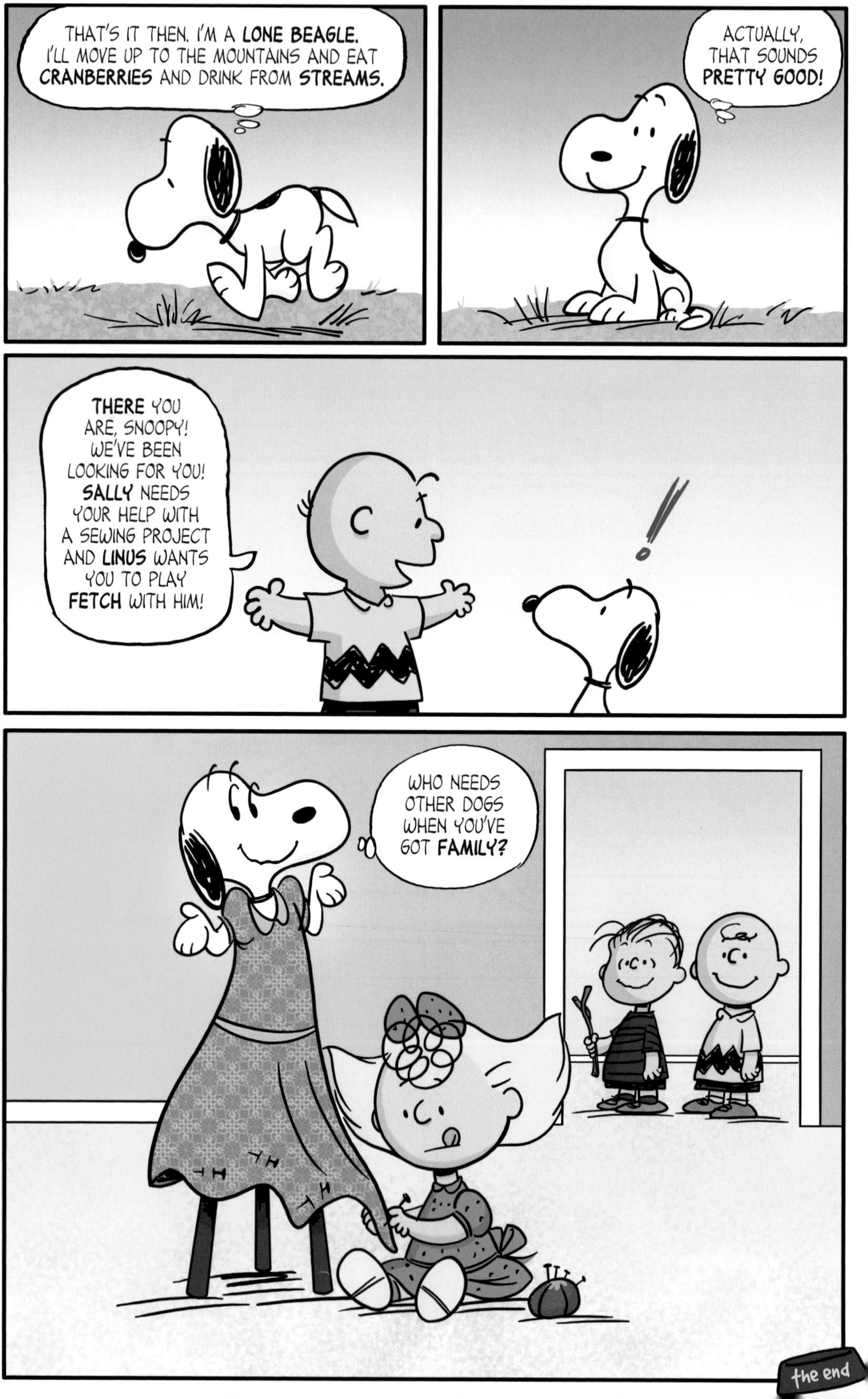
THAT'S IT THEN. I'M A LONE BEAGLE. I'LL MOVE UP TO THE MOUNTAINS AND EAT CRANBERRIES AND DRINK FROM STREAMS.
ACTUALLY, THAT SOUNDS PRETTY GOOD!
THERE YOU ARE, SNOOPY! WE'VE BEEN LOOKING FOR YOU! SALLY NEEDS YOUR HELP WITH A SEWING PROJECT AND LINUS WANTS YOU TO PLAY FETCH WITH HIM!
!
WHO NEEDS OTHER DOGS WHEN YOU'VE GOT FAMILY?
the end

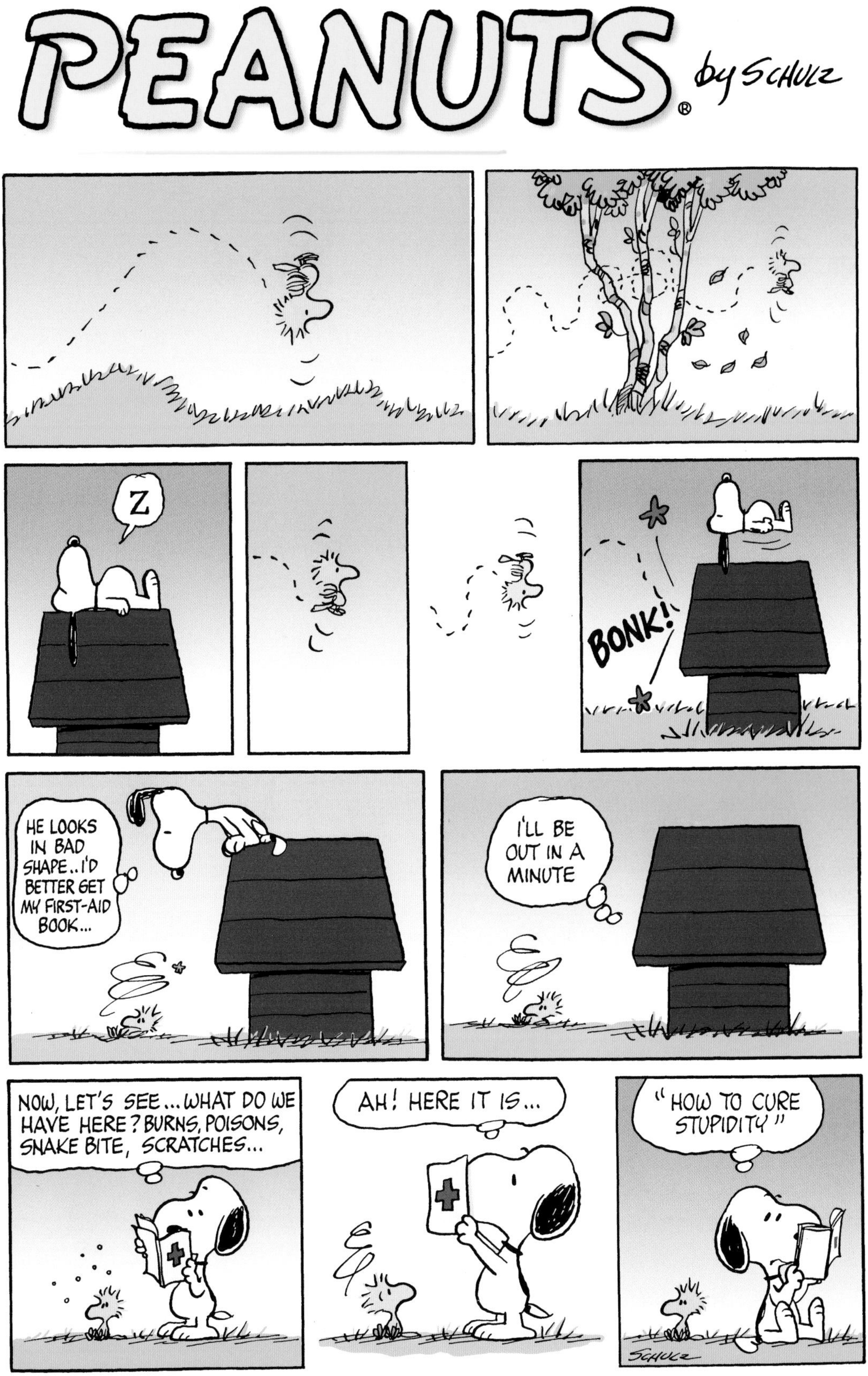
PEANUTS
by SCHULZ
Z
BONK!
HE LOOKS IN BAD SHAPE..I'D BETTER GET MY FIRST-AID BOOK...
I'LL BE OUT IN A MINUTE
NOW, LET'S SEE...WHAT DO WE HAVE HERE? BURNS, POISONS, SNAKE BITE, SCRATCHES...
AH! HERE IT IS...
"HOW TO CURE STUPIDITY"
SCHULZ

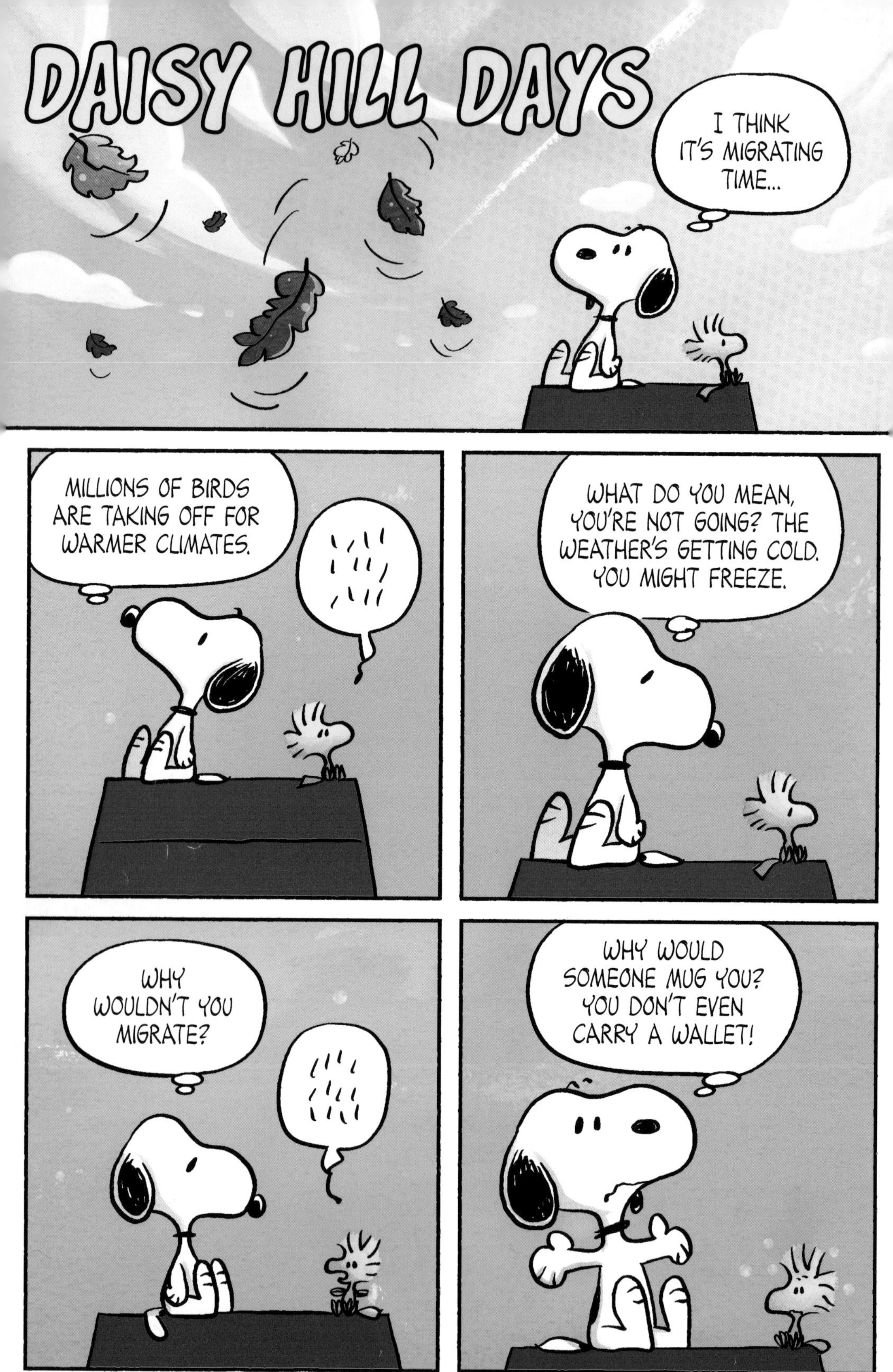
DAISY HILL DAYS
I THINK IT'S MIGRATING TIME...
MILLIONS OF BIRDS ARE TAKING OFF FOR WARMER CLIMATES.
WHAT DO YOU MEAN, YOU'RE NOT GOING? THE WEATHER'S GETTING COLD. YOU MIGHT FREEZE.
WHY WOULDN'T YOU MIGRATE?
WHY WOULD SOMEONE MUG YOU? YOU DON'T EVEN CARRY A WALLET!

Story by **Jason Cooper** Art & Letters by **Donna Almendrala** Colors by **Katharine Efird**

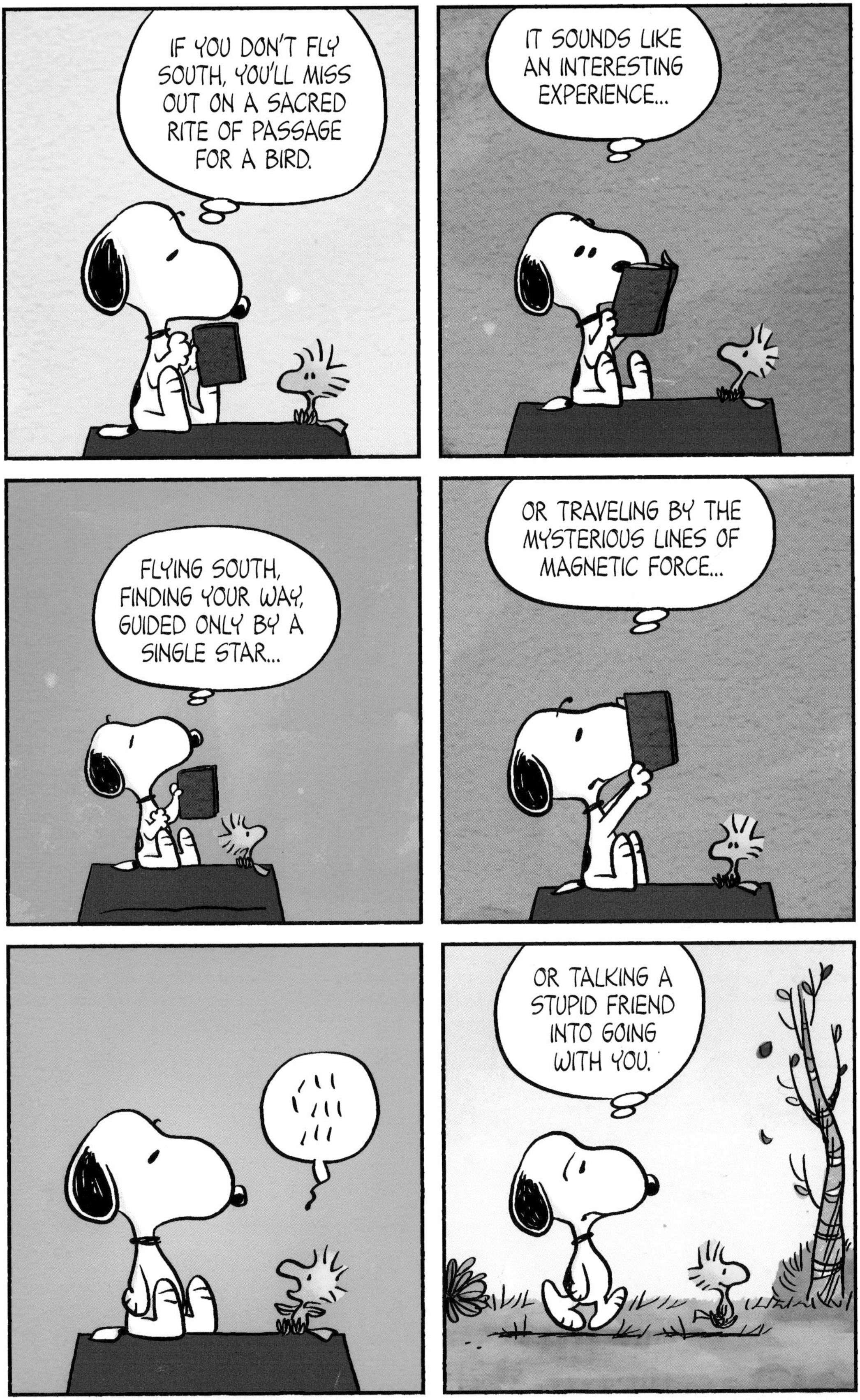
IF YOU DON'T FLY SOUTH, YOU'LL MISS OUT ON A SACRED RITE OF PASSAGE FOR A BIRD.
IT SOUNDS LIKE AN INTERESTING EXPERIENCE...
FLYING SOUTH, FINDING YOUR WAY, GUIDED ONLY BY A SINGLE STAR...
OR TRAVELING BY THE MYSTERIOUS LINES OF MAGNETIC FORCE...
OR TALKING A STUPID FRIEND INTO GOING WITH YOU.

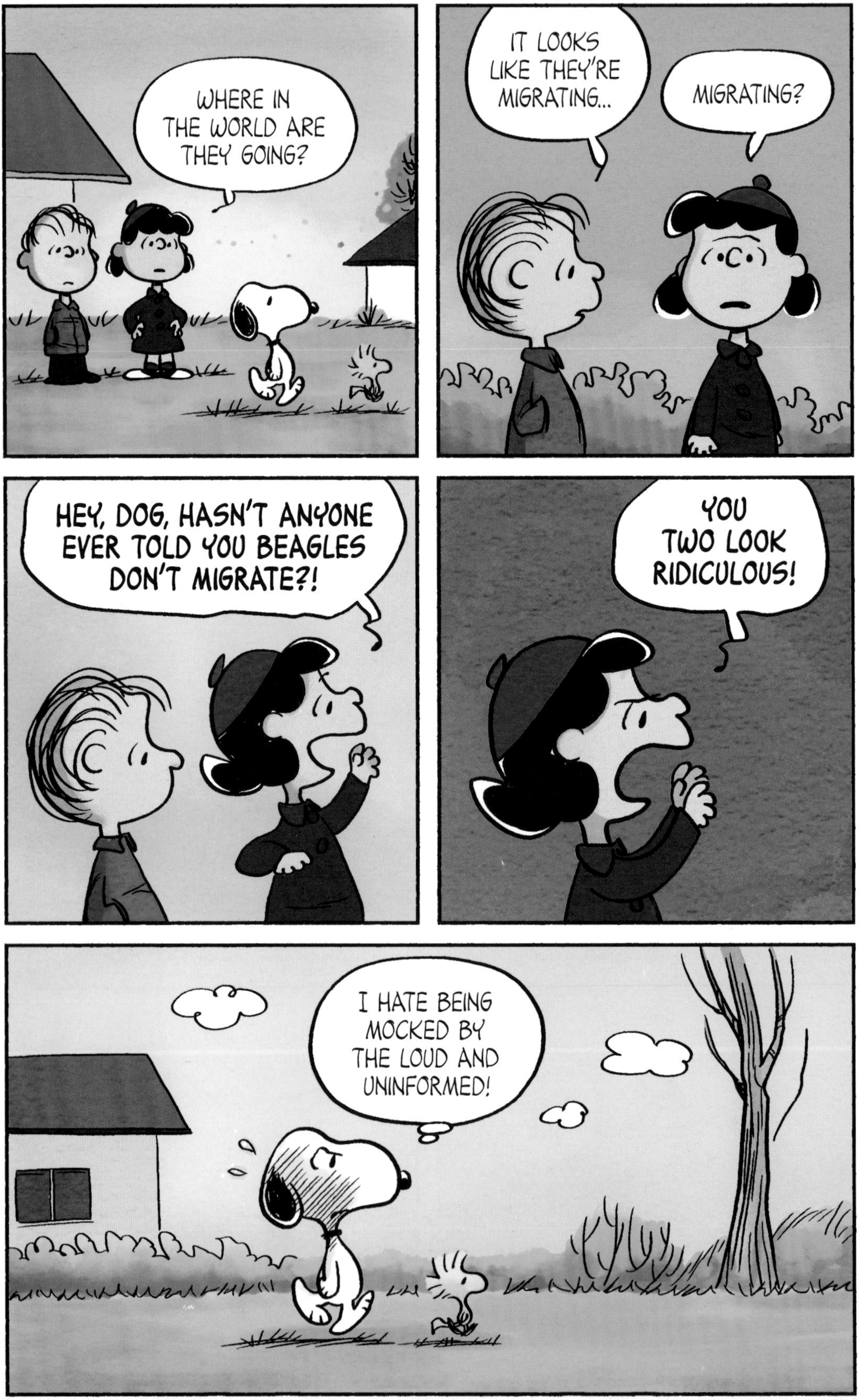
WHERE IN THE WORLD ARE THEY GOING?
IT LOOKS LIKE THEY'RE MIGRATING...
MIGRATING?
HEY, DOG, HASN'T ANYONE EVER TOLD YOU BEAGLES DON'T MIGRATE?!
YOU TWO LOOK RIDICULOUS!
I HATE BEING MOCKED BY THE LOUD AND UNINFORMED!

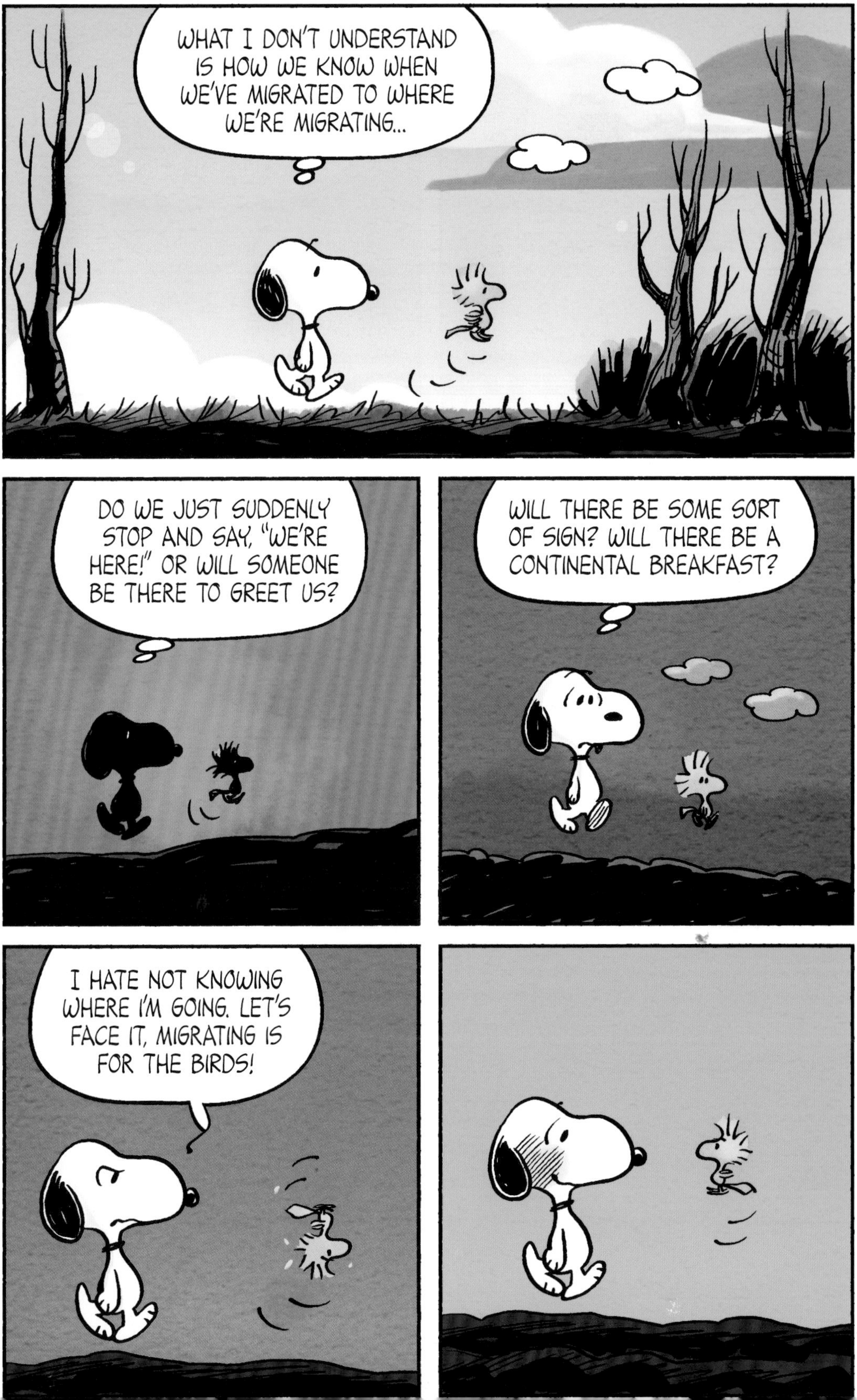
WHAT I DON'T UNDERSTAND IS HOW WE KNOW WHEN WE'VE MIGRATED TO WHERE WE'RE MIGRATING...
DO WE JUST SUDDENLY STOP AND SAY, "WE'RE HERE!" OR WILL SOMEONE BE THERE TO GREET US?
WILL THERE BE SOME SORT OF SIGN? WILL THERE BE A CONTINENTAL BREAKFAST?
I HATE NOT KNOWING WHERE I'M GOING. LET'S FACE IT, MIGRATING IS FOR THE BIRDS!

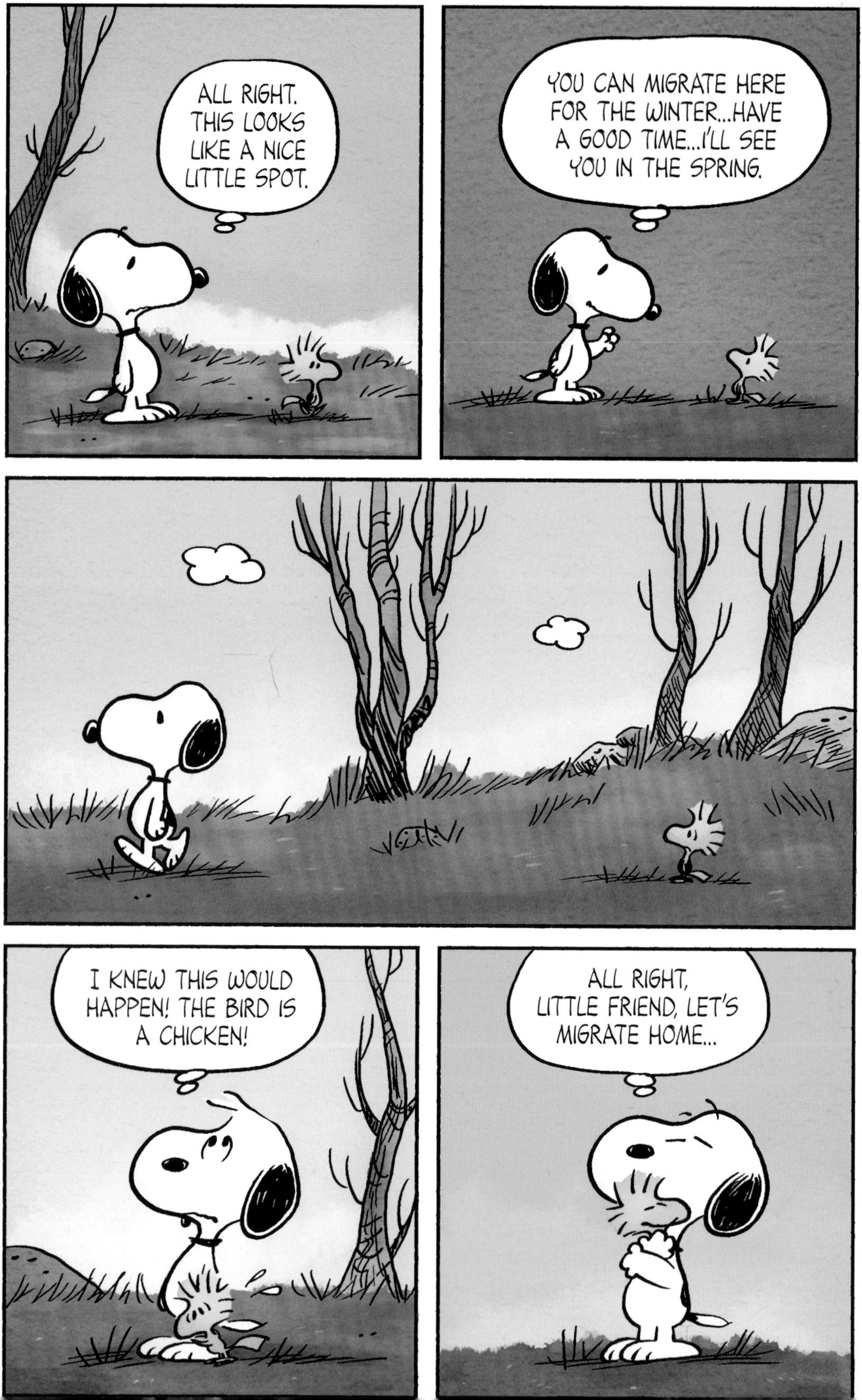
ALL RIGHT. THIS LOOKS LIKE A NICE LITTLE SPOT.
YOU CAN MIGRATE HERE FOR THE WINTER...HAVE A GOOD TIME...I'LL SEE YOU IN THE SPRING.
I KNEW THIS WOULD HAPPEN! THE BIRD IS A CHICKEN!
ALL RIGHT, LITTLE FRIEND, LET'S MIGRATE HOME...

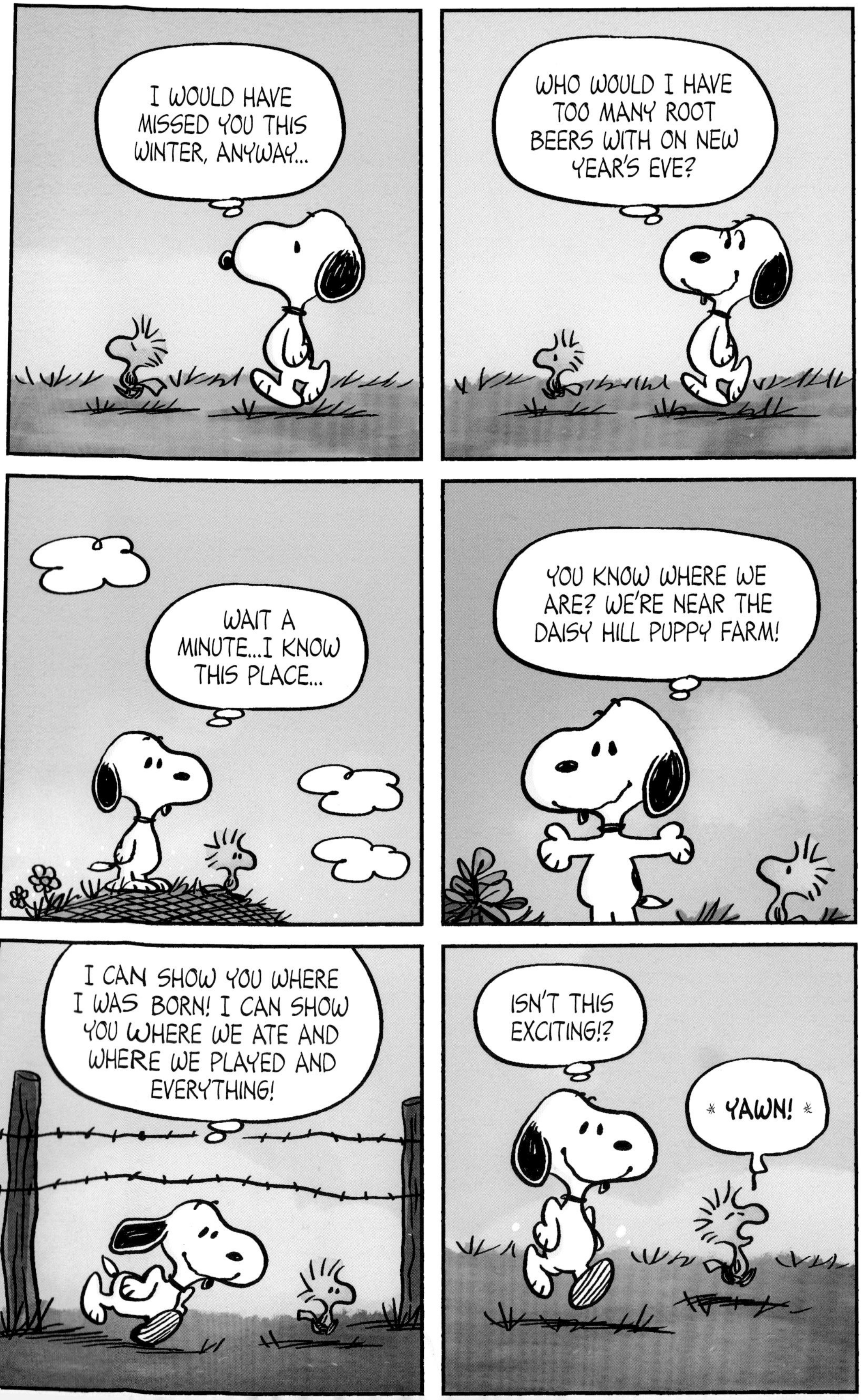
I WOULD HAVE MISSED YOU THIS WINTER, ANYWAY...
WHO WOULD I HAVE TOO MANY ROOT BEERS WITH ON NEW YEAR'S EVE?
WAIT A MINUTE...I KNOW THIS PLACE...
YOU KNOW WHERE WE ARE? WE'RE NEAR THE DAISY HILL PUPPY FARM!
I CAN SHOW YOU WHERE I WAS BORN! I CAN SHOW YOU WHERE WE ATE AND WHERE WE PLAYED AND EVERYTHING!
ISN'T THIS EXCITING!?
YAWN!

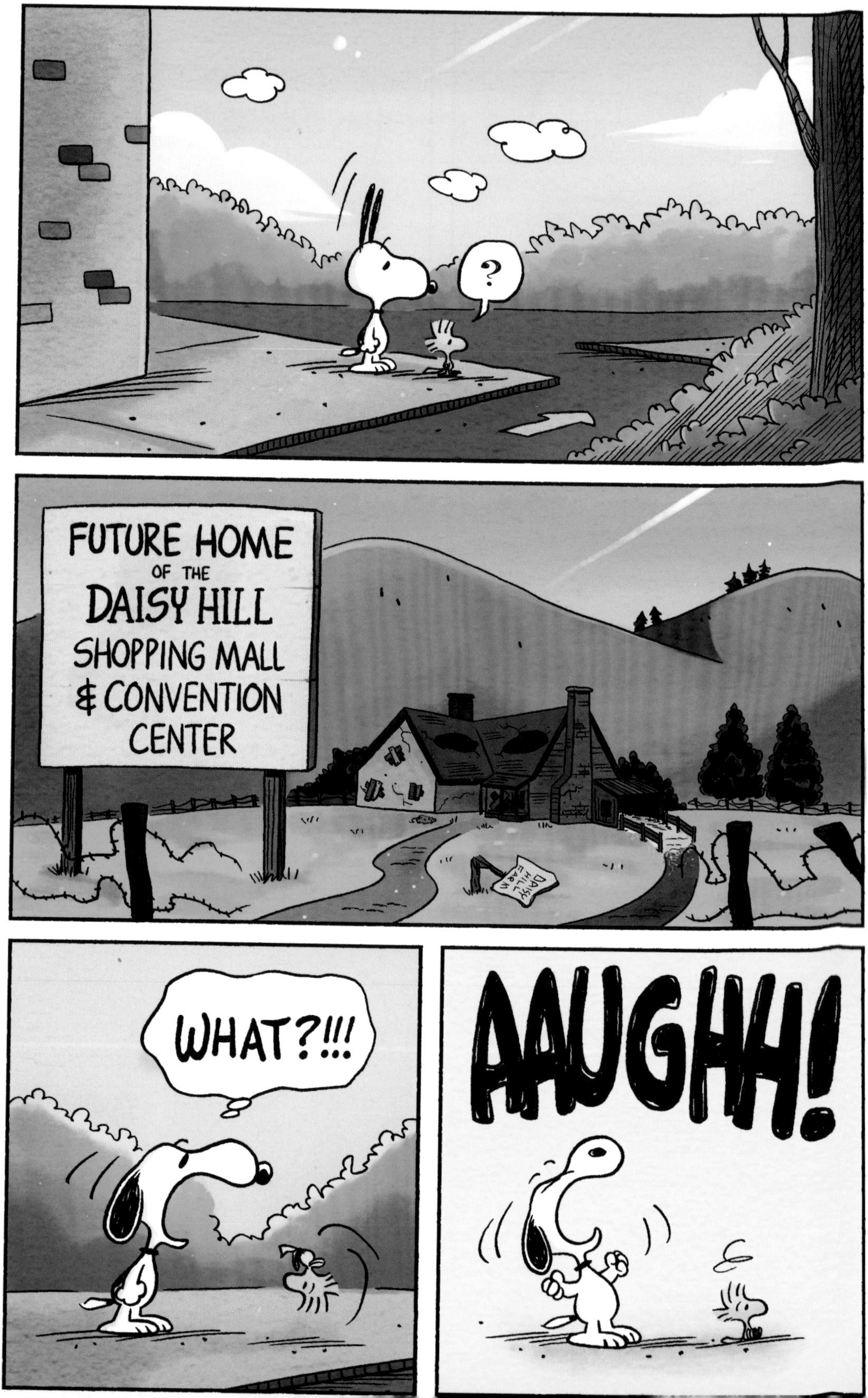
?
FUTURE HOME OF THE DAISY HILL SHOPPING MALL & CONVENTION CENTER
DAISY HILL FARM
WHAT?!!!
AAUGHH!

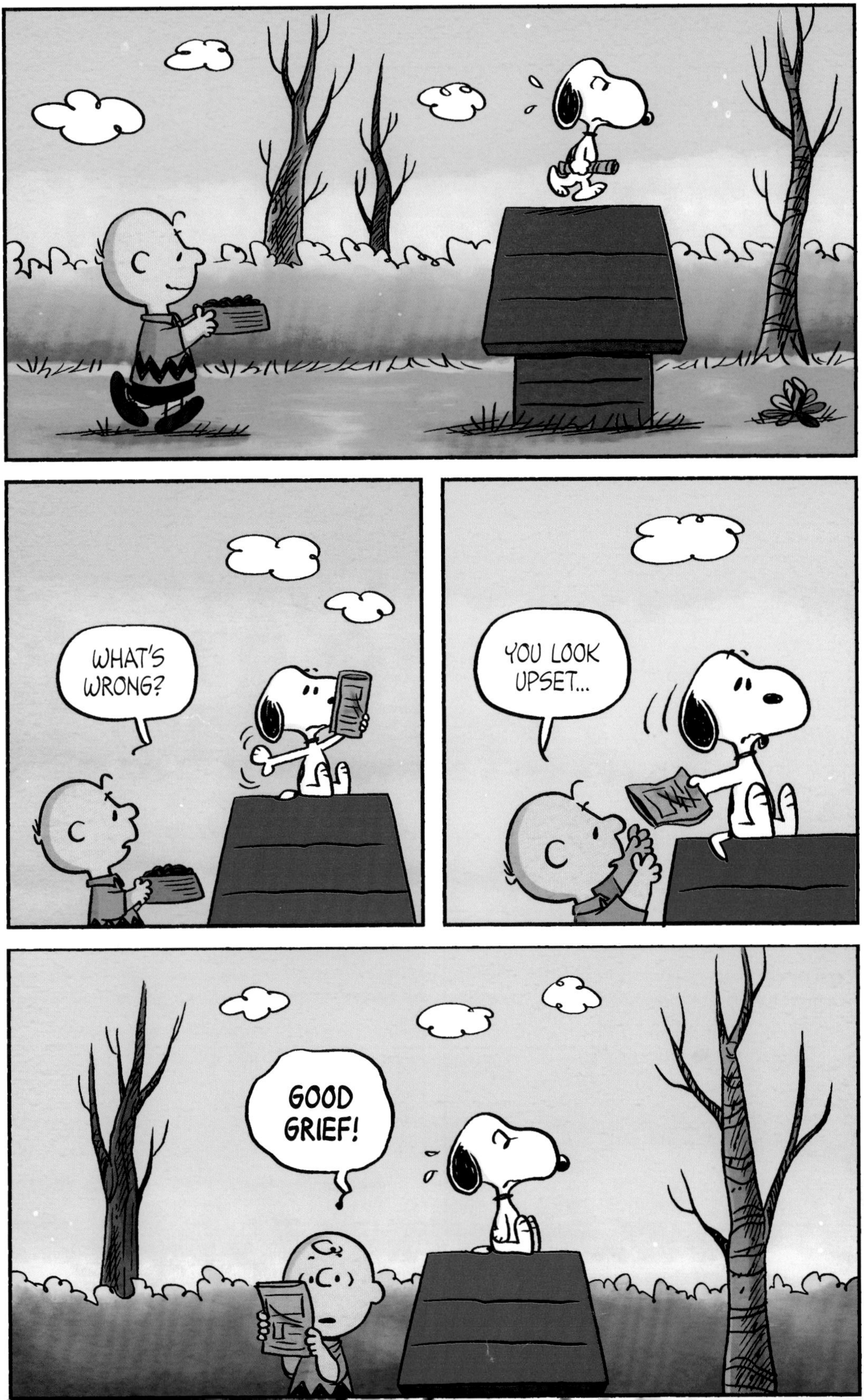
WHAT'S WRONG?
YOU LOOK UPSET...
GOOD GRIEF!

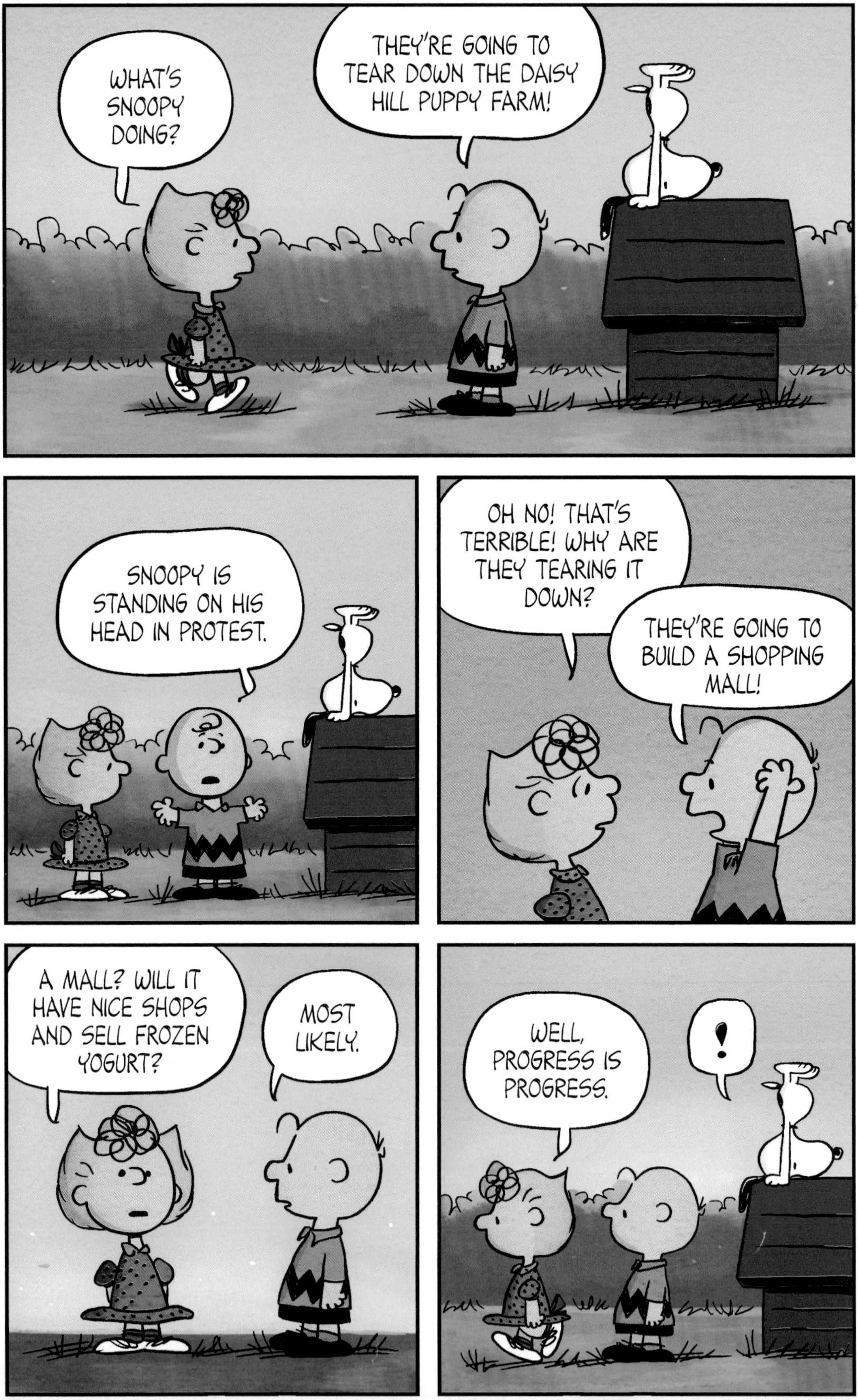
WHAT'S SNOOPY DOING?
THEY'RE GOING TO TEAR DOWN THE DAISY HILL PUPPY FARM!
SNOOPY IS STANDING ON HIS HEAD IN PROTEST.
OH NO! THAT'S TERRIBLE! WHY ARE THEY TEARING IT DOWN?
THEY'RE GOING TO BUILD A SHOPPING MALL!
A MALL? WILL IT HAVE NICE SHOPS AND SELL FROZEN YOGURT?
MOST LIKELY.
WELL, PROGRESS IS PROGRESS.
!

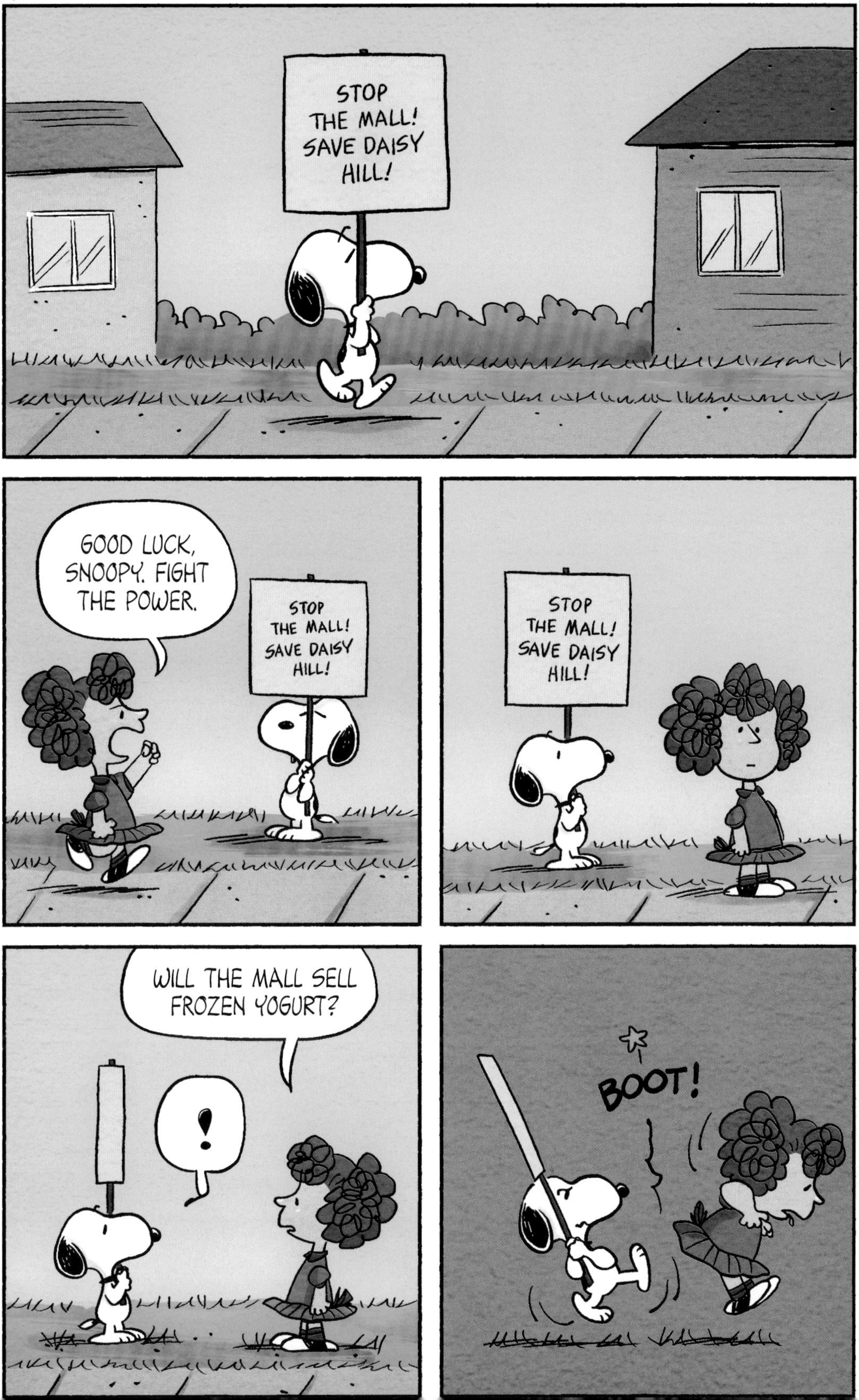
STOP THE MALL! SAVE DAISY HILL!
GOOD LUCK, SNOOPY. FIGHT THE POWER.
STOP THE MALL! SAVE DAISY HILL!
STOP THE MALL! SAVE DAISY HILL!
WILL THE MALL SELL FROZEN YOGURT?
!
BOOT!

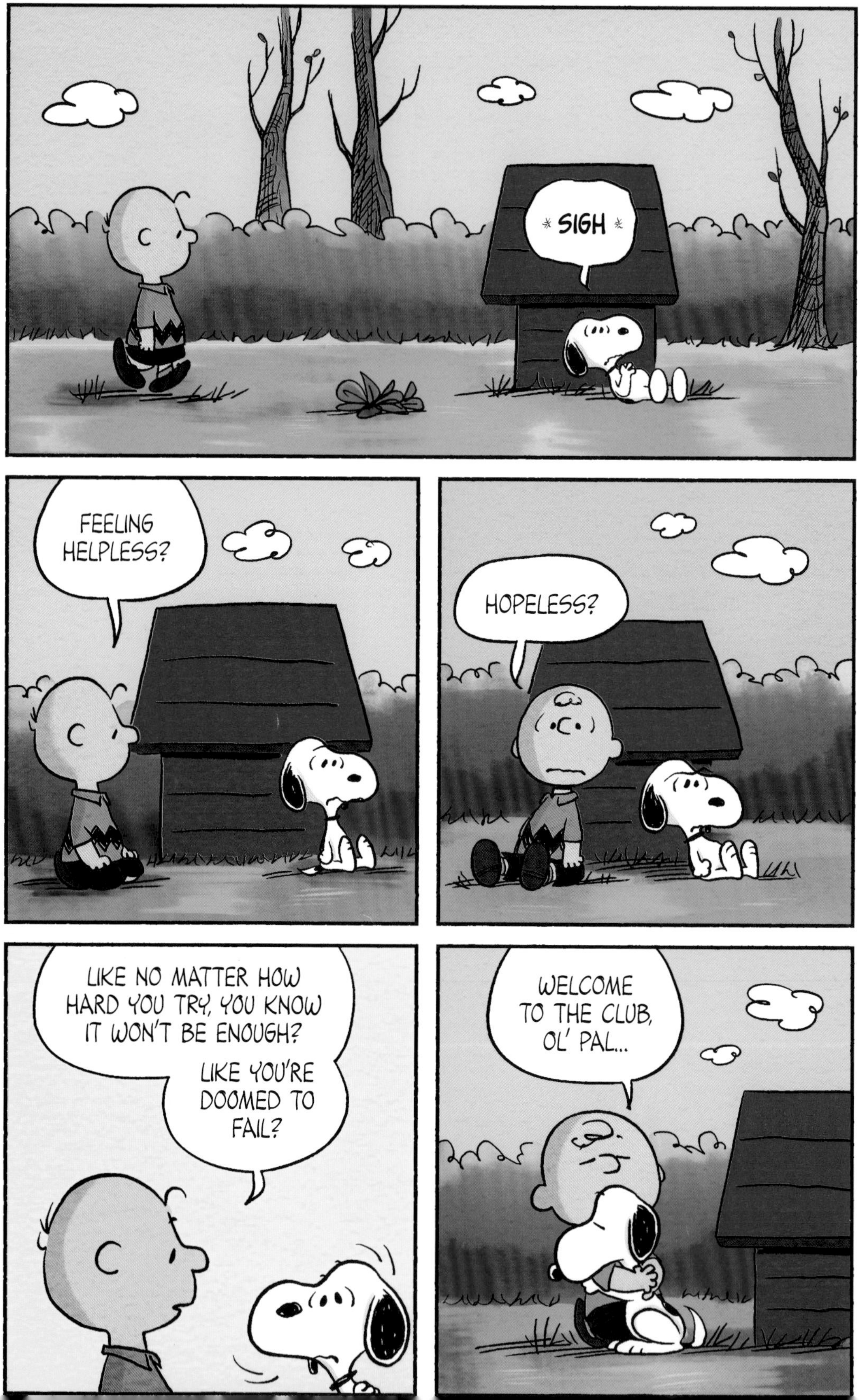
SIGH
FEELING HELPLESS?
HOPELESS?
LIKE NO MATTER HOW HARD YOU TRY, YOU KNOW IT WON'T BE ENOUGH?
LIKE YOU'RE DOOMED TO FAIL?
WELCOME TO THE CLUB, OL' PAL...

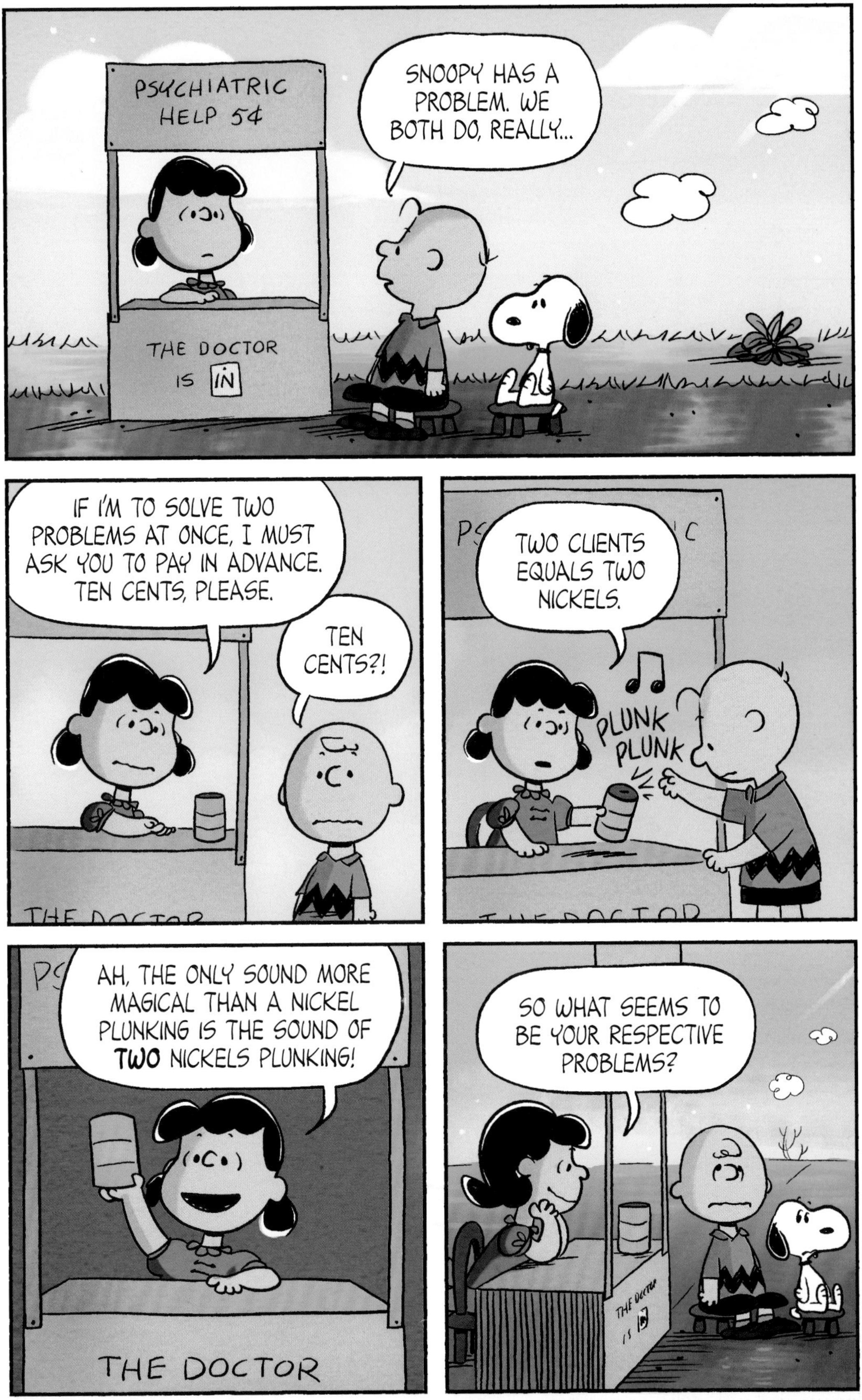
PSYCHIATRIC HELP 5¢
THE DOCTOR IS IN
SNOOPY HAS A PROBLEM. WE BOTH DO, REALLY...
IF I'M TO SOLVE TWO PROBLEMS AT ONCE, I MUST ASK YOU TO PAY IN ADVANCE. TEN CENTS, PLEASE.
TEN CENTS?!
TWO CLIENTS EQUALS TWO NICKELS.
PLUNK PLUNK
AH, THE ONLY SOUND MORE MAGICAL THAN A NICKEL PLUNKING IS THE SOUND OF **TWO** NICKELS PLUNKING!
THE DOCTOR
SO WHAT SEEMS TO BE YOUR RESPECTIVE PROBLEMS?

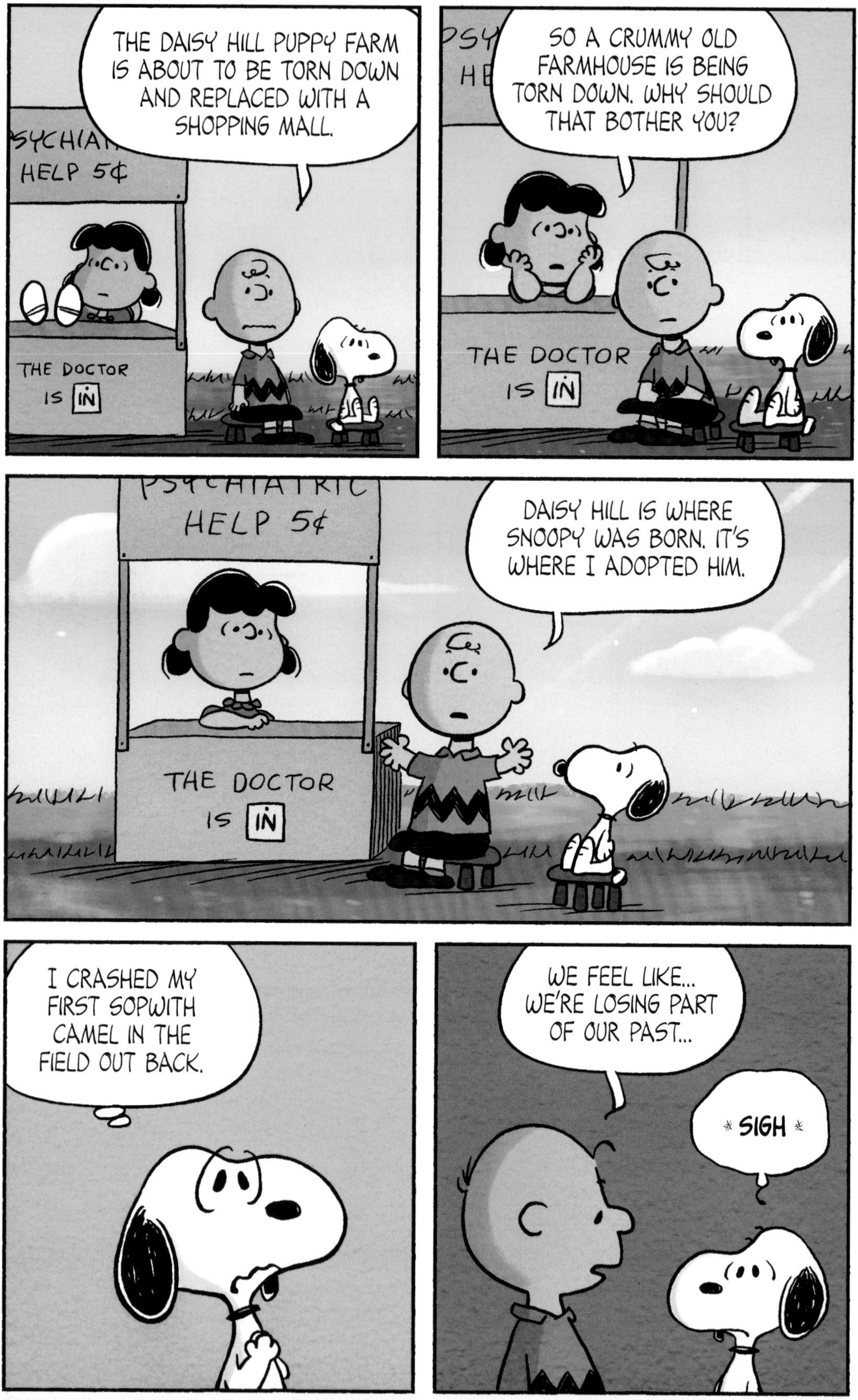
THE DAISY HILL PUPPY FARM IS ABOUT TO BE TORN DOWN AND REPLACED WITH A SHOPPING MALL.
PSYCHIATRIC HELP 5¢
THE DOCTOR IS IN
SO A CRUMMY OLD FARMHOUSE IS BEING TORN DOWN. WHY SHOULD THAT BOTHER YOU?
THE DOCTOR IS IN
PSYCHIATRIC HELP 5¢
DAISY HILL IS WHERE SNOOPY WAS BORN. IT'S WHERE I ADOPTED HIM.
THE DOCTOR IS IN
I CRASHED MY FIRST SOPWITH CAMEL IN THE FIELD OUT BACK.
WE FEEL LIKE... WE'RE LOSING PART OF OUR PAST...
SIGH

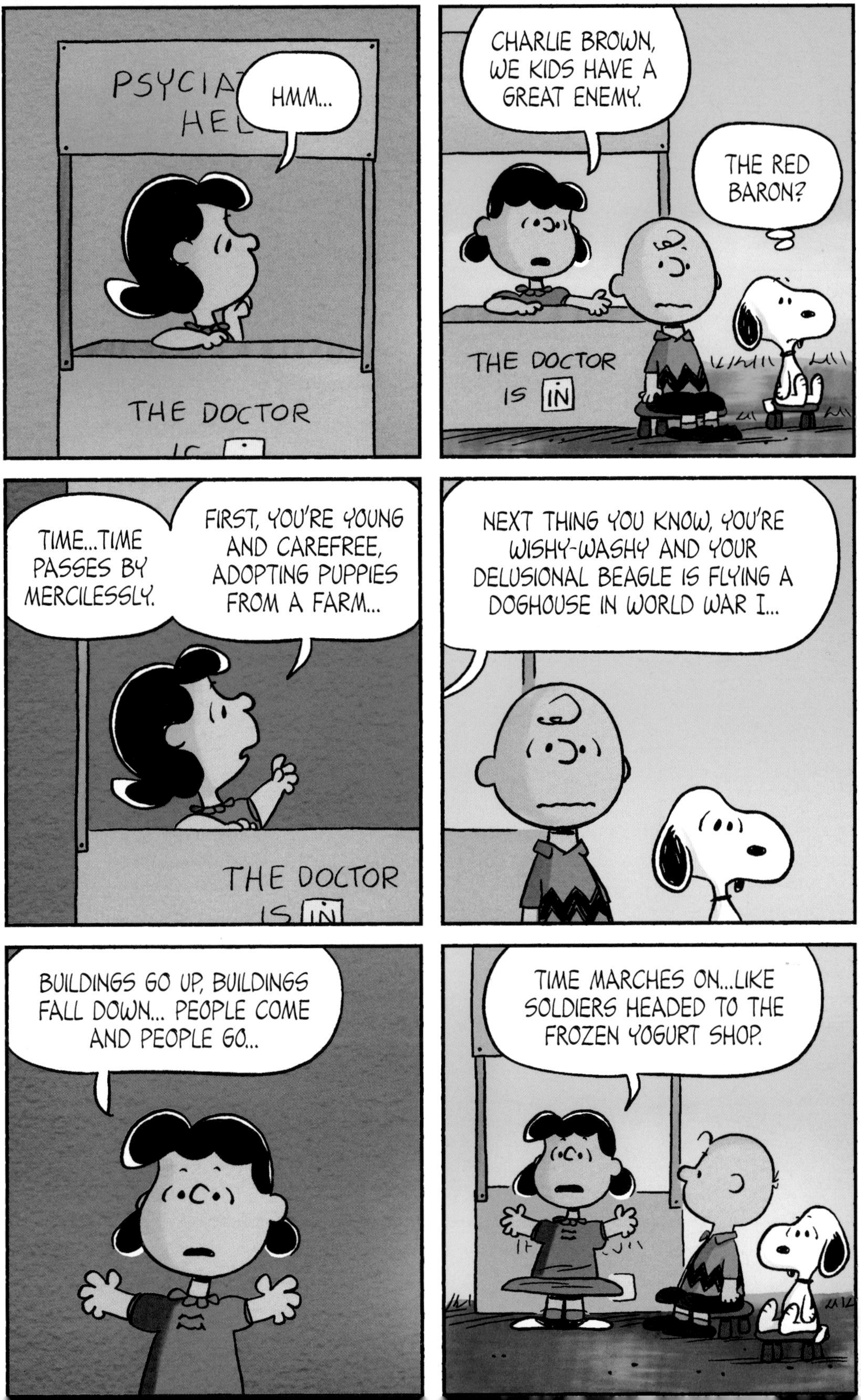
PSYCIA
HEL
HMM...
THE DOCTOR
CHARLIE BROWN, WE KIDS HAVE A GREAT ENEMY.
THE RED BARON?
THE DOCTOR IS IN
TIME...TIME PASSES BY MERCILESSLY.
FIRST, YOU'RE YOUNG AND CAREFREE, ADOPTING PUPPIES FROM A FARM...
THE DOCTOR
NEXT THING YOU KNOW, YOU'RE WISHY-WASHY AND YOUR DELUSIONAL BEAGLE IS FLYING A DOGHOUSE IN WORLD WAR I...
BUILDINGS GO UP, BUILDINGS FALL DOWN... PEOPLE COME AND PEOPLE GO...
TIME MARCHES ON...LIKE SOLDIERS HEADED TO THE FROZEN YOGURT SHOP.

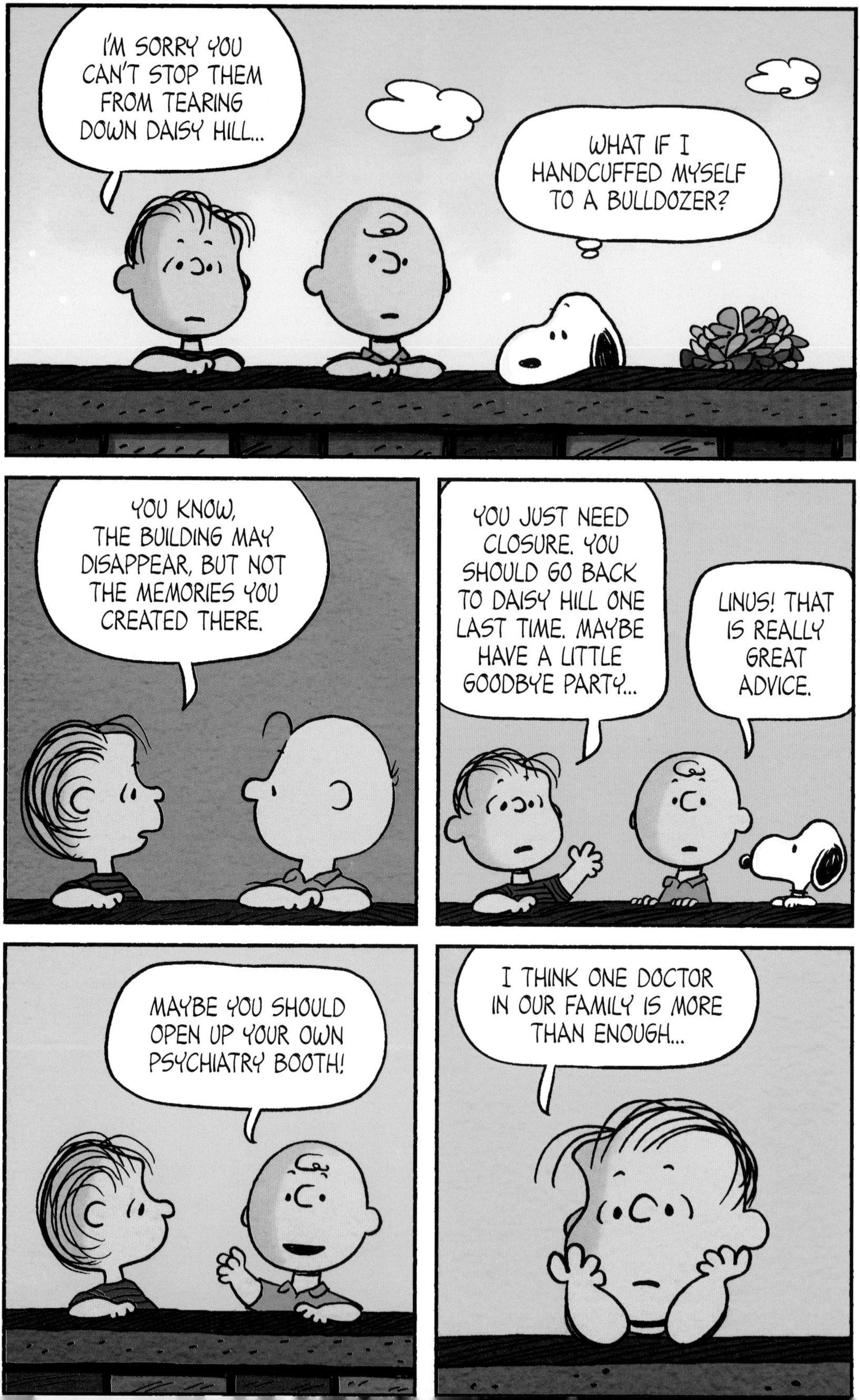
I'M SORRY YOU CAN'T STOP THEM FROM TEARING DOWN DAISY HILL...
WHAT IF I HANDCUFFED MYSELF TO A BULLDOZER?
YOU KNOW, THE BUILDING MAY DISAPPEAR, BUT NOT THE MEMORIES YOU CREATED THERE.
YOU JUST NEED CLOSURE. YOU SHOULD GO BACK TO DAISY HILL ONE LAST TIME. MAYBE HAVE A LITTLE GOODBYE PARTY...
LINUS! THAT IS REALLY GREAT ADVICE.
MAYBE YOU SHOULD OPEN UP YOUR OWN PSYCHIATRY BOOTH!
I THINK ONE DOCTOR IN OUR FAMILY IS MORE THAN ENOUGH...

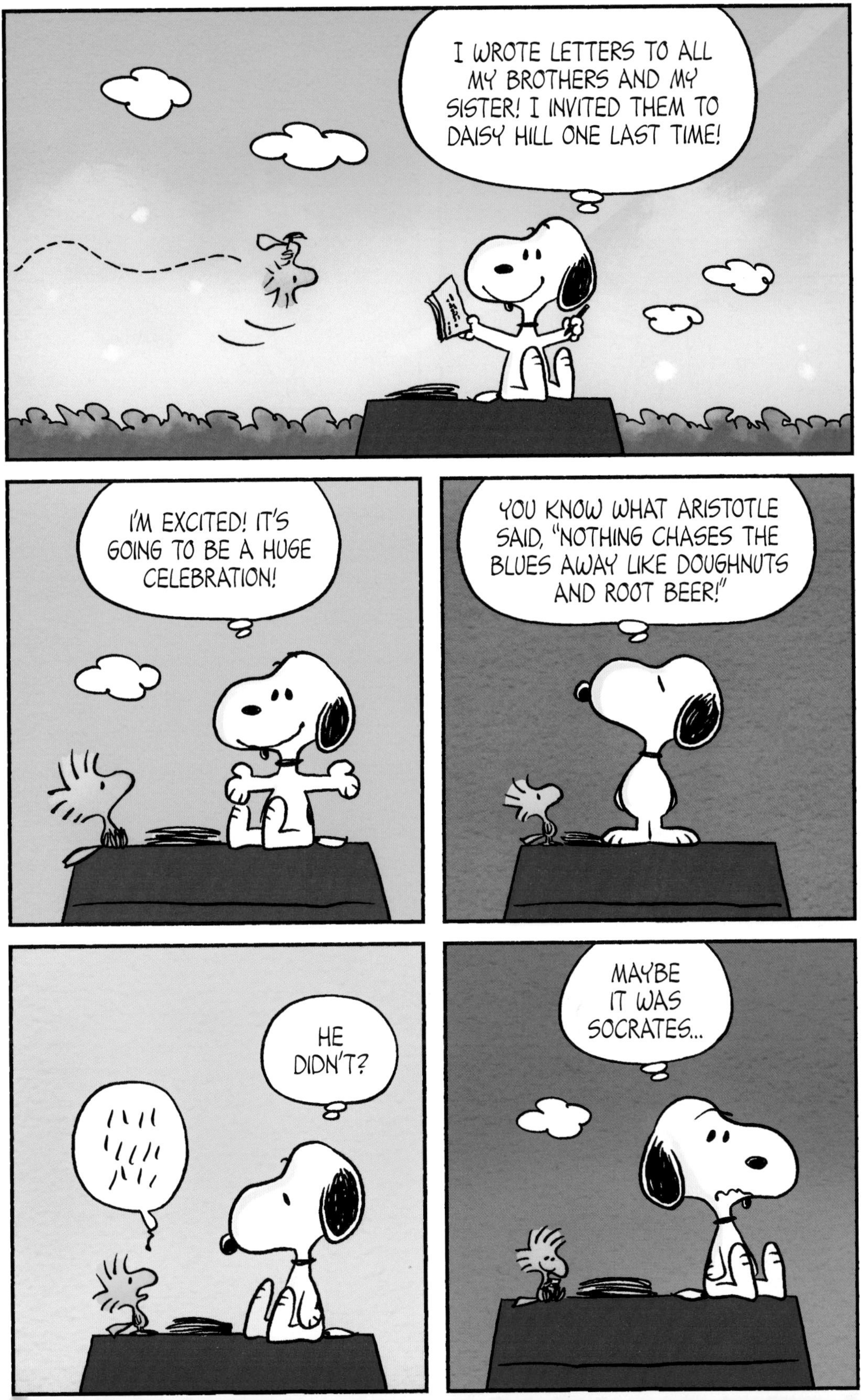
I WROTE LETTERS TO ALL MY BROTHERS AND MY SISTER! I INVITED THEM TO DAISY HILL ONE LAST TIME!
I'M EXCITED! IT'S GOING TO BE A HUGE CELEBRATION!
YOU KNOW WHAT ARISTOTLE SAID, "NOTHING CHASES THE BLUES AWAY LIKE DOUGHNUTS AND ROOT BEER!"
HE DIDN'T?
MAYBE IT WAS SOCRATES...

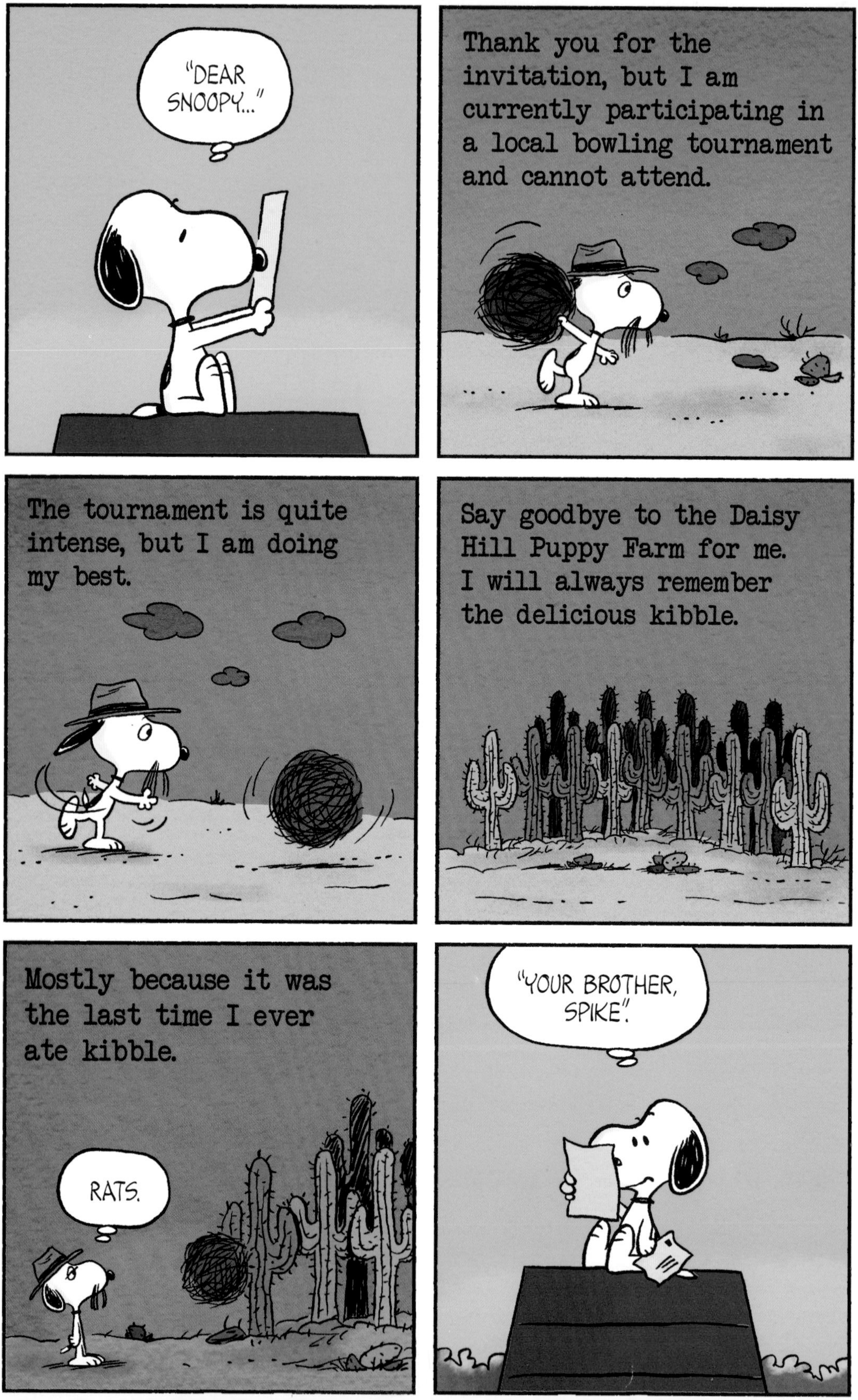
"DEAR SNOOPY..."
Thank you for the invitation, but I am currently participating in a local bowling tournament and cannot attend.
The tournament is quite intense, but I am doing my best.
Say goodbye to the Daisy Hill Puppy Farm for me. I will always remember the delicious kibble.
Mostly because it was the last time I ever ate kibble.
RATS.
"YOUR BROTHER, SPIKE".

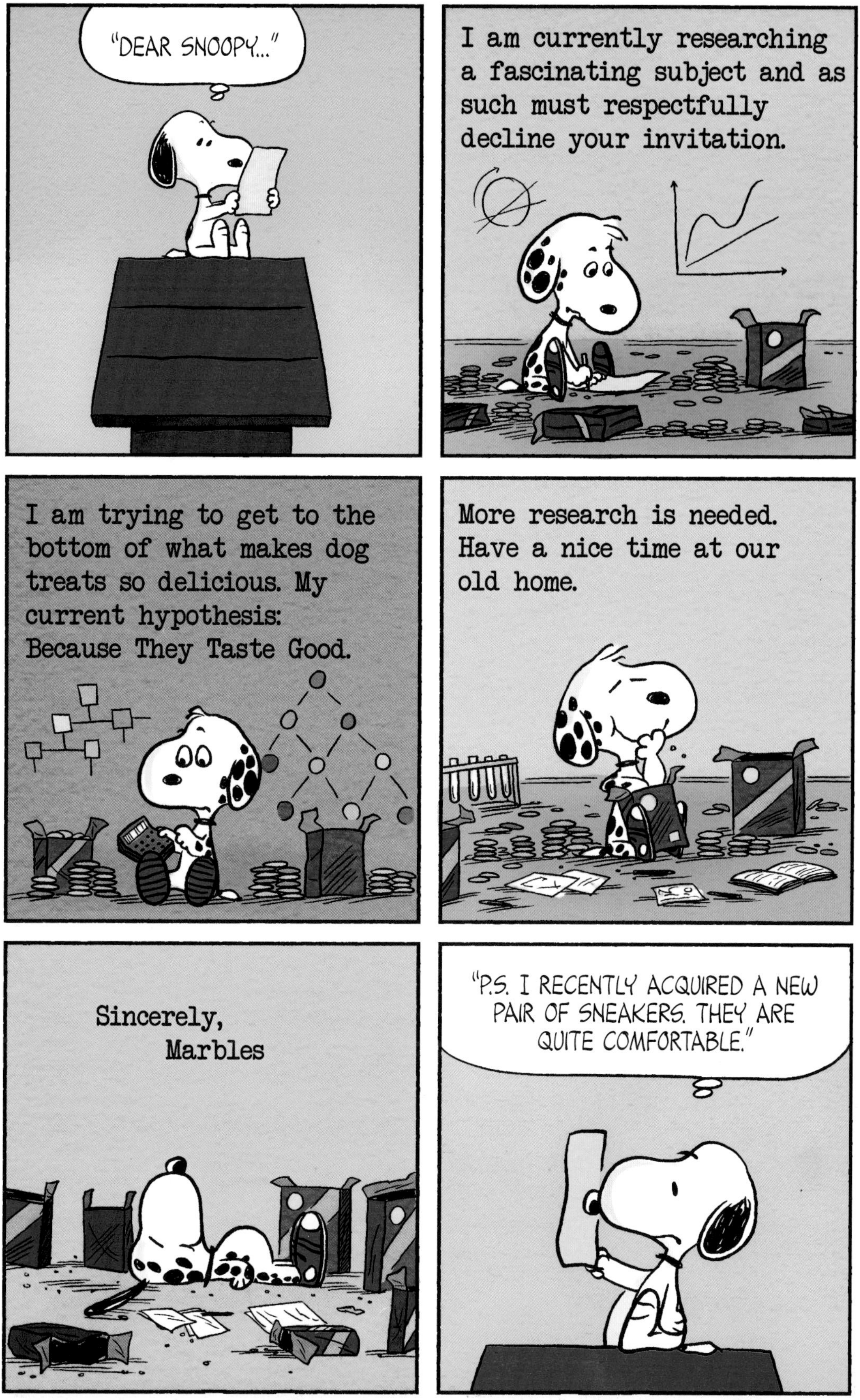
"DEAR SNOOPY..."
I am currently researching a fascinating subject and as such must respectfully decline your invitation.
I am trying to get to the bottom of what makes dog treats so delicious. My current hypothesis: Because They Taste Good.
More research is needed. Have a nice time at our old home.
Sincerely,
Marbles
"P.S. I RECENTLY ACQUIRED A NEW PAIR OF SNEAKERS. THEY ARE QUITE COMFORTABLE."

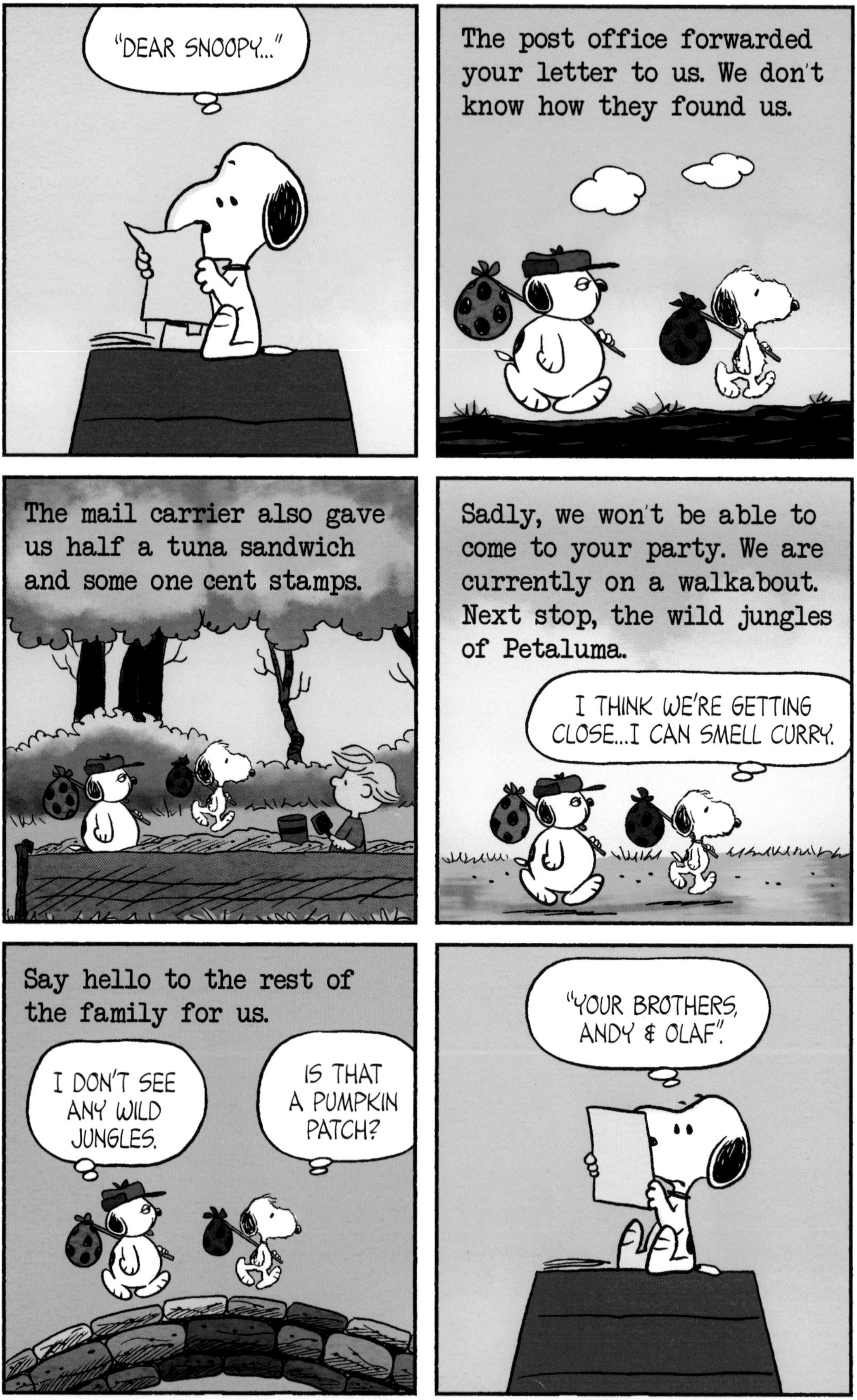
"DEAR SNOOPY..."
The post office forwarded your letter to us. We don't know how they found us.
The mail carrier also gave us half a tuna sandwich and some one cent stamps.
Sadly, we won't be able to come to your party. We are currently on a walkabout. Next stop, the wild jungles of Petaluma.
I THINK WE'RE GETTING CLOSE...I CAN SMELL CURRY.
Say hello to the rest of the family for us.
I DON'T SEE ANY WILD JUNGLES.
IS THAT A PUMPKIN PATCH?
"YOUR BROTHERS, ANDY & OLAF".

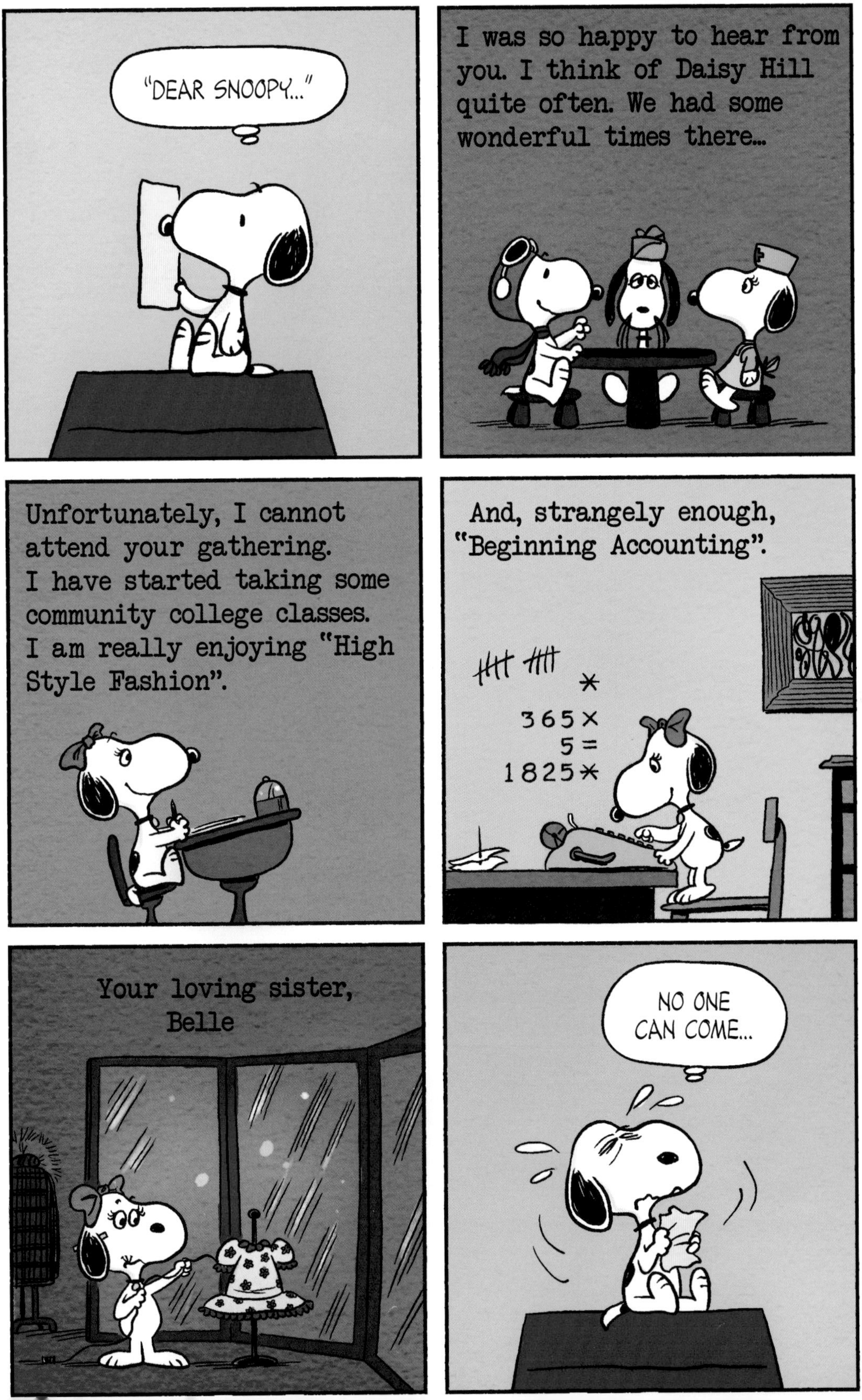
"DEAR SNOOPY..."
I was so happy to hear from you. I think of Daisy Hill quite often. We had some wonderful times there...
Unfortunately, I cannot attend your gathering. I have started taking some community college classes. I am really enjoying "High Style Fashion".
And, strangely enough, "Beginning Accounting".
365×
5=
1825*
Your loving sister, Belle
NO ONE CAN COME...

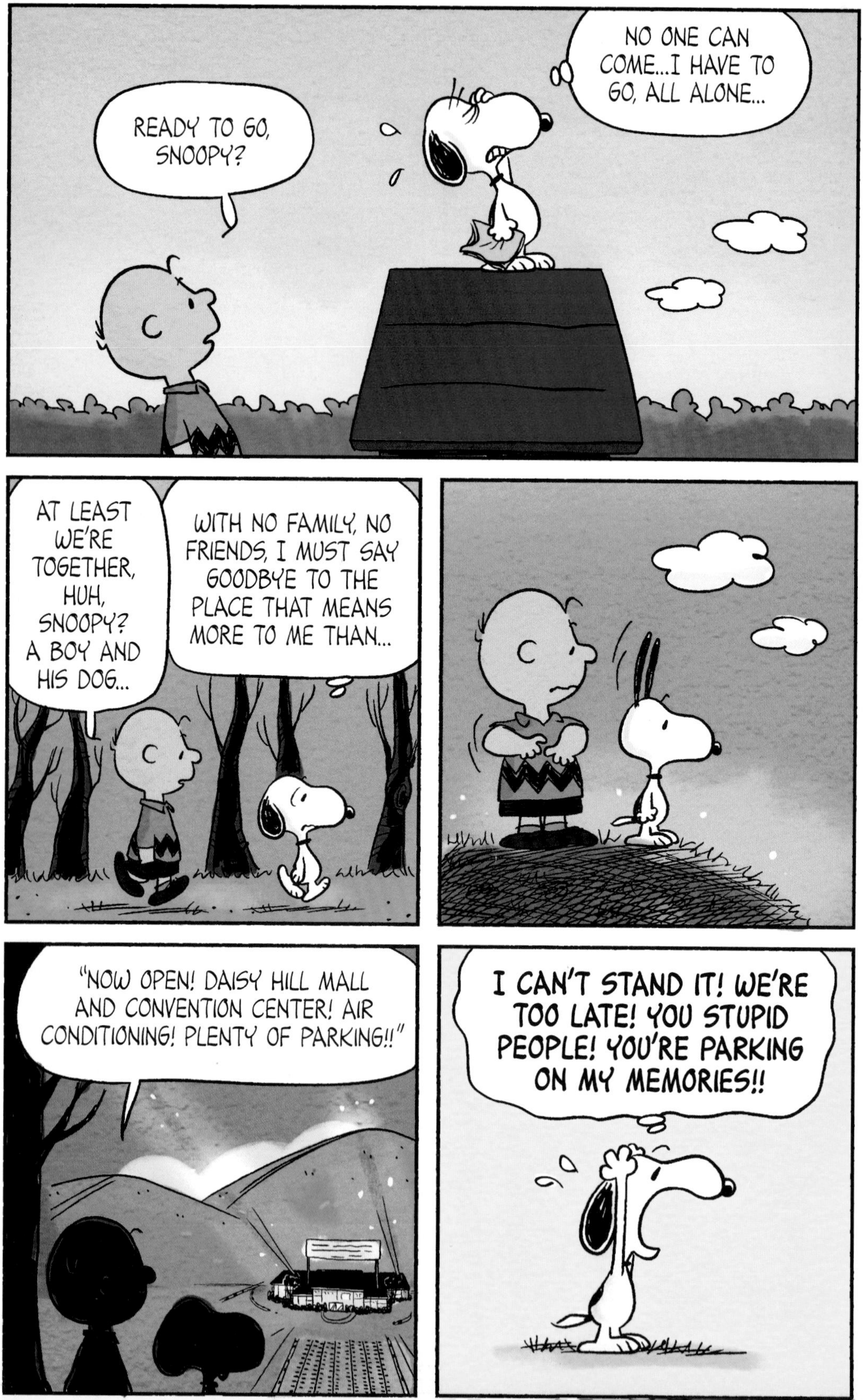
READY TO GO, SNOOPY?
NO ONE CAN COME...I HAVE TO GO, ALL ALONE...
AT LEAST WE'RE TOGETHER, HUH, SNOOPY? A BOY AND HIS DOG...
WITH NO FAMILY, NO FRIENDS, I MUST SAY GOODBYE TO THE PLACE THAT MEANS MORE TO ME THAN...
"NOW OPEN! DAISY HILL MALL AND CONVENTION CENTER! AIR CONDITIONING! PLENTY OF PARKING!!"
I CAN'T STAND IT! WE'RE TOO LATE! YOU STUPID PEOPLE! YOU'RE PARKING ON MY MEMORIES!!

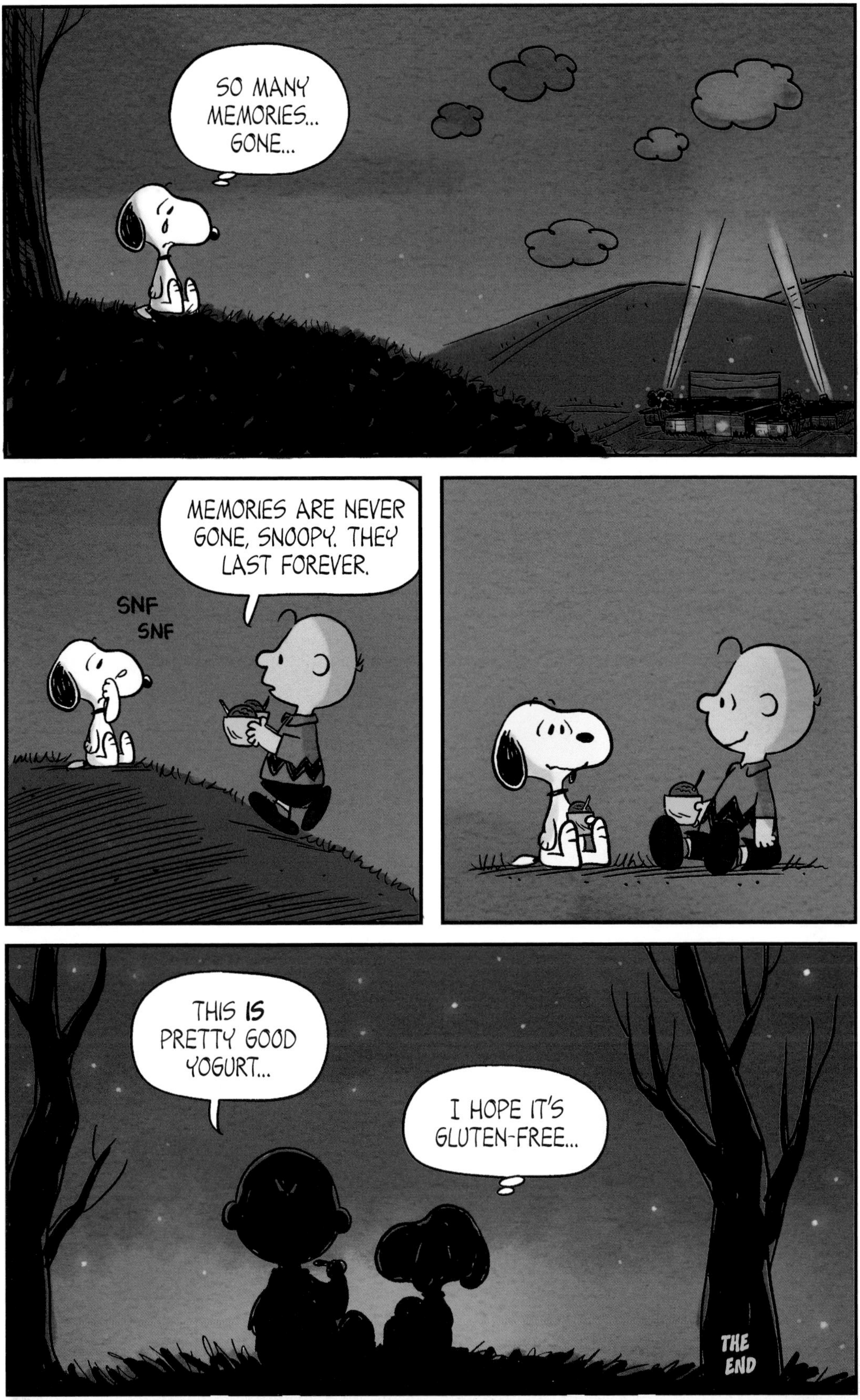
SO MANY MEMORIES... GONE...
MEMORIES ARE NEVER GONE, SNOOPY. THEY LAST FOREVER.
SNF SNF
THIS **IS** PRETTY GOOD YOGURT...
I HOPE IT'S GLUTEN-FREE...
THE END

DISCOVER
EXPLOSIVE NEW WORLDS

ADVENTURE TIME

Sam Sykes · Selina Espiritu · Sarah Stern
Brave Chef Brianna

KELLY THOMPSON BRIANNE DROUHARD M. VICTORIA ROBADO
MEGA PRINCESS

THE NOT-SO SECRET SOCIETY
DALEY · CRAFTS · CLARK · BRUNI

OVER THE GARDEN WALL

STEVEN UNIVERSE
VOLUME ONE

kaboom!™

AVAILABLE AT YOUR LOCAL COMICS SHOP AND BOOKSTORE

To find a comics shop in your area, call 1-888-266-4226

WWW.**BOOM-STUDIOS**.COM

Adventure Time
Pendleton Ward and Others
Volume 1
ISBN: 978-1-60886-280-1 | $14.99 US
Volume 2
ISBN: 978-1-60886-323-5 | $14.99 US
Adventure Time: Islands
ISBN: 978-1-60886-972-5 | $9.99 US

The Amazing World of Gumball
Ben Bocquelet and Others
Volume 1
ISBN: 978-1-60886-488-1 | $14.99 US
Volume 2
ISBN: 978-1-60886-793-6 | $14.99 US

Brave Chef Brianna
Sam Sykes, Selina Espiritu
ISBN: 978-1-68415-050-2 | $14.99 US

Mega Princess
Kelly Thompson, Brianne Drouhard
ISBN: 978-1-68415-007-6 | $14.99 US

The Not-So Secret Society
Matthew Daley, Arlene Daley, Wook Jin Clark
ISBN: 978-1-60886-997-8 | $9.99 US

Over the Garden Wall
Patrick McHale, Jim Campbell and Others
Volume 1
ISBN: 978-1-60886-940-4 | $14.99 US
Volume 2
ISBN: 978-1-68415-006-9 | $14.99 US

Steven Universe
Rebecca Sugar and Others
Volume 1
ISBN: 978-1-60886-706-6 | $14.99 US
Volume 2
ISBN: 978-1-60886-796-7 | $14.99 US

Steven Universe & The Crystal Gems
ISBN: 978-1-60886-921-3 | $14.99 US

Steven Universe: Too Cool for School
ISBN: 978-1-60886-771-4 | $14.99 US

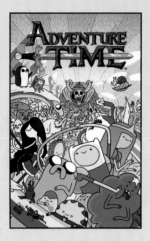

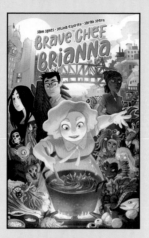

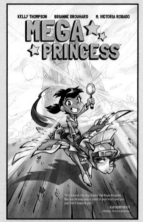

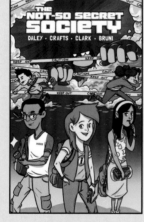

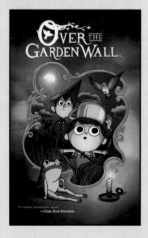

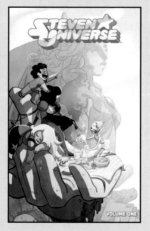

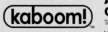